BAD TIMES

Book Three: Avenging Angels

Chuck Dixon

This is a work of fiction. Names, characters places and incidents are either the product of the author's imagination or are used fictitiously. Any resemblance to persons living or dead is entirly coincidental.

A Bruno Books Production
First Paperback Edition

Cover Design: Derek Murphy
Interior Design: JW Manus

Other Works by Chuck Dixon

Bad Times: Book One:
Cannibal Gold

Bad Times: Book Two:
Blood Red Tide

Seal Team Six: The Novel
(#1 in ongoing hit series)

Seal Team Six 2
(#2 in ongoing hit series)

Seal Team Six 3
(#3 in ongoing hit series)

Seal Team Six 4
(#4 in ongoing hit series)

Winterworld

Batgirl/Robin Year One

Batman Versus Bane

Jerusalem, AD 31

The sun had no mercy. It was a hammer and the Roman fort was the anvil.

It was noon and invisible fire rained down from a cloudless sky. The light shone painfully off of white-washed walls and tiled rooftops. There was a feeble breeze off the surrounding hills brushing over the ramparts of the fortress the invaders built at the corner of the great temple. The zephyr was scant relief to the soldiers on sentry there. It did little more than stir the inferno. They were at least above the stink of the streets below.

The tribune had gone indoors to enjoy the comforts of shade and so could not see centurion Aelius Sextus Antoninus removing his helmet to wipe the sweat from the band. The centurion enjoyed the momentary sensation of a gust in the sodden bristles atop his head before returning the foul-smelling leather bucket to its place.

This was his nineteenth year in the ranks. Fifteen with the Eighth and the last four with this pack of dogs in the Tenth. They were condemned to service in Palestine as a punishment for various offenses from gambling to sloth to minor theft. Aelius was here also, despite coming from a good, well, a *decent* family. His offense was his brutal efficiency. He was a tough and able commander and seen by his masters as the best choice to whip these scum into fighting condition. It was his penultimate year in service and so he kept his thoughts to himself.

Aelius buckled the strap beneath his chin and walked the walls. His century, eighty men representative of the worst the legions had to offer, stood in place sweltering in their armor, their pila in their fists, shields on their arms, and swords on their belts. They wore the lighter steer-hide kit and that was a mercy. Still, armor was armor and it hung from their shoulders heavy with sweat. The centurion allowed for regular water breaks. They could not have the rabble seeing any man of the Tenth faint in the ranks. It would not do. The projected power of Caesar Tiberius must appear indomitable. Fear of that power was all that kept these Jews in line.

And the Jews were becoming more troublesome all the time. Their own king could not control them. Their priests could not calm them. The filthy mob bridled under a Roman harness and no amount of the lash would calm them. They took umbrage at everything Roman. Every perceived slight was an excuse for riots. The day the eagles were raised over the newly constructed fortress a crowd gathered at the gates throwing stones and shouting. They were driven away at spear point and scores were taken away to be scourged. The next morning two soldiers were found murdered; probably caught drunk on their way back from whoring. Twenty Judeans were put on crosses the next day. Ten for each Roman dead. Things had settled down a bit since then. There were sullen looks and occasional squabbles and little else through the winter. Any fool could see it was a fragile peace, an illusion.

Now the city was crowded with pilgrims to the temple to celebrate the Jews' holiday of Passover. They were celebrating their emancipation from the Egyptians long ago. The yoke of servitude placed upon them by Rome was bitterly felt in these days of remembrance.

The tension was strained for all to feel. And today would be a high water mark.

"I am not one to question a prefect's wishes," Aelius said to a pimply optio whose name had slipped his mind. "But he might have held off on executions until this damned festival is over."

"What is this festival of theirs, sir?" the optio said. His voice was reedy from a parched throat.

"They celebrate leaving Egypt for this place, Optio," Aelius said.

"Why did they leave Egypt, sir?"

"I'll be damned and gone to hell if I know. I've been to Egypt and it looks much the same as this to me."

"Centurion!"

Aelius turned to see that the tribune had stepped back onto the ramparts from his quarters. The man was half Aelius's age but from a better family, though not exalted enough to keep him from duty in this pesthole. He wore immaculate armor that was more decorative than anything else. It shone with silver bosses and trim to mark his rank. It would also mark him for slings and bows were they in battle. His head was bare and Aelius envied him that.

"Have they nailed the bastards up yet?" The tribune stepped to the battlements and shielded his eyes to scan the hill at Calvariæ Locus.

"Not as yet, Tribune," Aelius replied. He suspected that the tribune's eyesight was not so keen. A shifting crowd was clearly visible on the flanks of the hillock but no crosses had been raised. Soldiers stood in a ring encircling the crest of the hill. As miserable as it was atop these walls, it would be pure hell standing down in the dust and suffering the invective of the mob.

"These Jews are mad," the tribune spat. "Only one god and they are afraid to even say his name. They build a temple without one statue to worship. What does their god even look like?"

"I hear that they believe he looks like a Jew," Aelius offered.

The tribune snorted at that.

"They're very wrought up over something, Tribune," Aelius said.

"This Jew they're nailing up today. He's something of a hero to them. He spoke against the raising of the eagles and incites the Jews to riot with his words." The tribune dipped a cupped hand in an urn of tepid water and dribbled it over his face.

"Should the prefect not have held off this execution, Tribune? At least until the pilgrims have departed the city."

"Pilate keeps his own counsel. The rebel dies today along with a pair of thieves."

A collective moan rose from the crowd about the hill as the first cross was raised. The sound broke up into shouts of anger. The words were not decipherable from here but then they would have been in that damned dog's bark of a language in any case. Still, the tone was plain and Aelius could see the ranks of the soldiers close up, their shields forming a seamless wall. A second and third cross were hauled upright. A naked male body hung from each, suspended from nails through wrists and ankles and supported by a rope about the torso to keep them upright and prolong the punishment.

The men would be hours dying. Tormented by thirst, scalded by the sun, in agony from long spikes driven through their wrists and ankles. Ropes were tied about their arms and beneath their ribs or else their own burden would tear them from the nails. Many in the crowd would be family or followers. Others stood in the glare to watch from morbid curiosity men slowly die. These last would drift away once the three men lost consciousness.

The man suspended on the center cross shouted in words indecipherable to the men on the walls. Was he pleading for mercy to his god or cursing the fate that brought him here? Perhaps he called out to loved ones or proclaimed his innocence to his tormentors. His face was turned to the sun and he howled upward, muscles straining against the fire in his limbs.

"What is the name of the rebel condemned today, Tribune?" Aelius asked.

"Yeshwah bar Abba," the tribune said. "The mob calls him Barabbas."

Paris Canal, St-Martin

"These are in extraordinary condition," the dealer said, squinting through a jeweler's loupe at the pair of coins in clear plastic cases.

"You say that like it's a problem," Lee Hammond said and gestured to the waiter for a refill. They sat on an open air veranda enjoying the cool night air a story above the street. They had a postcard view of the lights of the city and the cars and busses buzzing by. What made traffic so picturesque in Rome, London and Paris and such a pain in the ass everywhere else?

"Over two thousand years old. Stamped with a clear profile of Hamilcar Barca, the Carthaginian emperor. And uncirculated," the dealer said and removed the lens from his eye.

"*Les mêmes à nouveau. Deux doigts,*" Hammond said when the waiter reached him. Lee was holding two fingers clamped together to indicate the depth of Maker's Mark he desired. The waiter nodded and departed.

"They are heavily tarnished, of course. Exposed to water or dampness for a long period. You were wise not to clean them."

"Yeah. I watch *Pawn Stars.*"

The dealer squinted and pursed his lips.

"TV show in the states. So what are they worth?"

"These are heavy coins. Surprisingly heavy. They

were struck for a special purpose; perhaps as part of ransom or some other large transfer of funds."

"Uh huh."

"It is highly unusual to find coinage of this weight and quality. While a thinner coin might be kept as a keepsake or token, currency like this was most often melted down for its metal worth. To have two such examples survive..."

"Yeah. Yeah. How much?"

"By weight alone they are worth a touch over two thousand euros."

"So about three kay American. What's their collectible worth?" Hammond said, accepting the tumbler from the waiter. Liquid gold with a single ice cube sliding on the bottom.

"Two times their going troy ounce value. Perhaps three times that at auction."

"No auctions. This has to stay private. Very private. Secret even."

"Ah. Well, I know some collectors, of course. But I would have to remove one of the coins from its case and examine it more thoroughly. Strictly so that I might offer them my assurances."

"Sure. Take them both. Do whatever tests you need," Hammond said.

"You have more?" the dealer said with an arched eyebrow.

"A shitload."

The dealer squinted again and tilted his head.

"I have beaucoup. Mucho beaucoup," Hammond said, murdering two languages at one pass.

The dealer nodded with pleased smile and slipped

the plastic cases into a pocket of his jacket.

"I go then. Will you be departing? Perhaps we might share a taxi?"

"No," Hammond said, smiling and swirling the cube in the crystal tumbler. "I don't have a single place in the whole goddamned world I have to be."

Somewhere Sunny

"You don't want to know?" Dwayne Roenbach said.

"I don't," Caroline Tauber said with an easy smile.

They lay in the shade of a cabana on a sugar sand beach. Dwayne was propped on an elbow and running the palm of his hand gently over Caroline's swollen belly. She wore a maternity swimsuit they bought in Majorca that had a panel open to leave her, to Dwayne, beautiful belly exposed.

"Boy or girl. Doesn't matter?" he said.

"I didn't say that," she laughed.

"But you didn't ask. You were right there and you didn't say, 'Hey, am I having a girl or a boy?'"

"We'll know soon enough."

"I should have been there," Dwayne said.

"To check for a wee-wee?" she said.

"No son of mine will have a wee wee, Mama."

She laughed.

"Seriously, I should have been with you," he said and lay back on the chaise they shared.

"It was just an ultrasound. You had to be with the guys. You saw where the treasure was buried," Caroline said and used both hands to smooth out the sunblock Dwayne had been applying to her tummy.

He made a hmmph noise. But it was true. Dwayne had a vantage point on the day, two thousand years plus prior, when the crew of a Phoenician bireme pulled an iron bound chest ashore on an islet in the Aegean. Caroline witnessed them actually burying it at the foot of an escarpment but Dwayne would not allow her to travel; especially on an extra-legal trip to uncover a hidden fortune in gold coins. Especially since it was far from a hospital. Dwayne marked the spot on the charts she indicated. The *Ocean Raj*, the modified container ship they were leasing through a shell corporation, remained moored in the sea near Nisos Anaxis in the chain of tiny atolls on the diamond sea. This was the island where Dwayne and Caroline witnessed the arrival of the *Lion of Ba'al*, the pirate boat that dropped off the trove of coins two millennia before.

The treasure was buried in a pit on a beach that was now covered by twenty feet of water as ocean levels rose and land masses sank over time. It would be simple enough to retrieve it from the relative shallows. The difficulty came with doing so in secrecy. Many had hunted for the legendary gold coins over the centuries. The first to uncover them were entitled, legally, to bragging rights only. The Greek government would grab the goodies. So the scavenge work would have to be done on the down low.

The former SEAL, known to them only as Boats, devised a plan to literally suck the treasure out from under the world's nose. A suction device was ordered from Fukuwara, a Japanese firm specializing in undersea exploration gear. It was purchased through the same shell corporation that Lee Hammond formed to lease the *Raj*. The manufacturer in Kyoto questioned the need for an extra nine hundred meters of reinforced tubing but payment in cash quelled their objections as well as their curiosity. The *Raj* made for the port at Alexandria and picked up what Chaz Raleigh called "the world's biggest Hoover" in Alexandria. Boats and his

Ethiopian crew fit it at sea while they returned to Nisos Anaxis.

They moored a quarter mile off the west coast of a collection of rocky atolls spiraling north of the coast of the main island. After several dives they set up the steel framework needed to position and weight the business end of the hose on the sea bottom. Over several nights they hauled sand and debris through the hose and aboard the *Raj* where anything larger than a dime was sifted from the silt. On the second night the coins began to appear on the sifting screens. They came up in rust-colored sand; the oxidized remains of the iron-banded chest. The coins numbered in the thousands and looked like dirty gray discs. Jimbo Smalls struck the edge of one with the blade of a knife and the exposed metal gleamed with a rich yellow hue. When Boats was satisfied that they'd sucked up all they could they reeled in the hose and set course for anywhere but the scene of the crime.

Lee Hammond called the day before from Paris to let Dwayne and Caroline in their luxury hideaway know that the prize was going to add millions to their collective kitty.

"Well, I'm here now and I'm not going anywhere," Dwayne said, pressing her hand in his. He settled back on the chaise to listen to the gentle surf rolling in.

A shadow blotted out the sun and Dwayne opened his eyes to find a waiter from the hotel standing over him.

"Yes?" Caroline said.

"I am here to remind you of your luncheon reservations at Chiro's, sir and madame." The waiter smiled professionally.

"Reservations?" Dwayne said.

"In thirty minutes. Party of three." The waiter

bowed once and departed.

"Party of three?" Dwayne said.

They had enough time to go to their suite and change from swimsuits into clothes more appropriate for the hotel's main restaurant. The dining hall was mostly empty as it was mid-afternoon and well past lunch serving hours. The maître d' led them to a table at the rear of the room and partly sheltered by potted palms.

Seated at the table was a dark-haired man with eyes of the most unusual tarnished green. He half stood to greet them.

"Hello, Samuel," Dwayne said, pulling a chair out for Caroline.

GALILEE

"This is not my idea of a vacation," Hammond said and slapped a mosquito to leave a smear of his own blood down his arm.

"I thought you said you like adventure," Bat called back from a turn in the trail.

"That doesn't sound like me."

"Then what's your idea of a vacation?"

"Anywhere you are, sugar." He trotted to catch up to her but she moved fast through the trees ahead of him.

Bathsheba Jaffe laughed as she hiked on, the backpack swaying in counterpoint to her magnificent behind.

It was her idea to show Lee her country.

The Ranger pictured lazy days on the beach at Dado Zamir and nights bar-hopping around Tel Aviv. Instead, she picked a week on the Israel National Trail.

It all started as an easy walk along the beach at Netanya but they turned inland until they were in the forested high country. The mosquitos grew thick and the stinging nettles grew thicker. Often the trail vanished into dense trackless brush. Bat just dove in and Lee had no choice but to follow her, drawn by the vision of those incredible legs fully visible beneath her cut-offs and whipped on by male pride. Here he was a hard-charging former US Army Ranger and a damned skinny girl was kicking his ass.

She took the lead early and kept it. And each time they emerged from some fresh patch of spiny hell he looked like he'd been dragged behind a truck for ten miles of bad road. She looked like she was ready to pose for an L.L. Bean catalog shoot.

The forest they moved through was a mad mix of maples, oak, cypress, poplar and cedar. Bat explained that this forest was planted by the Trees for Israel program started in the 1950s. Jewish school kids from all over the world collected money and saved their pennies to buy saplings to replant the Promised Land. She told him that the north of the country was once carpeted with thick cedar woodlands. But they had been clear cut thousands of years ago to build ships for the Romans. So Jews from all over the world gave their lunch money so that the forests could return and the Galilee could be green once more. Those kids must have knocked on a crapperload of doors, Lee thought, because we've been hiking through this for two days with no end in sight.

The woods gave way to a banana plantation; neat rows of the broad-leafed plants ran over gentle hills under a deep blue sky. Another surprise for Lee. It was a country smaller than New Jersey and thinner across in spots than most counties in America but there was a tremendous variety of terrain and vegetation.

By late afternoon they reached a bluff where they could look back at grids of segmented farmland sloping gently down to the Mediterranean. The sea was visible only as a hazy greenish bar on the horizon. They decided to pitch camp right there to take advantage of a prevailing wind rising up the face of the bluff that cooled the air as the day closed.

They shared a cold meal of tinned salmon and naan bread with butter. Lee insisted on making a small fire to use some of their water to make two mugs of his nasty coffee.

"How do you drink this stuff?" she said, making a yucky face.

"It's cowboy coffee," he said.

"Because they used it to kill Indians?"

"Funny."

They were snuggled in the pop tent. The glow of the dying fire cast shadows over them through the translucent tent fabric. The air was chilling as night fell and Bat wiggled closer.

"What's your story, cowboy?" she said.

"Well, I'm not a cowboy. I just like their coffee."

"Well you're not a venture capitalist, a web millionaire, or a real estate speculator like you've told me the other times I asked about you."

"I said those things?" Lee said.

"You know, to be a good liar you need a good memory." She tapped his lips with a finger.

"I'll try to remember that. I was going to tell you I won the Powerball next."

She bopped him on the forehead with the heel of her hand.

"Hey!"

"We've been seeing each other over three months and the only thing I know about you is your name. I know you're ex-military because your tats don't lie. But I don't know shit about you beyond that. Money's not a problem for you and your time is your own except for your mysterious trips to who knows where."

"We have a good time, right?" Lee said. "And you know I like you."

"We have an awesome time. You fly us around on

chartered jets and spend like a Saudi. You know how to make a girl happy and you're good-looking in a rough kind of way."

"Sucks to be my girlfriend, huh?" he said and tried a smile.

"Is that what I am?" Her expression darkened. "How am I supposed to know that?"

"Hey, you sound like you're getting serious, Bat."

"Do I?" It was a challenge.

It was at this moment in every relationship where Lee would begin his exit strategy. He'd duck away at the earliest opportunity to evade that old velvet trap. Something stirred in his gut and he was moving on before he knew it, leaving a broken heart and, usually, a good number of his clothes behind. He was the type to flee without farewells. In his mind he'd never actually broken up with a woman. It was always just here, just tonight, and gone in the morning.

But not this time. No itch burned in his stomach. He didn't begin fantasizing his escape. There was no urge to slip away with no forwarding. He really liked Bat and wanted to stay with her for who knew how long. Maybe she was even The One. That struck him as a crazy thought as he'd never considered that The One ever existed. The notion of the perfect girl for Lee was like Big Foot or Santa Claus; a fun idea that never stood up to serious contemplation. Still, no warning jingles from his flight instinct.

Maybe because she was also a combat vet. She knew not to ask questions about that because she wouldn't want those questions asked of herself. And, he admitted, she was a combat vet who was as hot as a swimsuit model.

Besides, stuck in a pop-up tent two days from anywhere was not a great place for the "it's not you, it's me" speech.

"I think I deserve the truth," she said with a vise-like grip on his right ear lobe.

So, he told her the truth. The Tauber Tube and traveling back through time to prehistoric Nevada and the ancient Aegean and being hunted by the Russian *mafiya* some of the time and a mysterious multi-billionaire *all* of the time and how he and a bunch of ex-Army buddies made a fortune by finding treasure in locations they found on their visits to the past.

And the craziest part?

She believed him.

Caesarea Provincial, Capital of Judea, AD 16

It was beastly hot despite every effort to make it otherwise.

For prefect Valerius Gratus no effort was made at all. He left that to the slave boys who populated his coastal palace. And there were many of them and all had their function.

He reclined naked on a marble couch while slaves misted him with water from a clever device that sent liquid under pressure to a network of brass hoses positioned above him. Slaves worked a kind of bellows that sent the water through pipes to exit through pin-sized spicules to create a cooling vapor that descended upon him like the lightest rain. The chilling effect was aided by more boys working broad linen fans to fashion a wind to accompany the artificial drizzle.

And still Gratus sweated like a racehorse. He lay in a pool of his own effluvia that smelled like soup from the garlic-laced meal he'd eaten at last night's feasting. This damnable place felt as though it were shrinking around him in a cloying and unwelcome embrace. The office of prefect was given him as though a boon by edict of Tiberius himself. But Gratus was left to wonder what he had done to deserve such a slight as to be given the task of governing a sweltering land of swamps, sand, pestilence, and Jews. And its governance was not entirely under his aegis as he answered to the legate of Syria for all but the slightest decisions.

The single consolation of this unenviable office was that he was mostly left alone in his post. There was enough graft to more than satisfy his greed and enough pretty boys to satisfy his other needs. The boys were cheaper here than in Rome or Gaul and, while he still found Greeks to be the most beautiful, he appreciated Arab youths for their docile compliance to his every whim. Gratus raked off enough from taxes and tariffs and straight bribes to populate his home with a seraglio of young flesh.

He turned his head to regard through sleepy eyes the three boys working the fans. They were lean, dark, and free of the ugly muscle tone and body hair that signaled their coming into manhood. Diminutive bronze gods they were with sloe eyes and clever hands. Despite the crushing heat he felt himself becoming aroused and, having made his choice of an Arab lad, began to rise from his couch.

Gratus was motioning for the selected boy to lower the fan and come closer when Ravilla, his troublesome and annoying attendant, entered the open courtyard of the villa. Ravilla was assigned as his lictor and provided legal counsel that the prefect seldom heeded. The prefect suspected that Ravilla reported to the legate in Antioch.

"Honorable Prefect, you have a visitor," Ravilla said with the disapproving sneer that was a permanent fixture to his features.

"Tell them I am occupied with the business of the empire," Gratus grumbled.

"They insist they have an appointment," Ravilla insisted.

"My calendar is clear, lictor. Tell them to come another day." Gratus was standing now and taking the boy's hand in his. The boy looked up at him, smiling shyly. The smile the prefect returned was of a predatory nature.

"He brings gifts," Ravilla said.

Gratus dropped the boy's hand and whirled in fury.

"Why did you not say so as you entered, you troublesome excrescence?" Gratus roared. "See that he is attended to in my offices while I dress!"

Gratus stormed for his private chamber alone. He spared one remorseful glance back to the smiling Arab lad and that promising mouth. The business of the empire took precedence.

"And with what business do you petition the prefect?" Gratus proclaimed as he entered his official greeting room with its racks of unread scrolls and pedestal holding up a bust of Emperor Tiberius that was as inaccurate as it was flattering. The black marble walls, high lapis ceiling, and fine fixtures of brass and ivory were meant to intimidate visitors, and usually did.

This visitor was clearly not impressed. He stood before Gratus's enormous malachite table, dressed in an indigo robe of silk-trimmed linen, looking impatient but attempting to conceal it beneath a veneer of boredom.

"You may call me Sutra Vari," the man said with a nonchalant air. "I come from the east across the *harena maris* and many ranges of mountains."

The man's Latin was oddly accented and precise. He spoke it with no hesitation but there remained a sense of the rote in his tone. And that was not all that was odd about him. He was tall for a foreigner from these climes. His face was close-shaven and a crown of snow white hair atop his head. It appeared to be even whiter in comparison to his mahogany colored skin. His features were fine, even patrician, with a thin nose well set between black eyes. His most remarkable feature was his teeth. They were even and straight and as white as virgin marble. Gratus had to wrench his eyes away from betraying his fascination. But he'd never seen such perfection in teeth except perhaps on a prize chariot horse.

"Are you a man of position in your land?" Gratus asked while taking a seat in his own chair and gesturing for the visitor to do the same. The man did not take the invitation and remained standing.

"I am not, honorable Prefect. I am a man of considerable resources however."

"And what is your business in Caesarea, if I might be so bold as to inquire? And what result do you seek from this audience with me?"

"I am a trader in goods. Rare goods of excellent quality, wise Prefect. I dare say, items such as may be unknown within your empire."

"That answers my first query but not my second," Gratus said, growing impatient with this foreigner's evasive manner. Can no one east of Brundisium ever come straight to a point?

"As I told your servant, I bring gifts to honor you. In my lands it is customary to be generous with hosts and as I am a newcomer to these lands and you are, in effect, the host..."

"I see! I see!" Gratus said, fixing a smile on his face. The stranger returned it showing, once again, those magnificent *dentibus*.

The stranger snapped his fingers and a pair of Arabs, smelly adults with matted beards and rags for clothes, entered carrying a large cage of gleaming metal wire between them. Inside was a pair of birds that resembled pheasant but for iridescent blue wings and jet black bodies.

"A rare species from the mountains of my homeland. Their meat is tender and succulent. You may enjoy them as a meal but, as they are male and female, you may also breed them for sport."

"Yes, yes! Birds!" Gratus said and gestured impatiently.

The stranger snapped his fingers once more and two more Arabs more filthy and ragged than the first two entered carrying a basket piled full of a fruit that resembled apples of a yellowish hue.

"A fruit of my native land. Great pains were taken to keep it chilled and unbruised for your enjoyment. It is crisp like your own apples but sweet like pears."

"Hm." Gratus was unable to conceal how underwhelmed he was.

A single Arab was summoned and in his hands he held a slender ceramic bottle decorated with exquisite relief sculptures in iridescent blue of elephants and deer and monkeys.

"The wine of my land. It is crushed and fermented from a rare berry found only at the highest reaches of the ranges that ring the place of my birth. It brings comfort and relief from pain and remorse."

Gratus sat wrinkling his nose at the bottle as it was placed on the corner of his desk.

"And my last offering." The dark stranger clapped his hands once and yet another pair of odiferous Arabs entered bearing a rolled carpet on their shoulders.

"A carpet," Gratus said dryly. What was the obsession of all these black bastards with carpets? He had enough moldy rugs gifted him to cover the road back to Rome with their ornate hideousness.

The Arabs jerked at the binding ribbons and lifted one hem of the rug causing it to unravel, suddenly depositing a figure onto the floor of Gratus's office. A boy. A naked boy with tawny skin and flawless of limb with a shock of silken hair as black as a raven's wing. The boy rose to his knees and peered up at the stunned prefect with bold eyes that vowed for a passionate heart. Gratus felt breathless.

"As Cleopatra was delivered to your own Julius," the stranger proclaimed without irony or drama.

"Yes, yes..." Gratus said and reached out hands to take the boy's to help him to rise to his feet.

"I trust you are pleased, munificent Prefect," the stranger said and bowed his head.

"I am. Most pleased. But what is this in aid of? What do you anticipate in return for such generosity?" Gratus said, too enthralled with the vision before him to feel the least bit suspicious.

"Only your friendly regard should our paths cross again in business or in society," the stranger said and bowed once more as he backed away to make egress from the prefect's presence.

"Oh, you have it. You most assuredly have it," Gratus said, not turning from the boy's fixed gaze to watch the stranger depart. He could not now even recall the name of the visitor with the too-perfect smile.

Gratus awoke late the next day in a state of euphoria he could not explain. His sleep had been deep and dreamless and quite sudden. He had the new boy brought to his bed where they shared the strangely bottled wine—Gratus insisting the boy drink a full measure before his lips would touch the cup. This was the land of Herod and one must always be cautious when taking food or drink from an unfamiliar source. The boy became dreamy-eyed but there was no further ill effect and so Gratus drank greedily from the thick, sweet wine. Its effect was almost immediate and Gratus settled back on his bed as though carried on the wings of doves and watched the world swirl close about him while the splendid boy explored his body with daring hands.

And that was the last he could recall of the evening before. He awoke as though still in the embrace of the spirit's charms. He was warm within and cool without and had not a worry in the world. Certainly not at all like the rude awakenings he'd experienced on other mornings following a night of drinking. The haze of comforting bliss stayed with him even as he rose to find the corpse of the magnificent boy lying contorted and pale as a ghost on the floor at the foot of his bed. The lad lay with glassy eyes and foam flecked lips, his lifeless hands gripping the nap of the carpet that had served as his vessel.

The prefect stumbled naked about his house, aware that he should be alarmed but feeling untroubled by his discovery. A physician was summoned but found no symptom of poisoning in evidence but for the wild aspect of Gratus's eyes. The boy, the physician surmised, died as a result of ill favor from the gods.

Gratus thought no more about it beyond regret over not being able to recall what had occurred between himself and the gifted boy. Ravilla, his ever-present lictor, insisted that it was an attempted poisoning and that the strange visitor of the day before be brought before them to answer for his actions. Gratus acceded to this only to remove the noisome lictor from his presence.

No evidence was found of the visitor but soldiers located the Arabs who served in his caravan and brought them back to the palace where they were scourged and finally strangled with ropes. They knew nothing of the stranger except that he hired them in Seythopolis to carry him and his goods west to Caesarea. He paid them generously in silver and released them from his service. Beyond that they knew nothing and each went to their deaths protesting the same.

That was the end of the matter, or so Gratus believed.

Two nights later he made for his bed with a pair of his most treasured slaves to find a bottle much like the one given him by the stranger resting on a table. It was decorated as before in blue relief depicting jungle cats this time. And this bottle was smaller by half than the one before. He called the servants together and questioned each one. Not a one had any idea how the bottle had come to be in the prefect's rooms. He dismissed them all, even the pair he'd intended to bed.

Gratus's thirst and the memories of the delicious rapture the wine created in him overcame his trepidations. He poured a few sips into a cup and tasted it cautiously. It was thick and sweet as he remembered. He could feel the warmth of it creeping into his limbs and poured himself a more generous serving, draining the smaller bottle, and surrendered to the enveloping effect of the draught.

He awoke the following morning feeling the same jocund drowsiness as the time before and spent the day idly lying upon a chaise watching the shadows grow longer along the walls of the courtyard. The lictor tried to engage him in the business of the day but Gratus only waved him away to return to his study of the clouds scudding overhead like his own personal parade.

That evening he went to his bed chamber alone to find a new bottle upon the table. This one was even smaller than the night before and encrusted with images of braying donkeys. Gratus snickered at the jest though it held no significance to him. He drained the bottle in three long swallows and fell back upon the bed to plummet into Elysium.

This went on for several days. Each night a new, though increasingly more diminutive bottle was found on his bed table. And each day he felt the effect of the draught less and less as the volume of the bottles shrank.

The seventh day passed in distracted ennui and all the prefect could think of was the coming of night and his new bottle of the healing tonic. But that night he entered to find the table bare of a bottle of any size. On hands and knees he crawled about the floor looking for a vessel of any kind and found none. Exhausted, he dropped into a fretful sleep and was awake before the light of dawn tinged the mountains to the east. His mood was in stark contrast to the prior days. He was short with the slaves and even cuffed a body servant hard enough to draw blood from the boy's mouth. Gratus felt an unease as though stalked by a nameless dread. He was physically uncomfortable as well, alternately flushed and chilled, and had the disturbing sensation that his skin was growing tighter.

The following days and nights were hell made real as the prefect was racked with intense pains in his limbs and a crippling agony in his gut. He would not eat as all tasted like ashes no matter how sweet or seasoned the servants prepared it. He could not sleep or even sit or lie down for prolonged periods. His hands shook and his head pounded and no amount of wine would relieve his torment. Gratus's mind shrank to the solitary focus of those tiny bottles and his overpowering desire to feel their effect once more or die.

He lay on his couch, writhing in a lake of sweat,

when Ravilla entered to inform him that the mysterious stranger had returned to seek a second audience.

The prefect staggered into his office with hands clawing for the stranger who was standing cool and immaculate before him. Gratus fell to his knees before the man and begged for the gift of another bottle of the elixir.

"Honorable Prefect! Remember your station!" Ravilla cried in alarm but Gratus groveled and snuffled and kissed the hem of the stranger's robe.

"He does not wish your counsel," the stranger said boldly to Ravilla.

"Then perhaps the legate in Antioch will listen to me," Ravilla said, taken aback by this dark bastard's effrontery to an official and citizen of Rome.

"He will never hear you," the stranger said and withdrew his hand from within his robe to reveal a strange object in his fist. It gleamed darkly, a stubby rectangle of unknown design or purpose. Ravilla smirked as he looked into the circular hole in the device held out at him in the stranger's upheld grasp.

Ravilla began to ask how the stranger meant to prevent him when a sudden crack of thunder filled the room. The lictor felt something tap him in the chest and looked down to see a crimson blot spreading across the front of his white tunic. He raised his head to ask a second question but this was cut short by a second clap of thunder that went unheard by Ravilla as his skull flew apart.

Prefect Valerius Gratus took no note when the lifeless form of the lictor dropped to the tiles behind him. He was aware only of the agony twisting his innards and the man standing before him who could bring a cessation to his suffering. He felt the man's fingers grip his hair and pull his face from the cloth of the man's robe. Even Gratus's deadened senses could smell the stink of sulfur in the air.

"The wine is laced with a substance gifted to me by the god Morpheus," the stranger said in a soothing voice.

"You have more?" Gratus quavered.

"Much more. All you could want."

"What must I do to get it?" Gratus was weeping openly, his hunger was so great.

"Anything I ask," the stranger said and smiled revealing such teeth as must only be seen on Olympus.

Our Lunch With Samuel

"We have a lot of questions," Dwayne said.

"I don't have a lot of answers for you," Samuel said.

"And why don't I believe that?" Dwayne said.

"Can we start with why you're here?" Caroline said.

The restaurant remained empty except for wait staff preparing tables for the early dinner crowd. A carafe of chilled wine had been brought to their table along with a plate of finger food as ordered. Neither were touched.

"I need a favor," Samuel said.

"It's the least we can do after you saved our asses," Dwayne said.

"In the future," Caroline said.

Samuel said nothing. Caroline studied him. He was older than she first thought in their encounter somewhere in the days to come. The way he moved with the easy vitality of an athlete made her think he was perhaps in his twenties. But she could see now that he was older by ten years or more than that. Perhaps he was one of those lucky people who never quite looked their age.

"I wish you'd forget that," he said after a while.

"Kind of hard, buddy. Any tips on the Super Bowl? The Derby? Google?" Dwayne said.

"I can't help you with any of that even if I knew what you were talking about."

That gave Caroline a chill for some reason.

"So, this favor. It involves our special little machine, right?" Dwayne asked.

"It does. I need your team to make a trip. And soon."

"When and where?" Caroline said.

"The year 16 AD on your calendar. September. The location is Syria. Your device is located at this time in the eastern Mediterranean, am I correct?"

"On the money," Dwayne affirmed though he had a strong suspicion that Samuel already knew that or he wouldn't be here. He too studied this strange man with the pond green eyes. He reminded Dwayne of someone—someone Dwayne knew well. It was in the simple mannerisms and the way he held his head. Dwayne couldn't put his finger on it.

"You are perfectly situated for a manifestation on the coast of what is now Lebanon but in the year to which you will be traveling is the Syrian province of Rome," Samuel said.

"You say that like it's a trip to Atlantic City," Dwayne said.

"I would not ask but there is little choice and no time for an alternative strategy. You are in the unique position of being able to make a change for the better and thwart the plans of our mutual enemy."

"Sir Neal Harnesh," Caroline said.

"You seem to be able to pop up where and when you want, Sam. Why can't you handle this?" Dwayne said.

"I am alone. This requires a team effort to make happen. I would go along with you but that is not possible under the prevailing conditions."

"What's Harnesh up to in Roman history?" Caroline asked. She let the "prevailing conditions" remark pass.

"You must trust me on this. Sir Neal is something far more than you realize; far more than I told you the last time we met. He is, in effect, building a new future from the past. His grand scheme is to alter the history that you know in an attempt to create a world that he alone controls."

"Hold on. I thought this whole Butterfly Effect thing was bullshit," Dwayne said.

"There is a lot you do not understand. Effects in time are mostly local, confined spatially as well as temporally. They are like ripples on the surface of a defined body of water. The cause remains below the surface even though the ripples are gone. But the effect is only felt about the original causal event."

"You're right, Sam. I don't understand it." Dwayne shrugged.

"I get it. I'll explain it to you later, honey," Caroline said.

"With crayons and colored paper?" Dwayne said and reached for the carafe to fill a glass.

"So, paradoxes aren't created by altering the established timeline," Caroline said to Samuel. "You're saying that the continuum repairs itself in some way."

Dwayne took a long slug of red.

"Yes," Samuel said. "Otherwise each tiny occurrence that disturbed the past would have massive, catastrophic effects going forward and each excursion would cause more compounding alterations creating a chaotic environment for the traveler to return to, eventually resulting in a 'present' in which the traveler either no long existed or could not return to either because the means of his own conveyance was never created or he was simply never born."

Dwayne drained his glass and poured another.

"Then how the heck is Harnesh going to alter the past to his own advantage if none of the events impact his version of the future?" Caroline said.

"Because there are key moments of shift in the past; personalities or events that, if changed in any permanent way, would change the course of the time stream causing a split, an alternate reality branching away from the original to create a new timeline significantly different for the set pattern. Sir Neal has chosen such a moment that, if changed, will be a step toward creating that parallel existence that will be in his control."

"That's all just theory," Caroline said.

"Is it?" Samuel said and regarded her with those tarnished green eyes.

The chill returned only deeper and more intense. She shivered involuntarily. She took the glass from Dwayne's hand and drained it to the dregs.

"The baby. I thought..." Dwayne started.

"Trust me, daddy. The baby needs a drink too," Caroline said and poured a fresh glass while Dwayne spoke.

"Okay, so Harnesh has picked a big moment to go back to and fuck with the past. I get that. But what's his pick? When are we going back to?"

"Think about it, dumbass," Caroline said, setting the again-empty glass down. "The year Sixteen. Anno Domini. The Middle East. Romans."

Samuel said nothing.

Dwayne said, "Jesus Christ."

"Bingo," Caroline said and handed him a freshly filled glass and waved the waiter over for more.

Nazareth, AD 16

The march from the sea was the most arduous portion of the military action. Even though it was more leisurely than the soldiers were accustomed to as the prefect insisted on accompanying the legion. His litter and baggage train slowed them to a crawl and there were frequents rests. Even so, it was cruelly hot and they lathered under their armor.

At the end of their march the XXIII Legion Judaea reached the town of Nazareth under their own banner: a rearing bronze stallion even though they were strictly a foot unit. They marched down a hill road through a sadly parched fig orchard and into the bowl in which the miserable collection of hovels sat. Orders were relayed and they formed up in a square within sight of the crumbling wall that enclosed the village.

As was their custom, they immediately set about with mattock and spade to erect an earthwork square to fortify their camp. It was hard work after the dusty march but they were accustomed to it and each man dug and lifted to clear his own area of sand as long and wide as he was tall. Some of the old horses made the tired joke that they were digging a grave for two—one for the man they were and one for the man they would never be.

Decimus Munatius Purpurio, tribune of the XXIII, saw personally to the construction of the prefect's tent. He stood with his cloak about him to keep dust from his polished goatskin armor as he directed the men to speed. The armor was his finest dress outfit, kid leather lightened with lye and trimmed in silver. It was magnificent but showed every spot of dust like blood on a virgin's gown. The prefect's tent was an expansive contraption of colorfully striped cloth in comparison to the rough canvas tents the soldiers billeted in when, that is, they did not sleep in the open beneath ground sheets. Valerius Gratus himself remained within the draped interior of his litter to escape the sun and the dust.

The prefect was appearing and behaving oddly since last Purpurio saw him. The man was ever an odious pervert but now he took on the aspect of a dying man. He was lean to the point of emaciation with sallow skin and eyes that twitched like a rabbit's at bay. And Gratus's mental disposition was troubling as well. The tribune questioned the need and purpose for this current campaign and was shouted to silence by an angry Gratus. Purpurio considered sending a letter to the legate in Antioch detailing his doubts about the prefect's fitness for the post. He decided against what could turn out to be a rash move that might jeopardize his career. If these mad plans of the prefect's went to shit, Purpurio would remain unsullied. He was only following the orders of his superior as any good soldier was supposed to, was he not?

The town was not much to see. It was one of the purely Jewish towns, simply packed to the guard walls with the foul creatures. The houses were close to one another and each in need of a fresh coat of wash. The place stank as well. The smell of rancid piss reached the Roman camp from the tanneries at the far end of the place. There was either carpentry work or fresh construction going on within the walls as the sounds of saws and hammers could be heard even before they were within sight of Nazareth. One of the temples dominated the center of the town and was the only well-kept structure in sight. The burnished bronze dome atop its roof gleamed red in the setting sun. They'd enter the town tomorrow and Purpurio only wished he'd brought a horse so he would not have to soil his boots by trudging through their filthy streets. He considered for a moment being carried within the gate on a litter of his own but rejected that idea. In his current state, Prefect Gratus might react poorly to such a display of hubris.

The tent was erected and the stumbling prefect helped within by a gaggle of his pretty boys. Purpurio walked the earthworks to make certain they were up to form. It was night before the camp was complete and a heavily salted soup served to the hungry men. The tribune satisfied himself with cold lamb strips, dried apples, and a cup of wine before retiring to his own tent.

Tomorrow promised to be a long and tedious day.

The town smelt even worse within the walls. Tribune Purpurio kept a cloth soaked in vinegar handy to hold before his nose to take the stink from his nostrils and taste from his tongue. A greasy clinging smoke from cook fires created a fog in the narrow lane leading from the main gate. The odor of feces and urine, from goats and Jews, rose out of every alley and all was overhung by the dense stench from the tanneries.

With an aquilifer holding the legion banner aloft, he led the bulk of the XXIII to the dusty open square that lay before the temple. A token force was left behind to protect the encampment and as a personal guard for the prefect who remained asleep in his tent despite the late morning hour.

Such precautions were mere gestures, in Purpurio's opinion. There would be no trouble from these peasants who lined the streets watching the passage of the soldiers with the idle interest of sheep. The tribune wondered how these could be the same people who millennia before came screaming out of the hills to the north to build an empire of their own in these lands. They were crushed into submission after years of occupation by the Syrians, then the Greeks, and now the might of Rome. They were not sheep, he decided upon fresh appraisal, they were whipped dogs.

The soldiers, urged on by shouts from their centurions and echoed by optios, entered the area before the temple and formed in ranks four deep and twenty across in a hollow square of men and steel filling the center of the rutted square. Children followed along after the Romans until they were shooed away, urged to speed with taps from spear butts.

Purpurio strode through the settling cloud of dust raised by the hobnailed passage of his men toward the temple doors. His aquilifer, sweating beneath a wolf's head cowl, trotted after. His prime centurion, a gruff old lifer named Bachus, met him at the foot of the temple steps.

Bachus climbed the steps, drawing his sword. He beat upon the doors with the butt of his sword. The waiting Romans were rewarded a moment later by the creak of hinges. A bent old Jew shambled blinking into the sunlight. He wore a simple robe and a ludicrous cap balanced on his head. He was heavily bearded and appeared to Purprurio to be peeping from within a snowy hedge. He shared this thought in Latin with his aquilifer, who chuckled. Following the old man was a younger man with dark hair worn long under a skull-cap of white cloth. This one had eyes as alive as the old man's were insensible. The elder was the high priest and de facto headman of this town but the tribune suspected that it would be this younger man, with the eyes of a hungry wolf, that he would be speaking to.

"Greetings from Emperor Tiberius and the people and senate of Rome," Purpurio said in a rote manner. He was already tired of this farce.

"What brings the armies of the emperor to our city?" the younger man said. The old man remained mute.

"City?" Purpurio scoffed. "We are here under order of Valerius Gratus, the prefect of Judea, to see to the collection of all men within this... 'city' between the ages of fourteen and twenty years."

"Collection?" The young man spoke passable Latin for a native Jew. "To what purpose? You know that Jews are exempt from military conscription under edict from Herod Antipas."

The centurion snorted at that.

"Conscription?" Purpurio sneered. "As if I would pollute my ranks with your kind."

"Herod Antipas..." the young man began.

"Enough with your Herod," the tribune shouted. The Jews despised this Herod and his brothers as traitors to their faith yet invoked their names whenever they felt they were wronged. And they were perpetually wronged in their own eyes and never failed to be vocal about it. Purpurio always found Greeks the most argumentative until, gods help us, he met his first Jew.

"You will call the men of ages fourteen to twenty years as though to prayers," the tribune said. "You keep rolls of your followers along with their ages accurately demarked. I know this. I want those rolls presented to me. I shall check your numbers against the total of the men we count."

"Will we not be told of the reasons for this?" the young priest said.

"How old are you, lad?" Purpurio said smiling.

"I am twenty-two in years," the young priest said, his dark eyes flashing.

"I hope you can prove that," the tribune said, turning away.

A ram's horn was blown from the roof of the temple and the people of the town came to the temple square to gather at the steps. It was a mob of several hundreds of men, women and children. They shifted uneasily under the gaze of the surrounding soldiers leaning on heavy shields all about. The sight of a cloaked Roman officer standing atop the steps by their rebbe and his young student did nothing to calm them. The student held a book open in his hands that all recognized as the town ledger of Nazareth. This was all looking more ominous with each passing moment. A shouted order from behind the ranks of soldiers and the armored men took one step forward to further hem the crowd in.

The tribune stood on the highest step and looked over the mob pressed before him. He took a rough mental tally. He barked at the young man who called for silence in their language. When they had hushed, the tribune barked again and the young student called out again telling all women and children beneath the age of fourteen to return to their homes and school. When the square was occupied by men only, a Roman with a high-crested helmet called an order and the surrounding troops, as one man, took another step forward. Those that remained were pressed closer in upon one another.

The young man echoed another order from the Roman atop the steps that sent all men over the age of twenty back to their homes or mills or tanning. The crowd shrank by a third, leaving perhaps near a hundred men standing in a loose collection. The centurion called once again and the troops stepped three paces closer to form a seamless hedge about the men.

"These rest go with us," tribune Purpurio stated flatly and descended the steps.

The young man stood silent.

"Tell them!" Purpurio growled.

The young man left the old priest and walked down into the square and shouldered through the encircling soldiers. He joined the men and boys waiting there. He spoke to them in their own tongue. They would go with the Romans without protest or attempts to flee. Any trouble to their Roman masters would result in reprisals against their families.

The soldiers formed up in two columns before and behind the crowd of men and, following series of bayed orders, marched to the town gate with their charges between them.

The dark-haired student priest stepped along with the Nazoreans, offering prayers and comforting words. He walked with the village ledger beneath his arm.

The prisoners were brought into the Roman camp. The tents had been struck to create an open space. The men and boys were gathered at the center with soldiers standing at ease about them. A table was brought from the prefect's tent and set up with a camp chair for Titus Brocious, the prefect's new lictor, to sit. The ledger was taken from the young priest by the tribune and offered to the lictor who opened it to the current tally of male villagers with their birth dates marked in a column by their names. The young priest stood at his side offering assistance with the pronunciation of names and the numbers of the obtuse Jewish calendar. Lictor Titus had a sheet of vellum prepared to set down his own tally of the captives.

The prefect remained in his tent with his boys. Purpurio wondered if he was awake even though the sun was climbing to its highest point.

Names were called and written on the vellum sheet in Titus's careful hand. The soldiers were spelled by ranks and allowed a cup of watered vinegar and a handful of dried fruit. The tribune sipped diluted wine poured by his aquilifer. It was as tedious a process as Purpurio had anticipated.

At the end, when the last name was called and the final Jew had stepped forward, there was a discrepancy of six names between the ledger and the freshly penned list on the lictor's sheet.

The young priest was questioned but had no answers.

The tribune summoned old Bachus forward and told him to take three centuries into the town and find the six fugitives. The prisoners were ordered to sit on the ground. The remaining soldiers stood guard over them, leaning on shields and speaking quietly. The young priest was in agitated conversation with the lictor. Troublesome damned Jews, thought Purpurio, and repaired to his tent until Bachus returned with the slackers.

The troops dispatched to the town returned at sundown with only four of the missing six. Bachus reported that they indeed found all the fugitives but were forced to kill two as they resisted capture. A third man and a woman were killed as well when they protested the taking of their son. Bachus candidly added that the town was in a bit of an uproar since their young men were taken. The soldiers left under a hail of stones thrown by some of the town's children. The centurion decided to withdraw his men rather than make an issue of it.

"Best that you did," Purpurio agreed. "You'd be half the night pursuing the little bastards through that labyrinth. And even then not come up with one of them."

"Aye, sir." Bachus nodded. "What of the four we found?"

"Ligatures for them," the tribune sniffed. "They'll be the first to die."

The four miscreant Jews were dragged before the others and strangled with bow strings until their tongues turned black and legs ceased kicking. A moan of terror rose amongst the Jews and they backed from the executions until halted by the spear points at their spines.

"What is this?" The young priest rushed forward spouting his atrocious Latin.

"What did you think this was?" Purpurio snarled. "I told you they were not to be conscripted. To what other purpose do you think we would put this filthy lot? They are to be executed."

"By whose order? What have they done?" the young priest cried, turning to the lictor crossing six names from his list with the stroke of a stylus.

"It is by order of the prefect Gratus and therefore the Syrian legate and through him the command of Tiberius Rex himself!" Purpurio said heatedly.

"I would speak with this prefect!" the young priest proclaimed.

"What is your name, Jew?" the lictor asked, stylus poised above vellum.

"I am Yusef Kayifas."

The lictor spelled the name as best he could at the bottom of his tally.

Joseph Caiaphas.

Titus wished to recall the name of this Jew. He was intelligent yet pliable, qualities valuable in the law and politics. A political Jew of some standing might be of use one day to Titus either in his service as lictor or in any higher post he sought.

"I am of the priestly course of the Sadduccees and so passively interested in the affairs of Rome. I offer no offense other than to ask for what crime these men will be murdered!" Kayifas demanded.

"Executed," came a quavering voice.

Valerius Gratus exited his tent, walking like a man twice his age. His eyes shone black as polished ebony and his skin appeared like candle-lit parchment in the failing sun.

"They are to be executed for crimes against the Empire," Gratus said, stepping up to Kayifas and holding himself in a parody of the decorum expected from a man of his station.

"What crimes?" Kayifas demanded.

"They are Jews. And Jews cause no end of trouble. These will be done away with as a reprisal for those crimes; as an object lesson in the dangers of defying the will of Tiberius and all who hold his imprimatur." Gratus's voice trailed away at the end into a wracking cough.

"But execution." Kayifas stepped closer to the prefect. Purpurio made to grab the Jew's arm but Gratus waved him away.

"Allow him to speak, Tribune. These Jews provide

me distraction with all their talk and his accent is amusing for now." Gratus tittered. "Tell us, Jew. What alternative do you offer?"

"They might be sold as slaves," Kayifas offered. "Near a hundred able young men you hold here. They are worth a fortune to flesh traders."

Gratus's eyes swam in his head at this. He put a hand to the back of the lictor's chair to steady himself.

The wily young Jew had discerned the weakness in their prefect, Purpurio realized. He suspected this current action was motivated by a payment of some kind. Now Gratus's mind was whirling with the possibility of compounding the graft in his purse with the sale of these captives.

"You speak well and you speak plain, Jew." Gratus nodded slowly. "I will sleep upon this decision. These prisoners live until morning at the very least. We shall see with the sun's rise whether my mercy will be further strained."

With that the cagey old pedophile stumbled back to his tent.

Kayifas turned to the huddled men and spoke honeyed words. Each man dropped to his knees, keening prayers in their mongrel language until shouted into silence by Bachus. The soldiers laughed at this. Purpurio ordered the prisoners be hobbled with lengths of rope and be fed a single bowl of watered gruel. A full sentry would be kept that night to prevent escape.

Late the following morning, prefect Gratus stepped from his tent to pronounce that the captives would be marched across Galilee to the slave market in Philippi. Three centuries of the XXIII would take them there along with the lictor Titus to see to the sale. Those men would be paid a bonus from the proceeds of the sale with the balance going into the coffers of the prefecture.

The remainder of the legion, under command of the tribune Purpurio, would see the prefect and entourage safely back to his palace.

The young prisoners—tanners, metalsmiths, orchard workers, students, and carpenters—were unhobbled and marched from the camp under guard to follow the road north to Syria and slavery.

The prefect watched the growing dust cloud with what Purpurio thought was a fragile smile of avarice.

THE OCEAN RAJ, SOMEWHERE SOUTH OF CYPRUS

Morris Tauber was incredulous at the level of credulity his sister expected from him.

"You expect me to believe this?" He laughed.

"With everything we've been through the past year I would have expected you to have a more open mind," Caroline said.

"Having an open mind doesn't mean I can't still be analytical, Sis. I can be broad-minded and still know sheer insanity when I hear it."

"Samuel saved us from those Harnesh guys who took us to the future. *To the future*, Mo! You believe that, right?"

"I believe that. As incredible as it is, that's the only explanation that makes sense."

"It's not an explanation," Dwayne put in. "It happened. To us. In the future."

They were down in Morris's lab below decks aboard the *Ocean Raj*. It was fashioned from the walls of Conex containers and reinforced by girders welded in place by the ship's crew. To any casual inspection, the main deck and holds below were filled with stacks of the steel cargo containers. But they formed a shell that covered a multi-level lab complex including a control center, mainframe computer cold room, a shielded mini-reactor, and the large chamber where the Tauber Tube rested around its raised walkway.

While the rest of the team vanished to the four

corners of the world, Dr. Tauber remained on board to take advantage of the solitude to fine tune the time-challenging device he and his little sister had created. And, in any case, someone with the know-how needed to keep an eye on the mini-reactor had to be on hand. Parviz and Quebat, the ex-pat Iranians with a fatwa on their heads, were taking a train tour of Scandinavia. Morris monitored their stolen nuclear device.

The big container ship was anchored in international waters well away from the shipping lanes. Boats and his mostly Ethiopian crew were here as well and collecting their paychecks doing light maintenance and spending the rest of their days loafing.

"So, Samuel knows things, Mo," Caroline said. "He's from the future. He's seen stuff we can't imagine and he already knows how the movie ends if we don't act."

"If he can travel through time so easily then why doesn't he do this himself? Why does he need the help of a bunch of wildcat treasure hunters?" Morris said and took at a seat at his computer console and began fiddling with connections inside a CPU tower he'd taken apart.

Caroline grabbed the seat back and yanked him away from the console. She spun him in the chair and leaned on the arms to put her face inches from his.

"We're off the grid, brother. Our movements through space and time are unaccounted for by Sir Neal and his people. They *know* about Samuel and it's all he can do to stay one step ahead of them. I'm not asking you to *believe* anything. But this is major or I wouldn't be asking you to set it up. It's important and we need to do it."

"But those men on Rhodes who took you and Dwayne," Morris said quietly. "They knew about us."

"And they're dead," Dwayne said. "For them, the trail went cold right there. That timeline is a dead end for Harnesh and his group. We are still off their radar."

"Have you asked the other Rangers if they want to involve themselves in this? There's no treasure this time," Morris said.

"We haven't put it to them yet." Dwayne shrugged. "But they have plenty of cash. They might agree to a freebie. I know Jimmy will. He's still disappointed he bailed on our last outing."

"Well, we still have operating capital. So, if you can convince the others..." Morris said.

"I love you, bro!" Caroline leaned closer and kissed him on the forehead.

"Only because I always give in to you eventually," he said as she stood up, releasing his chair to roll back.

"It's the basis of our relationship." She grinned.

"If this Samuel really knows about future events, did you ask him any questions?" Morris said.

"Like what?" Dwayne said.

"Like whether Sis is having a boy or a girl."

With a groan, Dwayne smacked himself on the forehead.

Berne, Switzerland

The guys agreed to meet Dwayne in Berne and Caroline finally agreed to check into the private clinic there.

"I don't like hospitals," she said.

"It's more like a resort, babe," he assured her. "You put your feet up and concentrate on making our baby."

"I like making our baby but I don't want to *be* babied," she said before he left her in the lobby in the care of a concierge.

"Give it a chance. I'll be back in three hours," he promised and went back to the limo.

After being shown around her private suite, a needle hot shower followed by a massage, pedicure, and lunch of fruit cup, mahi-mahi bruschetta and herb tea, Caroline decided that being babied wasn't so bad after all.

Lee Hammond booked the Rangers a sub-basement conference room at Von Spettenfried Privatbanc, a very, very private bank in the city. None of them had an account there but the bank's state-of-the-science secure meeting rooms could be rented at ten thousand euro a day. The intense privacy that was once guaranteed by Swiss banks was being slowly eroded by world intelligence agencies and changing finance laws in the United States and other cash-starved world economies. So a lot of the banks were adding to their bottom line by monetizing their greatest asset: secrecy. They opened their super-shielded offices and meeting rooms to high-roller consumers who wanted the nature and attendees of their meetings kept from prying eyes and ears. "You can never be too careful," was their unspoken motto.

The four former Rangers took seats around the black granite-topped table in the windowless room blasted from Alpine bedrock. Bottles of Bitburger Pilsner were chilling in a silver ice bucket on a banquet. A platter of cold meat and cheeses and a selection of breads lay by it.

Dwayne laid out the mission for them.

"Holy shit," James "Jimbo" Smalls said.

Chaz Raleigh spit out a mouthful of his sandwich.

"This sounds like a clusterfuck in the making," Lee said.

"We're in the right place at the right time," Dwayne said. "We're the only ones who can make this happen."

"Sounds like the wrong place and the way-wrong time to me," Lee said.

"I'm in," Chaz said after a swallow of beer.

"You are?" Lee looked at him wide-eyed. "That easy?"

"You ask me if I want to go back and save Jesus," Chaz said. "Yeah, I want to go back and save Jesus."

"Then why not just go back and pull him down off the cross?" Lee said.

"I take you've never read the Bible," Chaz said.

"I read Bill O'Reilly's book. Does that count?"

"No."

"I'll make this plain," Dwayne cut in. "This Sir Neal, the same fucker who nearly had me and Caroline killed, has his own version of the Tauber Tube. He's using it to change the rules. His people are going back in time and affecting key events. Or that appears to be the strategy, anyhow."

"So how does someone kidnapping teenaged Jesus change things?" Lee asked.

"Samuel doesn't think it's a kidnapping. He thinks it was supposed to be murder but there was some kind of fuckery and Sir Neal didn't get what he paid for," Dwayne said.

"Okay," Lee said, waving a hand before him. "This Samuel guy. He's from the future? He knows all this shit for sure? Like it's already happened and he's reading it in yesterday's newspaper. How can we believe all this?"

"Do you believe me? Do you believe me and Caroline entered the field and then showed up four days later in Rhodes with Caroline six months pregnant?"

Lee raised his hands in surrender.

"You may be an agnostic on all this, Lee. But Jesus Christ *did* exist. And even if you *don't* buy the son of God thing, you have to admit that the man influenced the world. A lot. And taking him out of the picture before he's twenty-one means he doesn't walk the road he was supposed to and none of what we know about him ever happened."

"So, no Christmas or Easter," Lee said.

"You can't be this dumb, man," Chaz said with some heat. "Jesus changed the world. We'd still be worshipping trees and shit. There'd be no Christianity or America or nothing. I don't want to *live* in that world, bro. I *won't* live in that world if there's something I can do about it."

"Okay, if this is the real messiah then wouldn't his father be intervening here to make it right?" Lee said. "You telling me this Harnesh guy is fucking with God's plan? And getting away with it?"

"Maybe we're part of God's plan," Dwayne said.

"Avenging angels." Chaz smiled.

"We're on a mission from God," Jimbo proclaimed, speaking for only the second time since the mission was sketched out. "Elwood Blues, right?"

"Whatever changes get made, they'll make a world where Sir Neal calls the shots," Dwayne said. "Whatever this is and whatever it means, it's what that fucker wants. That can't be good for anyone and particularly not us."

"It hasn't changed, has it? We're sitting here talking about Jesus right now," Lee said.

"Because there's still time to change what happened," Dwayne said and lifted a laptop onto the table and opened it. "But there'll be a point where it's too late to fix what's broken."

"We know this how?" Lee said.

"Samuel. It's all way over my head but, the way he explains it, time doesn't act in the cause and effect way that we think it does," Dwayne said as he tapped keys. "He said that traveling back in time is like lifting a sheet from a bed and dropping it back in place. The sheet's in the same position, the fabric is the same but the wrinkles are different."

The three men regarded Dwayne with blank expressions.

"Yeah, I don't get it either."

"Shit, as long as you promise to stop trying to explain it, I'm in too." Lee shrugged. "Color me curious."

"Jimbo?" Dwayne said to the silent Pima nursing a beer at the end of the table.

"And miss a second chance to play gladiator?" Jimbo grinned. "No fucking way, Maximus."

Dwayne turned the laptop so they could see the screen.

"This is our area of operations." Dwayne stood to

touch the screen and bring up details. "Our rescue target should still be in transit from here to here." His finger touched the screen to highlight a winding north/south road that stretched from what was now northern Israel and into southern Lebanon.

"We make an amphibious landing here along the Lebanese coast and move overland to intercept the slave caravan. We swim in or take motorized transport depending on how close Boats can bring the *Raj* to shore without any questions."

"Not many with the IDF patrolling those waters for Hamas," Lee said. "We couldn't have picked a worse time for this op."

"We'll work that out. Now the mission objective is to free all the slaves in that caravan. We are not, repeat not, singling out our primary. One, we have no way of identifying him. Two, we can't risk interfering with the string of events any more than they've already been dicked with. We free the captives and it's up to them from there."

"God's will," Chaz said.

"What kind of force are we looking at? What's our opposition?" Lee asked.

"Roman infantry."

The other three shared a look. Jimbo was grinning ear to ear.

"What's their strength?" Chaz said.

"I have nothing on that right now. Expect at least a century."

"That's a hundred guys, right?" Chaz said.

"Actually, more like eighty," Lee said and the others looked at him. "What? I *read*, all right?

"This caravan, what's their final destination?" Jimbo said.

"Most likely a slave market. Here." Dwayne

touched the screen, zooming on a place called Philippi.

"That sounds familiar for some reason," Chaz said.

"I'm looking at the distances here," Lee said and pointed at the screen. "This caravan has a shorter distance to travel than we do. How do we intercept them before they get where they're going?"

"We'll be on horseback," Dwayne said.

They had all had horse-riding as part of their Ranger training for Afghanistan and even been on a few old school ops in the mountains of the Kush. Jimbo's grin broadened. He'd been practically born on the back of a pony back on the reservation. Chaz was glum. He could ride but he didn't like it. Lee began to ask a question but Dwayne held up his hand.

"The horse situation is being worked out. I promise," Dwayne said.

"Clusterfuck," Lee said under his breath.

"There's a question of languages," Dwayne said, ignoring him. "We all have Arabic but it's the Egyptian dialect. It may not be of a lot of use. Languages change a lot over time. Same for Farsi. They're both old languages but they've changed since then. We'll need to wing it."

"Too bad none of us know a dead language," Jimbo said. "Latin or Hebrew. They haven't changed at all since the time we're going to."

"I may be able to help with that." Lee smiled one of his secret smiles that the rest knew usually meant trouble.

The Stranger Returns

Valerius Gratus awoke with a hand over his mouth. His first thought, upon struggling up from the well of sleep, was that one of his cherubs was being playful. He pushed his tongue between his lips to run it over the palm.

His next sensation was of the hand being swiftly withdrawn followed by the sharp sting of a slap across his jaw. He started awake, sitting up to find a hooded figure dressed in inky black by his bed. The room was dark, the lanterns extinguished. Gratus inhaled to cry out. He felt a hand of alarming strength close about his throat locking all sound within.

The black wraith dropped the hood to reveal the white-haired stranger with one knee on his bed and a hand slowly crushing the life from him.

"I told you to execute them," the stranger—what was his name?—hissed.

The hand leapt from Gratus's throat. The prefect sat up gasping and was then wracked with coughs. The man's hand was like a rope noose.

"Tell me why you defied me. Why you did not do as you promised." The stranger stood glaring at him, eye whites gleaming like pearl in the muted moonlight.

"How could you know?" Gratus managed to croak at last.

"Do you understand the concept of eventualities, Prefect?"

Gratus stared at him dumbly.

"History, all of human existence, is built upon countless moments. Each rests atop another as numerous as grains of sand upon a beach. But these moments are not equal in size nor import. Some are dust motes while others are boulders."

What *was* this madman on about?

"And each one rests upon the other to bring us here, to this very moment, this precise eventuality. By betraying me you began a chain of events leading to this very moment with you unguarded and me considering whether or not I should kill you."

"If I might explain..." Gratus began.

"No more lies. I will not kill you. Not because I do not want to, because, believe me as you believe nothing else in your rotten soul, I most dearly wish to kill you in as prolonged and painful way that I can imagine."

Gratus made no sound but to swallow.

"You will live but only because you are the only means by which I may rectify this catastrophe you have created. You will remain alive as long as you are useful to me as an agent."

"What am I to do?" Gratus asked, no, begged. He would do anything to save his life.

"You will send a runner after the caravan. This runner will carry a message written in your own hand addressed to—who commands the escort taking the slaves to market?"

"Bach—Bachus. Centurion prime to the Twenty-third."

"A message to Bachus. You are to tell him that, no matter what else happens, he must stay with the company of slaves. His soldiers must make certain that none escape. None. That means not one single captive may go missing."

"Yes. Yes. I will have my lictor..."

"You will write it by your own hand. Now. Before me. I will dictate each word."

"Yes. Of course."

"And it must reach the caravan before they reach Philippi. You will choose your fastest runner. And you will pray to whichever of your gods you believe favors you that they make this runner as fleet as a gazelle."

"I will. I swear."

The stranger reached out once more. He made a fist in Gratus's hair and pulled him from the bed. The prefect gained his feet uncertainly before being walked like a disobedient hound from his bed chamber and into his office. His feet barely touched the tiles as he was held painfully aloft by the stranger's grip. Gratus was thrust to his table.

"Write what I say," the stranger growled.

"Um... first might I ask about the wine...?" Gratus tried not to mewl but his voice came out in a broken whine.

"The morphea?" The stranger smiled without humor. "Yes, I have brought more of the wine. It will only be yours if you do as I say."

Gratus's chin quivered and he felt hot tears pool in his eyes. This man was equally his poisoner and benefactor. It sickened even as weak a man as Valerius Gratus that he had come to be in thrall to as cold a master as this. With shaking hand he dipped a stylus in a pot of ink.

"Say on," he whispered and placed the quill upon the vellum.

Another Time, Another Place

"Blue City, Station One in thirty minutes. Thirty minutes to Station One, Blue City."

The loudspeakers in each car repeated the message again in Gallic and then in high German.

The train was passing through a tunnel bored through the base of the mountains for ten leagues in length. The last tunnel before the Blue City. Samuel sat alone in his seat and looked at his ebon reflection in the glass. He chose the late train because he knew it would be mostly empty. The risk was greater traveling at this time. There was no sheltering anonymity of a crowd. His singularity might call attention to itself. But it also made it easier to spot pursuit. And he knew that there were many assigned to hunt him here.

A book lay open but unread on his knee. The Rise of Cnossus in Empire II. It was a boring tome but germane to the task at hand. Cnossus was proclaimed emperor in 1583 a.u.c. Born of a Roman father and Dalmatian mother, the reign of Cnossus and his heirs marked almost three centuries of decline. This dark period led directly to the Third Republic which remained in place for over a millennia until it was replaced in a violent coup followed by a series of military tyrants.

The world was more ordered now. Nationality had been erased in the West. The cities had been renamed using colors to erase any sense of heritage or fealty to past associations of race or heritage. The world was now one without the silly contrivances that held man back before the Age of Science.

You became a citizen either by birth or by bribe. And if you were not a citizen then you were nothing. And you would serve in the mines, fields, and factories that remained out of sight and mind of the citizens in their gleaming cities of steel and glass.

Samuel turned from his reflection to see a man watching him. The man was seated ten rows from Samuel on the opposite side of the car's center aisle. The man turned away after holding Samuel's gaze for a heartbeat. It could be nothing. Samuel studied the man. The watcher was in dark clothing of fine fabric. A crimson collar encircled the man's throat. A patrician then. He was an older man with deep creases in his face that told the truth of his age while the black-dyed hair atop his head was little more than a vain attempt to extend his youth. Despite his age he appeared to be a hard man. Perhaps he earned his way into his class in the military or the guard. He was certainly not born to it. Samuel could tell that by the large rough hands resting on the man's knees.

It was either professional or idle interest that made the man concerned with him. Samuel turned away for a moment. When he turned back the man was watching him once again, boldly appraising Samuel and not caring that his subject was aware of it. It could still be the professional interest that a lawman takes in everyone he sees. And, in the nearly empty car Samuel was naturally a target for appraisal.

Samuel had planned to get off the train at Station Three, closer to his intended target area deep in the heart of the city. But he would alter that and get off at the next stop to see if the hard man followed.

The train emerged from the tunnel and rose toward

the starlight of towers at the city center. Tallest of these was the Castra; the stolid block rising eighty stories above the streets and housing the guardsmen who enforced the will of the current tyrant: Hiram Galba. The towers were limned with blue to acknowledge the name of the city in lights. This was the Blue City. *In Civitatem Hyacintho*. The Castra gleamed darkly with a deeper hue of indigo neon in homage to the uniform of the guard.

The elevated tracks spanned over the low rooftops of plebian homes set in orderly grids about the center. The streets below were dark now. After curfew traffic was restricted to state approved vehicles only. Samuel regretted his decision to take this later train. Better he had joined the early morning crush in the Red City the day before in order to arrive here as just another faceless traveler in the mob.

The train slowed as it glided into the shelter of the station. It came to a full stop and set itself down with a metallic rasp as the magnetic field that supported and propelled it was powered down. He waited until the arrival in Station One had been announced a third time before leaping from his seat for the exit furthest from his watcher.

He sensed rather than saw the watcher rise to follow. The few passengers who had gotten off were already making their way to the escalators that would take them down to the street. This was a fully automated station. No officials were in sight. And, thankfully, no guardsmen either. Samuel walked swiftly from the train and crossed the platform to slide his plastic travel pass over the sensor at the exit kiosk.

The kiosk's speaker beeped. The circular datum screen lit up to inform him that he was exiting in error. His pass was for travel to Station Three, Blue City as his final destination. The bars of the exit kiosk remained closed. He ran the pass over the sensor again. The screen blinked and reiterated its original message. The bars stayed closed.

An ozone smell reached him. He glanced to see that the train had shut its doors and was rising on its electrified field for departure. The watcher stood alone on the platform regarding him. Samuel slid the pass over the glass plate again. A human voice came on the speaker and asked him to please wait until an attendant could arrive to assist him. The voice asked him his full name, province, and departure city.

"Remember to speak clearly and include your prenomen, nomen, and cognomen. Help will be with you momentarily."

He threw himself over the exit bars, landed on his feet, and ran for the escalators. He heard the scrape of shoe leather behind him. He turned to see the watcher, the hard man, rushing from between the open bars of the kiosk. Of course, a patrician would have a Visa Europan. All doors were open to the privileged.

Samuel reached the head of the bank of descending escalators. All three flights were clogged at the center with the passengers who had exited the train. He changed direction and made for the ascending escalators. They were closed for the night as his was the last train arriving until morning. He vaulted the barrier and lost his footing on the slick metal steps. He tumbled down a few painful steps then gripped the hand rail to right himself.

The watcher was stepping under the raised barrier and trotting down the steps toward him. Samuel rolled over the balustrade separating his current flight from the next. The watcher raced down the steps to catch him. Samuel leapt the next balustrade and landed hard on the escalator steps to find that the steps on this flight had been collapsed for the night leaving a smooth, uninterrupted slide to the bottom. He released his grip and allowed gravity to carry him toward the street exit. He felt an impact beneath him relayed through the metal plates. The watcher was on the slick, inclined surface with feet sliding as he gripped the handrail like a drowning man. His feet gave way and the watcher crashed to the ramp and began a toppling descent in Samuel's wake. The heels of his shoes yipped in protest as the watcher tried to control his slide.

Samuel gave in to the downward momentum, tucking his knees to his chest and slipping down the final length of the four story grade at alarming speed. He left the watcher behind but at a cost.

He reached the bottom of the escalator and skidded under the lower barrier to a painful stop against a wall. He hobbled toward an exit arch only to see a guard vehicle parked at the curb. Two guards, in their indigo uniforms and face-concealing helmets, stood by the armored truck in idle conversation.

Samuel's abrupt arrival and disheveled clothing would be certain to draw their attention. He quickly stepped back into the arch and made his way along the wall toward a row of dark stores within the station itself. He'd made it into the shadows just as he heard the squeaking of the watcher's heels come to a stop on the escalator ramp. Samuel broke into a run. The watcher was sure to alert the guardsmen who would call for backup and seal off the station area.

The entrance to a pedestrian subway opened before him and he raced down the stone steps into a greater darkness. He heard no outcry and no pursuit. Down in the subway he could lose himself in the great mall that lay beneath Blue City. The mall came to life each winter when the deep snows came to the city above. It was high summer now and the place would be mostly deserted and its shops and eateries shuttered. From the mall he could take any number of paths and lose himself in the maze of tunnels that ran in every direction under the streets to every corner of the metropolis.

He slowed to a casual walk. These passageways would be patrolled by night and a running man would draw suspicion. There was enough risk that some bored guardsman might stop him to answer questions simply because he was alone and abroad so late at night.

Samuel was almost to the mall when he heard the scuff of a shoe. Behind him, black shadows pooled between the intermittent electric lanterns mounted on the tile walls. The hard man from the train could be standing in one of those dark places watching him.

Continuing on at a pace that Samuel hoped would make him look like nothing more than a man in a hurry to get home, he trotted into the mall. No footsteps followed.

There were voices from somewhere off to his right. He could not see their source through the forest of support columns spaced across the area surrounding the mall's central rotunda. They were male voices and he heard a tinny electronic response.

Guardsmen.

He slowed to a walk, keeping the columns between him and where he thought the voices were echoing. The words weren't decipherable. One still sounded professional but not urgent. Routine communications perhaps.

Samuel let out a breath and slowed his walk to a deliberate but unhurried stride. He was almost to the exit that would take him up to street level close to his target point. The voices grew fainter behind him, the cavern of the mall swallowing them up.

The man from the train stepped out from behind a column just in front of Samuel. He was smiling easily now. From within his coat he drew a pugio, a broad bladed dagger. Its steel gleamed like quicksilver in the artificial light. A ceremonial weapon given for meritorious service to the empire. No less deadly for its beauty.

The hard man stepped forward, blade held low and free arm up to shield himself. He moved like a man who had been in knife fights before. As he closed, Samuel could see the criss-crossed white of scar tissue across the backs of his hands. This man had survived many encounters like this one. That meant that Samuel could expect to bleed. The first rule of fighting with blades: expect to be cut.

Samuel did not break stride or even slow. He walked to meet his attacker. If this was to end well it would have to end quickly. One outcry and the guards would come running. They were not yet out of earshot. The squawk of the radio voice reached him as a distant echo.

He raised an arm in defense and the watcher stabbed out. The tip of the blade caught metal beneath the fabric of the sleeve and slid off to slash a long tear in the flesh to Samuel's elbow. Before the other man could bring the blade back for a return slash, Samuel ducked under the defensive arm. He drew his own weapon at the same time, a needle-like rondel with a triangular blade. A favorite among Gaulish assassins.

Samuel drove the blade up in a short piston movement to puncture the soft flesh behind the point of the other man's jaw. He could feel the impact then yielding through the ivory handle as the force of the point punctured the man's palate and drove into the soft meat of the brain. Samuel gave the dagger a savage twist. His opponent went limp. Samuel embraced the man to take his weight and lowered the corpse to the tiles without a sound. Even in death the man kept a grip on his own blade so that it did not fall to create a clatter on the tiles.

He wiped his blade on the dark fabric of the man's clothing and returned the rondel to the scabbard cleverly concealed in the lining of his jacket. He then plucked the pugio from the man's dead grip. Standing astraddle the corpse, Samuel thrust the point of the pugio into the man's throat to follow the path of the wound made by his own weapon. It might appear to be a suicide long enough for Samuel to accomplish his business in the Blue City and move on.

Taking the dead man beneath the arms, Samuel dragged man into a shadowy recess between two shop fronts and propped him against a wall. He made a quick search of the body. The man wore a medallion beneath his shirt front. A golden bull on a chain. A former soldier and probably a guard when his service was done. He stuck the medallion into the man's slack mouth and left the chain dangling from the teeth. The final gesture of a man faced with no other escape from dishonor.

Samuel stood and inspected himself. There was no blood on him but his own. The other man died too swiftly to bleed. He took his jacket off and draped it over the wounded arm and continued on his way toward his appointment.

As he exited the mall he was joined by the first of the commuters making their way toward their places of work or stops for surface transit. The sun was just beginning to show over the surrounding mountain peaks. A shaft found the head of the massive brass eagle that towered ten stories above the central plaza.

Samuel imagined that the gargantuan bird had its

predator gaze on him alone as he crossed the broad space. There were others walking here as well. He lost himself among them on the way to meet an appointment he was already thirty years late for.

The War Room

Time meant everything when you moved in it. It meant nothing when you moved *through* it.

The Rangers would get there when they got there. They picked a date of September 1, 16 AD for their arrival target back in The Then. That was the Nones of Sextilis by the lunar calendar that the Romans used. That was two weeks ahead of the abduction of the Nazarenes and enough time to get ashore and cover the ground they'd need to cover to set up an ambush along the road which the slave caravan would travel. Jimmy Smalls argued for more time in-country but Dwayne and the other nixed the idea. The less exposure the better. For once Morris Tauber agreed with the Ranger consensus.

That was the last time they'd all agree.

They gave themselves thirty days in The Now to plan, prep and deploy.

Lee handled procuring all the ordnance expect for body armor. Jimbo said he had a guy for that. Boats charted a course for them using their standard bullshit excuse of the *Raj* being a science vessel involved in a study of ocean temperatures. Dr. Tauber managed to locate Parviz and Quebat in Copenhagen. He asked if they could cut their vacation short by a week and return aboard the *Raj* to look after "the baby." The infant in question was the nuclear mini-reactor concealed and shielded in the hold of the container ship.

Boats offered a two-week leave to his crew of Ethiopians. To a man, they opted to stay on. The pay was good and in cash. They all preferred to stay on and build their bankrolls doing needed maintenance on board. His first mate, a wiry man of indeterminate age behind a black hedgerow of beard, was named Geteye. He made sure all hands earned that pay. Every ocean-going vessel had an endless chore list and the *Raj* was not a new ship by any means.

Dwayne and Lee worked up a rough timeline for the mission and presented it to the team for suggestions.

"Not to take a dump in your chili," Boats broke in on the presentation in the *Raj's* chartroom. "But we're going to have to anchor in deep water, guys. The Israelis are all over the Med in the region you want to go into. They're going to be on us at the first sign of fireworks."

"How far off shore?" Lee asked the red-bearded former SEAL.

"Twenty miles or more. And that's cutting it close."

"The surge needed for manifestation looks like a natural weather event for the most part," Morris Tauber offered.

"Those Jews are twitchy, Doc. And they have every right to be," Boats said. "They'll use any excuse to board us and you can bet your ass they'd sweep us for any kind of threat including radiation. And all the explaining in the world wouldn't get our asses out of that."

"We'll make it thirty miles and you can take us in on the motor launch," Dwayne said.

"That means I go with you? *Back* with you?" Boats said.

"I don't see another way," Lee said.

"I'm not waiting with the fucking boat," Boats said.

His usual smile was gone.

"No. You'll be on mission with us. You up for that?" Dwayne said.

"Shit, yeah!" Boats said, the grin returning.

"That will make us five," Chaz said.

"Four," Lee said.

"How do you figure that?" Dwayne said.

"Because you're not going," Lee said and looked at Dwayne flatly. The others shut down to let these two sort it out.

"Bullshit," Dwayne said.

"Caroline will be having the baby between now and mission start. She needs you there. And we would need all of your head in the game. Your head will be with her and the baby. And there's another reason," Lee said.

"Can I ask what that is?" Dwayne's face was darkening.

"If Boats goes back to The Then with us we'll need someone on this side who can go tactical if the shit hits the fan. That will be you." Lee said.

"Makes sense, D," Jimbo said.

"Yeah. It does," Dwayne said. "That's the way it has to be."

But it hurt.

The meet went on for another hour or so with Morris giving his usual warnings about maintaining temporal integrity and the Rangers pushing back with the needs for objective priorities.

"You can't be polluting the past with current technology," Morris urged. "You'll be entering an age closer to our own and possibly be encountering literate inhabitants. Any anachronistic technology you expose them to could be recorded. Dwayne and my sister had a few close calls on their last outing. All risks have to be minimized."

"We tried it your way once, Doc. We got our asses kicked," Chaz said, referring to their first trip to the past when they went with eco-friendly weaponry that failed against an army of man-eating proto-humans.

"The more gear we carry the more chance of success and the least exposure time. The best way to go is to go hard and fast and get the hell out," Lee said.

"Trust us, Mo. We'll take every precaution," Dwayne said, putting a hand to Morris's shoulder.

"Every precaution that doesn't add to our personal risk," Lee added.

A New Member of the Club

A week into mission prep the *Raj* had moved into an anchorage off of Limassol on Cyprus. It was a nothing-special port of call with the usual half-moon of blockish white condos and hotels standing along the shoreline. The container ship sat at anchor in the azure water away from the approach lanes of the big cruise ships that crawled in and out of port daily.

Even though they were not seeking a berth in the harbor there was business to attend to. Boats paid a premium to have a tanker come out to them to top their reserves off with diesel. Customs came aboard and the ex-SEAL sent them away with a few cartons of Marlboros, a case of Ron Rico, and some folding money.

Since the skipper was occupied, Lee Hammond went ashore on the motor launch with a couple of his crewmen to restock their food and freshwater stores. Dwayne Roenbach tagged along to catch a shuttle to Athens and then on to Berne to join Caroline.

Lee returned in the late afternoon with Parviz and Quebat and their luggage. There was another passenger aboard. Lee was at the gangway with a bag under each arm as Bathsheba Jaffe climbed the ladder to the sally port. The crew lined the rails to watch the raven-haired beauty in tank top and cargo shorts come aboard.

"Who's this?" Jimbo said.

"Our Hebrew teacher, bro." Chaz grinned.

*   *   *

"We figure our Arabic will get us by for the most part," Lee said to the Rangers and the SEAL as they shared beers in the captain's quarters with the AC on full. "But some Hebrew would come in helpful. Just a few dozen phrases we can memorize. Directions. Trading. Greetings. Just general tourist stuff."

"I can do that," Bat said. "But you guys don't exactly look like you're in the tribe. And a little of the old language does not go a long way. When things get tight you need to let me do the talking."

"Wait, what?" Lee said.

"I think the lady thinks she's going with us," Chaz said.

"No. Fucking. Way. Ain't gonna happen," Lee said.

"Hold on now. She knows everything?" Jimbo said.

"You mean all about your wayback machine?" Bat said. "Uh huh. Your boy here likes to talk after sex."

"Shit, Hammond!" Chaz slammed his bottle of Luxor on the table, creating a geyser of beer.

"She's all right! I vouch for her!" Lee shouted back; a rare display for him.

"You thought I was going to come out here and hold *shul* for you guys and not ask any questions?" Bat laughed.

"That didn't include an invite to the mission," Chaz said.

"I'm going. You need someone fluent. If you run into serious trouble then 'where is the nearest bathroom' is not going to be much help," Bat said.

"It's not all talk, baby. We're there to run and gun. Can you hack all that?" Chaz said.

"I've got seven years with the IDF. I'm a trained sniper with a Galil and an M14. I've been in combat and I know the country we'll be crossing better than any of you."

"Combat? So you've heard some hostile fire. You have any kills?" Chaz said, locking eyes with her.

"Three confirmed. Lebanon." She met his eyes unblinking and with no resentment. They had a right to know her bona fides.

"And if we don't take you along?" Jimbo said.

"What? I'll tell the world about a bunch of vets traveling through time making trouble in the past? Try and turn you in to the time cops? And have everyone think I'm nuts?" She laughed.

"But we make you stay here and no more sugar for Hammond, right?" Chaz smiled showing plenty of teeth.

"You can bet on that," Bat said, returning the feral smile with gusto.

"Guys..." Lee was not enjoying this turn in the confrontation. He felt like the table had turned against him and he was outnumbered.

"I vote for Bat." Chaz raised his bottle. Jimbo and Boats raised theirs as well.

Hammond shrugged and raised his.

"You're going to need a membership card, girl," Chaz said.

"To your little group?"

"To Jews for Jesus," Chaz said and clinked a bottle with her.

They took stock of the ordnance they had on board. The last mission was a clusterfuck despite its positive outcome but had required no firepower in the end. They still had more than enough small arms and case lots of ammo for each. Jimmy Smalls had a second Winchester Model 70 to loan to Bat. She could familiarize herself with it when they put back to sea. They'd all be putting in some range time then.

The team took to the common room to do regular maintenance on their armory. Bat impressed the guys by stripping down the gifted Winchester, oiling it, and reassembling it within ten minutes. Not bad for her first time with the weapon. She stripped down a Sig P-226 she'd be using as a sidearm. She also picked a 380 Colt snubby from the collection on the long table. A stainless job with no hammer.

"This anyone's?" She raised an eyebrow.

"Mine," Chaz said. "My pocket rocket for party night. It's yours if you want it."

"A girl can't have enough surprises," she said.

"I have a strap holster for it somewhere," Chaz said and sorted through a plastic tub of accessories.

They were all sharing Irish coffee and bullshitting over a table lined with a row of oil-slick rifles and shotguns when Morris Tauber walked in with an empty carafe. He went to the counter and emptied a pot of coffee into it followed by a long stream of sugar. Morris looked like he'd combed his hair with a pitchfork and had a week's growth of ginger on his chin. He rarely came topside and that was usually at night. He was the only one in the room without a deep tan.

"Our Iranian friends settled in?" Lee asked.

"They went right down to the nuke and never left it," Morris said and poured a cup from the dregs. "They're checking levels and running a diagnostic in sandals and shorts. Here's to us nerds, huh?"

He stopped mid-sip and blinked at Bathsheba.

"You're a woman," he said.

"Thanks. You're nice," she said.

"I mean. I don't know you and here I am talking about—"

"She's hip, Mo," Chaz said. "She's coming with us."

"I'm Bat Jaffe. I'm teaching the guys Hebrew."

"Oh. Well. I suppose. Yes," Morris said and retreated, cup and carafe in hand.

"That was the brain behind all this, right?" Bat said.

"One of them. Dr. Morris Tauber, engineer and theoretical physicist," Jimbo said. "But not a whiz at the social niceties."

"He's interesting," Bat said.

"He's gonna get more interesting when that coffee hits him," Boats said. "I put four fingers of Maker's Mark in the pot."

The Order of March

The runner reached the slave caravan where they camped the second night. Or rather, the third runner reached them as the message was relayed from one station to another along the road. Every Roman citizen bragged that these roads allowed a message to travel from any point in the empire to another within two weeks.

The caravan of slaves and their minders had made slow progress yet passed forty mile markers since departing Nazareth the day before.

The runner used his medallion from the *cursus publicus,* the official messenger service authorized throughout the empire, to make his way past the sentries posted about the fortified camp. In the moonlight of the Ides of Sextilis, he trotted along the rows of tents until he found the tent where the centurion Bachus slept. An optio offered to take the packet from the messenger.

"I am under orders of the prefect of Judea to deliver this into the hands of centurion Trivian Bachus and only him," the messenger, a slim boy of fourteen years insisted with the imperious attitude of a Claudian. The boy was a slave and in the hierarchy of the imperium a slave was empowered by the office of his master. Thus the legion optio was obligated to obey this lowly youth as though ordered by prefect Gratus himself.

The messenger was admitted to the tent. The optio spoke softly and the centurion stirred naked on his cot. Bachus sat up with a mumbled curse and took the packet from the runner's hand. It was held closed by a blob of wax embossed with the prefect's seal: a pair of swans with necks entwined. He tore it open and read by the light of a lamp held overhead by the optio.

Ut Cen. Mettius Trivian Bachus
De Valerius Epidus
Gratus, prefectus Judaica

Be warned that word has reached this office of an attack by rebels meant to halt your progress toward Philippi. You are to take refuge at the nearest fortifiable location and arrange for any reinforcements necessary to its defense. At all costs, the lives of the slaves in your charge are to be protected from harm and prevented from escape until further word from me.

The note was in the prefect's own hand. The letters were poorly formed and the words ran together in a way that made them almost illegible. His signature, a simple VEG, was scrawled across the bottom accompanied by another wax seal.

Bachus allowed his optio prime to read the message aloud as he sat at his campaign desk to pen an acknowledgment. The terse words of a soldier were written and sealed with Bachus's legion signet ring; a crude horse beneath the numeral XXIII. The runner was given drink and a place to sleep on the floor of a tent. Bachus dispatched one of his own men to run south to the next station to carry his reply, by relay, back to the prefect's villa in Caesarea.

"What are your orders, sir?" the optio said.

"Dispatch scouts to search the road ahead for a

defensible position," Bachus said. "We'll march at first light to follow. Half rations of water and food for the soldiers. Nothing for the slaves until we reach our goal. I have no idea how long we must hold before relief arrives."

"The Jews must have grown bold to seek to face three centuries on the march, sir."

"Perhaps there is someone in our charge they prize," Bachus said, running a hand over the bristles sprouting on his jaw. "There could be one or more of their leaders among the slaves we escort."

"Then why not execute them all and have done with it?" the optio said bitterly.

"I do not know and I cannot guess. But I know this: Gratus may very well be mad which only means that his commands must be carried out to the letter. I've no wish to incur the wrath of a lunatic with his power and influence."

"And when shall I have the men roused to break camp?" the optio said.

"Now, Sextus," Bachus said, stooping to reach for his boots. "We will march to greet the sun's rise."

Warrior Princess

It was a boy.

After eighteen hours of labor, Caroline Tauber gave birth to an eight-pound, twenty-one inch howler.

"We're not naming him Maximus," she said just before the drugs took affect and whisked her away to Happy Mommy Land.

Dwayne held the squealing red bundle in his arms and just stared.

"What are you going to name it, sir?" a nurse asked him.

"Damned if I know," he said and allowed another nurse to gently pluck his son from his arms to place him in a plastic-walled bassinet and wheel him away. He then numbly followed an orderly back to the suite to await Caroline and his son after the post-op clean-up had been completed.

The biggest flower arrangement he'd ever seen was there on a table. Next to it was a huge teddy bear in Ranger camouflage and sergeant's stripes. He'd phoned Morris when they wheeled Caroline into the delivery room. Plenty of time for his bros to call the order in to a local florist.

He sank down into a chair physically and emotionally drained. He could swear that bear was laughing at him.

"Hooah, Sergeant Teddy."

* * *

"I'm not wearing that," Lee said.

"I had it custom made for this op," Jimmy Smalls said.

"Maybe you want to look like a Dollar Store Spartacus. I'll stick with my Dragon armor," Lee said.

The team was on the main deck of the *Raj* unloading the crates Jimbo had brought back on the launch. The crates were drop-shipped to the port in Limassol care of Praxus Enterprises, the shell corporation the team used as an avatar for their dealing with the outside world. They even paid taxes. Sort of.

"This is the same as Dragon," Jimbo insisted. "Bob Tosches made these up for me at his shop."

"What did you tell him? He must think you've lost your damned mind." Chaz laughed.

"This looks like a fucking dress!" Lee said, holding up something that looked like a skirt fashioned from old school, pre-digital desert camouflage.

"It's a utili-kilt. Guys in construction wear them. The goddamn Scots highlanders wore kilts and they were badasses," Jimbo said. "Besides, they'll help us blend."

"At a gay pride parade?" Lee said in disgust and threw the kilt down.

"Buckles, my man? Where's the Velcro?" Chaz said, holding up a layered torso armor with steel studs in rows.

"It's a *lorica segmenta*. Standard issue for the Roman army. It's better than the shit we wore in Iraq. There's shoulder protection and straps that hang down to protect your balls." Jimbo held up a set of the torso armor manufactured in black Kevlar. "It's layered so it breathes. This shit is awesome. You'll see when you try it on."

"Buckles, bro?" Chaz said, jiggling a belt strap with a steel buckle jangling at the end of it.

"We can't be having Velcro and plastic fasteners back in The Then," Jimbo said. He was losing patience.

"I think they're cute," Bat said and held a set up against her as if she were at Neiman's.

Jimbo sagged.

"You'll look like Xena," Lee snorted.

"And that's a bad thing?" Bat said.

"I think he was talking to me," Jimbo said.

"I'm wearing my BDUs and Dragons," Lee said and walked away forward to the bridge.

"Oh, hell no," Chaz said and pulled a helmet from within a box. Packing peanuts spilled to the deck.

He held the helmet up. It was a recreation of a Roman *galea* in black ballistic cloth over a high-impact plastic dome. It was accented with brass bosses and had cheek guards and a bill at the rear for protection to the back of the neck.

"It's optional, okay?" Jimbo snatched the helmet from Chaz's hand. He didn't mention that he'd ordered greaves to cover their shins as well. Bat laughed.

"Fuck, yeah!" They all turned to see Boats standing in his cut-offs with the retro armor strapped on. With his wild red hair and beard he would have looked at home in the German *auxilla*.

"At my signal, unleash hell," Boats intoned gravely.

Now they all laughed.

Transit: the Med

All personnel and gear aboard, the *Ocean Raj* weighed anchor and moved out into the Mediterranean. They'd take their time to bring the ship to its new anchorage roughly thirty miles off Haifa in waters almost two thousand meters deep. The team would use the transit time to shake down their equipment and make any last minute adjustments to the mission plan.

Most strategies don't survive long once the boots hit the ground. The team worked out countless contingencies and tried to anticipate as many surprises as they could imagine. The law of unintended consequences was squared and then cubed by traveling into the past. Where every op had its share of gotchas, the world of the ancient past was mostly unknown. They would be making landfall at a strip of beach south of what was today the port of Haifa. Back in 16 AD it was Caesarea: the seat of imperial power in Judea. Their research informed them that they could lose themselves in the crowd of a bustling port city and also readily buy the horses they needed.

Of course, their research could be bullshit. One variable and the whole op was turned ass up. The city could be in the grip of a plague or famine. It could suffering the aftereffects of an earthquake or fire. Maybe the legions were there clamping down after a week of riots. They could motor their rubber raft right through an imperial fleet. Doc Tauber worked at fine-tuning the tube but he still couldn't guarantee what time of day they'd pop out—high noon or the middle of the night. They could drop into mirror seas or the middle of a hundred-year storm. There was just no way to know. It was impossible to be prepared for every eventuality but they'd be ready enough to stay flexible when, not if, things went sideways.

They had enough of the Carthaginian coins on board to live like kings in First Century Rome. They'd only take enough to buy mounts and incidentals. Lee Hammond took care of the currency they'd need for paying their way. A few days in a lemon juice solution removed the centuries of patina from the coins so they'd look closer to the right vintage in the eyes of anyone they met back in The Then.

Jimbo rolled a fifty-gallon drum off the lower rear deck of the *Raj*. Bat stood by with one of the Winchester 70s. The sea was as flat and calm as a tablecloth. The sun was low to port making the sea glimmer in copper and deepest green. The ship was moving slow. The barrel rose and fell on the rolling creamy wake.

"Let it drift on out," Jimbo said.

"Okay," Bat said and dropped her Ray Bans onto her freckled nose to cut down the glare off the water. She stood rocking easy with the slight movement of the deck. Three weeks on board and she had her sea legs back. But striking a moving target from a moving deck was still going to be a challenge.

The barrel bobbed away until it was a good two hundred yards out. It was a crimson dot catching light as it dipped and rose in the gentle current.

"Find your target," Jimbo said. He had a pair of binoculars to his eyes.

Bat rode the slight rise of the deck and sighted over the scope to locate the barrel. She lowered her eye to the scope cup. The drum seemed to leap within touching distance.

"Got it," she said.

"All yours then," Jimbo said.

She locked the reticules on the barrel and held that position as the deck fell beneath the soles of her sneakers. Holding her breath, Bat waited until the deck climbed up and the barrel was in view again. She let her breath out slow and squeezed firm and steady on the trigger.

Jimbo saw a geyser of foam six feet in front of the barrel.

"That an honest miss?" he said.

"If you mean, was I on it, I was," she said.

"You're hitting short."

She lowered the rifle and twiddled a dial atop the scope then raised it again to find the barrel now drifting closer to three football fields distant. Breathe in, ride the roll, squeeze.

Through the lenses, Jimbo saw a hole punched in the metal skin of the barrel. The force made the drum take a quarter spin.

"Money," he said with a grin.

She jacked a fresh round and retrained the 30x and nailed the barrel again. Four more times she worked the bolt and brought the crosshairs down and drilled the steel drum clean each time. The barrel was five hundred yards aft on her last strike and sinking low in the water.

"Nice," Jimbo said. "How'd that feel?"

"Like holding my first puppy." She smiled.

"What's your best?"

"In the rings from a thousand meters."

"On a range?" he asked.

"A place called Qana. Took a Hezbollah sapper

through the head," she said and pulled the bolt from the rifle with an expert tug.

"Head shots are a bitch."

"He didn't give me much choice," she said. "I'm going forward to clean the Winchester if that's okay with you."

"Sure," the Pima nodded. "Far as I'm concerned that rifle's yours from now on."

"Thanks." She flashed a smile and walked to a ladder with the rifle under her arm.

Damn, Jimbo thought, Lee better watch his ass around this girl. He wouldn't want to do anything to piss off someone who could shoot like that.

Bat found Chaz in the cabin they used for meetings and as a day room. He had buds in his ears from an iPod and listened to his tunes while running the blade of a combat knife, an eight-inch Bowie type with a brass tang, over the surface of a whet stone.

"What're you listening to?"

"Right now? Gorillaz. Part of a mix," he said.

"They're okay. You like Bonde do Rolê?"

"Brazilian, right? Yeah. I have some of them on here."

"Death to your speakers. Death to your speakersssss..." she growled in an exaggerated basso.

Chaz laughed. Bat poured some coffee from a pot warming on a hot plate.

"Hey, while I'm putting an edge on my blade, you need your knife sharpened?" He nodded to the bayonet in a web scabbard on the belt of her cut-offs.

"Thanks, but I promised my dad I'd always do that." She sat across the table from him, shaking a paper packet of Equal in her fingers.

"A Kabar. Your dad a jarhead?"

"First Marines. Semper fi, do or die. He carried it in Vietnam. He was at Hue City after Tet."

"So that's where you get it," Chaz said.

"My mom's tougher. Public school teacher in Cleveland. She's been in more fights than me *or* Dad." She took a sip.

"So why this fight, girl? You coming along to be with Lee or for the action?"

"A chance to see what you guys have seen? Like I could pass that up? Besides, you could use my help."

"A chance to visit your holy lands the way they used to be. Kind of a pilgrimage."

"Same for you, Chaz. I'm sensing this is more than just another op for you."

Chaz examined the razor edge of the blade in the light from the ceiling lamp.

"My dad was a deacon. Church of Christ. I turned my back on all that," he said, studying the silvery gleam off the polished metal. "Thought I had all the answers. Then I joined the army, got deployed and had my world rocked. I saw shit I couldn't handle; shit that drinking couldn't make me unsee. You have to deal with that, right? Well, I went back to my father and begged for his help. I found peace there in The Word with his guidance. Cancer took him three years back."

"I'm sorry to hear that, Chaz," Bat said.

"It's okay. He went easy. He was right with God. And knowing I was the same gave him his own peace. It was good between us in those last years. I'm thankful for that." Chaz slid the oiled blade into a leather scabbard.

"He must have been proud of you," she said.

"I just wish he could see what we're about to see." Chaz smiled easy. "The way I look at it, Jesus saved me and now I'm returning the favor."

STATION FIVE

The mist was growing to fill the well at the center of the chamber.

The tension was high as the technicians waited for whatever would emerge from the veil of icy mist spreading from the black steel array. Any opening of the field was a cause for anxiety. There were so many imponderables, so many opportunities for disaster. They were, after all, playing with the building blocks of the universe here. What lay beyond the chilling fog, growing denser with each passing second, was no abstract mystery. It was real and it was dangerous.

That's why armed and armored security waited at the base of the ramp with weapons trained and ready for whatever may exit from the field.

To the more learned technicians these precautions were childish. The true horror they might unleash by punching a hole into the fabric of time could not be subdued with bullets or bombs. It was the unimaginable power of existence itself that could suck them all into an endless void or cause them to vanish in an instantaneous torrent of light.

Today the strain was from a more particular, more localized, source.

Sir Neal Harnesh himself was visiting the Gallant Temporal Transference Field Generator at Station Five.

The man in the flesh.

The man who financed the experimentation and the

construction of the facility and recruited the staff at the costs of billions of euros sat sipping oolong in an observation room set in the mezzanine above the well in which the generator sat. No one could recall Harnesh ever visiting before, let alone sitting down to watch the device in operation. He was accompanied by Augustus Martin whom they were familiar with.

It was Martin who descended upon them when they "cocked it up" as he phrased it in his parlance. Like the time they were all herded from the generator well by a gunman and locked out of the facility. When security had cut their way in they found two men dead on the rampway and a control console had been vandalized to the point where it had to be entirely replaced. That was when paramilitary security was brought in from Gallant Security Solutions LTD. From that day on the facility felt more like an armed camp than a scientific operation.

The pressure was on from the plant managers that today's field opening must be flawless.

They worked through each step and felt the palpable frisson of static in the air, raising the hair on scalp and arms, as the initiating jolt from the shielded reactor in the sub-basement powered the carbon steel rings with mega-joules of free magnetic power. The rings vibrated and hummed. A fresh gout of white vapor descended from the ramp. The security men at the bottom of the ramp stiffened. They thrust the butts of their rifles into their shoulders and held the sights unwavering into the cavity of the ring array.

A single figure emerged from the chilled cloud. A man with white hair that was in severe contrast with his deep mocha complexion and silken robes of gold-trimmed indigo. The man wore the costume with authority and gestured impatiently for the guards to lower their weapons as he strode off the ramp. They parted to make a path for him. He stopped to glance up and sighted Sir Neal now standing at a window of the observation room. The robed man climbed the stairs to the mezzanine in a series of eager bounds to be shown into Harnesh's presence.

"Something to drink, Sumesh?" Sir Neal said softly.

"Anything with ice!" the newcomer proclaimed and Gus Martin stepped to a rolling bar cart to prepare a cold drink.

"I take it you have returned with news I will not like," Sir Neal said.

"What is that saying? 'You can't buy an Afghan but you can rent one?'" Sumesh Khan accepted without comment a crystal tumbler filled with an amber liquid in ice.

"I take it then that the Nazarene is not dead," Sir Neale said.

"He is not. Neither are any of them. He has been sold into slavery with all the captives. I have taken steps to make certain that the company he travels in remains together. It would not do to have him sold away to persons unknown and taken to places unheard of." Khan drained a long swallow from the tumbler.

"I wanted to avoid the task of finding and identifying him," Sir Neal said. "I wanted his death to be not a singular event but a statistic."

"They may still all be executed as you wish." Khan gathered the hem of his robe and took a seat. "We have him. It's only a matter of taking a more direct hand."

"Something I avoid when possible. I dislike actions that create interest in me. Though we deal in anomalies, I wish for them to remain unseen and unnoticed."

"Then I will return and see it done," Khan said and held out the empty tumbler for Martin to take.

"No," Sir Neal said. "I have another task for you. Something closer to home. Closer to the present."

"I thought this operation in Judea was priority," Khan said.

"It is. It is at the core of all I have planned. But you know this is a complicated game we play. Time is everything and nothing to us. You will return to Judea another day and it will be as though you were only absent a moment."

"As you wish, of course, Sir Neal. All I ask is to take a hot shower and I am at your complete disposal," Khan said, standing.

"Take all the time you need," Sir Neal said with a trace of a smile.

Sumesh Khan departed with a swirl of his dark robes.

"I don't like him, sir. He's dangerous," Augustus Martin said when Khan was out of earshot on the other side of the heavily insulated door.

"Said one predator of another," Sir Neal said. "It is that precise attribute that makes yourself and Mr. Khan valuable to me."

At Home

"Stephen. I like it," Dwayne said.

"It was my father's name." Caroline was smiling, beaming really, where she reclined in the bed nursing their son. The sun that streamed into the room seemed to be shining just for them. Dwayne couldn't remember being this happy or this at peace.

"Then your brother will like it, too," Dwayne said, standing by her and holding her hand.

"You're sure? You don't want to make a suggestion?" she said.

"I thought maybe Richard for his middle name."

"For Rick Renzi?"

"Yeah," he said and squeezed her hand.

They both thought that fitting. Rick Renzi was one of the Rangers who went with Dwayne and the others through the Tauber Tube to prehistoric Nevada to find Caroline and return her to the present. Renzi stayed behind to man a machine gun and cover their escape against a horde of blood-mad cannibals. But, as Caroline learned from a study of his ossified remains, Rick Renzi did not die that day long ago. He lived on for another forty years, trapped in the alien world of the distant past.

"It's good. Stephen Richard..." Caroline trailed away.

"We're going to have to do something about a last name," Dwayne said.

"He can take yours." She shrugged.

"Only if you take it first."

She looked at him, brows knitted.

"Well?" He smiled.

"Of course!" she said and clutched his arm to draw him closer to share a kiss while their son suckled away.

"It will have to be between the two of us until we can use our own names again," he said when they broke the kiss. "I mean, we can take the vows in our own name but the paperwork is going to have to be..."

"Shut up, dummy," she said, placing her fingers on his lips. "You're spoiling the moment with operational details."

They sat quietly and enjoyed the quiet, appreciating that it was fleeting and therefore precious.

After a while, Stephen Richard Roenbach broke contact with a look of sleepy contentment. He needed to be burped. Dad took the chore on like a champ and soon the little guy was asleep in his father's arms.

"We need to get one of these," Dwayne said, rocking the dozing infant in the glider chair by the bed.

"For our nursery on the *Raj*?" Caroline smiled weakly.

"We'll have a house. We have the cash. We'll move anywhere you want."

"Or anytime. Maybe Louis the Fourteenth would like some house guests for the summer." She levered herself from the bed and stepped into slippers. "Mommy has to tinkle."

"When can you and junior here move to the hotel?" He began to stand to help her but she waved him back down.

"Please don't call him 'Junior.' Mo is the one who called me 'Sis' and it stuck." She shuffled to the bathroom. "And I guess we can be discharged tomorrow."

"I'll make sure you're settled in before I head back to the guys."

"No need for that." Her voice echoed off the tiles in the bathroom. "I have a live-in nanny arranged and a concierge doctor on call."

"You're sure about that?"

"The team needs you. And I know Morris is losing his mind. He'll need you to hold his hand when they manifest."

"I hate leaving you like that."

"Leave me like what?" The toilet flushed and she was back in the room and taking her time getting onto the bed. "A five-star Swiss hotel with twenty-four-hour room service and a small army of staff members to take care of every little thing? You make it sound like you're abandoning me in a trailer park."

"You're spoiling our son already."

"Damn straight I am," she said and bent to kiss the baby's forehead then Dwayne's.

"All right. I'll book the evening flight to Athens," Dwayne said.

Forward into the Past

The manifestation went smoothly.

The weather was cooperating with an overcast sky and gathering thunderheads out on the Med.

The *Ocean Raj* had been custom-fitted to transform much of the superstructure and the entire engine deck into a Faraday box. Electronics and radio equipment were shielded from the powerful electro-magnetic field that would soon engulf the ship and surrounding water.

The ten-foot diameter balloon was inflated and rose on a nano-carbon cable high above the deck. It climbed into the night sky, dully reflecting the roiling clouds on its ebon surface. The line grew taut as it swayed at its maximum height of five hundred feet. Weighted cables, secured to davits port and starboard, were thrown into the water.

Below decks, in their shielded control room, Parviz and Quebat waited in Tyvek bunny suits for the signal that all was green for go. With the "all ready" sign from above, they fired a mega-joule charge down the line. The cables in the water crackled. A blue field of incandescent electricity climbed the balloon cable into the sky, singeing the air with fingers of sapphire flame. Within a second the balloon was swallowed up in a wriggling mass of static power drawn from the air around it. The coruscating field raced down the cable and along the deck of the Raj. Within seconds the entire ship glowed in a ghostly blaze of cold fire.

Down below the main deck, in a chamber built of, and concealed within, a five-story stack of Conex containers the titanium rings of the Tauber Tube bled frozen sheets and filled the chamber with a carpet of dense, chilled gas. Four men and one woman rushed through the mist, pushing before them a Zodiac inflatable boat loaded with gear. The boat trundled easily on the rollers of the loadmaster platform installed on the floor of the ramp. Pushing the Zodiac ahead, they vanished under the rings and into the fog and were gone.

The team leapt into the boat as one and clung to any handhold they could find. The raft was momentarily submerged in salt water end-to-end, then surfaced in broad daylight under a cloudless sky. The boat swayed in the light chop, adding to what the guys knew as the Tauber Effect: a disorienting nausea that momentarily left travelers through the tube as helpless as kittens. The guys knew what to expect. As a manifestation virgin, it struck Bat harder. She fought to maintain consciousness after spewing the contents of her stomach onto the rising deck.

"Sound off!" Lee said.

The count was complete at five. All present and combat ready if still a bit pukey.

They were in the Aegean on the open sea with no indication that they had fallen back millennia in time. Not a sail on the horizon. The mist still bleeding through the open field hung on the water behind them. That meant the rip in time was still there with the day and time they left in the future still accessible on the other side of the drifting cloud.

Using the transmitter Lee sent a text back through. He confirmed that they arrived safely along with the estimated time of day. Three in the afternoon. They would establish the exact date later when they could take a star reading. He received an acknowledging text from Dwayne before the mist evaporated, leaving them alone on the sea.

Boats made an inspection to make certain their vessel was intact and the gear still securely dogged down. The center of the boat was piled with waterproof gear bags. They were made of oiled leather and bore no markings and closed with straps and standard steel buckles. Theoretically they would not draw the attention of the curious.

"Well, skipper, what are our orders?" Jimbo asked.

Boats stood on the deck and dropped the pair of electric outboard motors into the water. He then scanned the uninterrupted horizon all around.

"We have a few more hours of light. I say we make for the mainland at quarter speed to get there at last light. There'll be more traffic closer the shore. Best we weren't spotted."

He started the engines up and turned the tiller to point the bow dead east. The twin ELCOs purred, pushing them through the water at ten knots. Just a goose on the throttle and Boats could bring enough horsies on line to have them skimming over the water at sixty. The humble little raft was the fastest vessel in the world right now—land or sea.

The sun was sinking in a magnificent burnt orange sky behind them as they sighted the shore as a darker line along the horizon. They had still not seen another sail on their entire trip.

"Shouldn't we have seen something?" Bat asked.

"These ancient mariners were pussies!" Boats proclaimed. "They didn't like to sail far from land or at night. They probably all put in somewhere by now. We have the sea to ourselves."

"Are you sure we didn't go back too far?" she said.

"If a dinosaur pops its head out of the water then we'll know," Chaz said.

The only animal life they saw was the growing number of gulls and terns in the air. A long flight of herons skimmed the water near them, heading for their perches on land before the sky grew full dark.

"I don't see a beach," Jimbo said, standing at the prow.

"Shouldn't we hear breakers by now?" Bat said.

Boats stood and raised a pair of binoculars to his eyes.

"Shit."

"What is it?" Lee asked.

"There ain't no beach. No surf. It's a tidal marsh," the SEAL said with disgust.

They rode swells to where the water shallowed. Boats tilted the motor shafts from the water as the bottom was thick with vegetation. The shoreline north and south was a thick forest of mangrove alive with clouds of mosquitoes and biting flies. An impenetrable tangle of roots grew into the black water.

"This was all a beach. I've been here," Bat said.

"The topography changes," Jimbo said. "Especially near the water line."

"Change of plans," Lee said. "We'll have to make landing closer to the port than we planned. We follow the shore north."

"And we'll do it deeper waters," Boats said. "Grab an oar everyone. We need to paddle clear of this shit before I put our screws back in."

Two to each gunwale, the team stroked away from the shore and the nasty fog of stinging insects until they were free of the undertow. Boats dropped the motors and steered them north, the dark mainland rolling along to their right.

Within an hour they saw a wooded headland rising from the shore. The scopes showed a narrow beach at the foot of a steep bluff choked with scrub pines and brush. No place to conceal the raft.

Boats gave the headland a wide berth and they came around it to find the city of Caesarea, the seat of power in Roman Judea, rising from the curve of a sheltered harbor. The full extent of the city was lost in the gloom of the moonless night. The structures they could see were mostly dark with only the soft amber glow of lanterns from within some of the buildings. Smoke rose from cook fires. A lighthouse of sorts sat at the end of a long jetty that bowed out from the headland to enclose the harbor. A fire burned in a large brazier atop a stout tower to provide a beacon. It was more symbolic than anything else. Few sailors in this age sailed by night. No torches lined the jetty.

"There's no sentry posted," Lee said, scanning the jetty with a night vision scope.

"What's in port?" Jimbo asked.

"I see masts. Tall ones. There's a few big ships in there," Lee said, shifting his gaze to glass the long waterfront. There was a forest of shorter masts swaying at one end of the harbor. "Looks like a fishing fleet. Maybe some merchant vessels."

"We need a place to get our feet on land and hide the Zodiac. Do you see anything like that?" Boats said.

"You're the specialist here," Lee said, handing off the NODs scope to the SEAL.

After a quick study Boats suggested they paddle into the harbor and scout for a place to hide the raft where they could find it again but no one else would be snooping. By unanimous agreement the team got the paddles out again and rowed inland.

They drifted silently past the base of the lighthouse and around the jetty toward the wharves lining the harbor. The large masts that Lee spotted belonged to a pair of Roman warships that towered over the smacks and barques anchored up and down the pier. The masts on the Roman ships were clewed up tight to their cross spars. The decks were dark and the hulls lined with the openings for four rows of oars. The ships were quiet. The only sign of movement were the shadows from the lines swaying in the wind. Otherwise the men and woman on the Zodiac might be the only living things in the city.

"They must all be at the orgy," Chaz whispered.

Boats shifted the tiller and they veered to starboard toward a place where an embarcadero described the curve of the shoreline. There were broad archways in the face of the harbor wall between stout stone supports that seemed to grow from the water. The rowers lifted their oars and the Zodiac drifted under one of the arches into a dark enclosure that ended in a wall forty feet within.

"Is this some kind of boathouse?" Chaz said.

In answer, Boats took a waterproof lantern and slipped over the wale into the black water. They watched over the sides as the glow of the lantern shifted back and forth beneath the Zodiac. The light died and Boats resurfaced seconds later.

"It's a good twenty feet deep here with an upward sloping floor," he said. "We can hide the Zodiac here."

"With a triangular structure of stone and iron?" Jimbo asked.

"Yeah. How'd you know that?" Boats said.

"I saw it on Wikipedia. These alcoves are where they stored the rams for their warships when they weren't needed."

"Then the Romans might be using them," Lee said.

"This structure is too old to be Roman," Jimbo reached out and ran a hand down the stones. "It was built before them. Phoenicians. This port was theirs once."

"You did a shitload of research for this op," Chaz said.

"I read up to prep for the last trip back. The one I had to bail on," Jimbo said. "Got back into it when we started this one."

"Ancient trivia for two hundred, Alex." Bat grinned.

"We'll off-load the gear and Boats can hide the raft," Lee said.

They paddled from the alcove and followed the wall to where it was joined by a broad set of stone steps rising from the water to the embarcadero. Forming a chain, they removed the oiled leather gear bags from the Zodiac and stacked them. Dark buildings lined the wide quayside. Nets were drying on racks. There were no sentries patrolling. A pair of turbaned drunks approached them with palms out. Chaz told them to fuck off in Arabic and they scuttled away muttering slurred curses.

Jimbo paddled and Boats steered the raft to the eighth alcove along the sea wall and entered. They removed the outboards and wrapped them in heavy plastic and sealed the bags with duct tape. Any remaining gear was strapped down tight and Boats released the cocks to allow water into the air cells inside the rigid hull. The raft sank lower in the water. The SEAL had modified the Zodiac for this purpose. He installed compressed air tanks so the hull could be re-inflated in minutes. Even with the hull flooded with water the Zodiac's closed-cell foam inserts kept it at neutral buoyancy. Jimbo and Boats dropped into the water and swam below to run lines from the raft through encrusted iron rings set in the ram carriage. They braced their feet on the floor of the alcove and pulled on the lines. As the raft above them lost buoyancy they pulled it under the water until it was suspended a few feet from the bottom.

Two minutes was all Jimbo could do underwater. He re-surfaced three times to gasp in a lungful of air. Boats came up only once. The guy was part fish. Jimbo dog-paddled while Boats secured and tied off lines fore and aft as well as on either side. The Zodiac's black hull was invisible against the dark floor of the alcove. They swam for the steps to rejoin the others.

The five travelers each hefted a seventy-pound gear bag and humped them into Caesarea and the land of the prophets.

THINGS CHANGE

The only thing missing was Dwayne.

All Caroline had to do was rest and nurse little Stephen. The rotating nannies did the rest. And anything else she wished was a phone call away. The Villa Kummer Grand had a full spa, in-room massages, and a kitchen of top chefs capable of preparing anything from haute cuisine to New York-style pizza. There was a sixty-inch TV in a private media room that was part of the suite. Caroline felt guilty as she thought of how much Dwayne would have liked that feature. She spent much of her time reading from some of her books and the huge selection she'd downloaded onto her Kindle in anticipation of the downtime. The rest of her days were spent sleeping and admiring the miracle that only days before was an uncomfortable bulge in her midsection.

The baby was a marvel. The emotions she felt for it surprised her. She understood it had everything to do with hormones but she felt it had to be more than that. Giving birth to a child of her own opened a new world to her every bit as surprising and enveloping as her trips into the past. Dwayne was part of both and she wondered about that.

Was the Army Ranger a true partner or just part of the adventure? When she was with him she didn't question what they had. When they were apart the analytical side of her kicked in hard. They had nothing in common but their experiences. Dwayne was smart but not an intellectual. He was a doer. And that appealed to her as she was impulsive herself. But she couldn't help but ask if they were right for one another in the long term. He would always be a chance taker and now that she was a mother she was looking to conserve risk and live whatever a 'normal' life was supposed to be. At least that's how she felt right now. Tomorrow might be different.

Caroline put down her book, a favorite volume of Richard Feynman essays she was reading for the umpteenth time, when she heard the baby crying in the next room. She rose and entered the master bedroom where she found the nanny had arrived before her. Greta was lifting the squalling and kicking bundle from the bassinet. Caroline held out her arms.

"He needs to be changed," the nanny said.

"I have to start sometime," Caroline said, taking Stephen in her arms. "You can supervise."

Together they cleaned, ointmented and slipped the infant into a brand new diaper.

"It's time for him to nurse," Caroline said and took a seat in an upholstered glider Dwayne ordered and had delivered before he left.

"Is there anything you'd like me to get for you?" Greta said once she'd handed the baby off.

"A cup of tea would be nice." Caroline smiled. "Decaffeinated, of course."

"Of course. One moment." And Greta was gone.

Caroline entered a waking dream state as Stephen nursed. This was pure contentment. She thought briefly of her feminist acquaintances when she was at school in London and Chicago. They'd be horrified to see her in such a state of reactionary oppression.

The door opened and Caroline was surprised that

Greta could be back so quickly with her tea.

Only it wasn't Greta. It was the man she knew only as Samuel in a strangely cut dark suit with a blood-stained tear in the right sleeve. She noted that he looked younger than the last time they met. It had to be her imagination.

"You have to come with me. Both of you. Now."

Greta returned with a steaming cup of tea and a plate of vanilla biscuits on a tray only to find the master bedroom empty. No Mrs. Nesbitt and no baby anywhere to be seen. She searched the rest of the suite and found she was entirely alone.

Though not for long. She was startled when a man stormed into the suite from the hallway with a gun in his hand. The man was lean and handsome with white hair set off by a nut-brown complexion.

"Where are they?" he said coolly, making the pistol vanish under his jacket as though it never existed.

"I don't know," Greta said. "They were here just a moment ago and then..."

She trailed away as the man fixed her in his gaze, calmly assessing her as though using what he saw and heard to come to a decision. Without another word or gesture, the man turned and left the suite.

Her grandmother used to explain away a sudden chill by saying that someone had just walked across her grave. Now Greta knew exactly what that felt like.

She also knew that she craved something stronger than tea.

Pax Romanica

They wound up letting Bat Jaffe do the horse-trading. They picked out ten sturdy mounts. Most of the traders spoke Aramaic only. But Bat found a toothless old bastard with a good string and haggled with him in rapid-fire Hebrew for what seemed like days. Other men stood by to witness the exchange and the tall strangers with their odd dress and aspects. A woman speaking for men in a matter of trade? And what army did these men march in?

"Just pay him what he wants," Lee growled.

"This isn't Walmart, honey," she snapped back. "You back down and they'll tell everyone they know. We're making enough of an impression as it is."

They eventually settled on three of the gold coins from their hoard. The horse trader seemed pleased and shouted god's blessings on them as they led the horses away.

"We still got ripped off," Bat said bitterly.

The horses were Nisaeans, a Persian animal bred for stamina but fast enough to get them out of trouble if it came to that. Jimbo knew horses best and picked out each one. He chose all mares and judged them to be two- and three-year-olds.

The scene was repeated at a saddle maker's. Bat and the stall-keeper going round and round. Five saddles and five pack frames for their gear.

"Where's the stirrups?" Chaz bitched.

"Come back in a few hundred years," Jimbo said. "No stirrups here until Attila arrives in the neighborhood."

"Well that's just fucking stupid," Chaz said. "How am I supposed to get up on this animal? And stay on? Should've brought our own saddles."

"Chronal integrity, bro." Jimbo smiled.

"Shit," Chaz said and looked around for something to use as a step.

The pack animals were saddled and the gear secured on their backs. The travelers decided to walk the horses until they were beyond the city walls. Caesarea was a trade center and so was a polyglot of peoples from all over the region. There were Jews, Arabs, Greeks, Armenians, Macedonians, Dacians, Parthians, Dalmatians, and every other people and race that lived beneath the rule of Tiberius Rex. There was enough variety of custom, dress, and appearance that four American men in t-shirts, oddly patterned kilts (Lee in his BDUs), and boots did not rate any special attention. Their weapons and armor were concealed on the animals' backs. They wore knives on their belts as the only visible means of protection. Bat had her Sig in a cross-draw holster concealed under a loose linen blouse that also hid her figure.

Bat was surprised at how little Roman presence she saw as they made their way along the dusty streets. From the wharfs to the market they saw only a few Roman soldiers and those seemed to be more interested in shopping. She naively expected the past to be like the movies: stolid legionnaires tramping everywhere behind their shields and columns of slaves in chains being urged on by lashes from a bullwhip. Except for some of the architecture there was no sign that this city was under imperial rule of any kind. It looked like any bustling seaside town in stark contrast to the tomb-like atmosphere they'd encountered the night before. There was no sense of either tyranny or rebellion in the air. No one seemed to be rankling under the yoke of oppression. She remembered that slaves did not wear any outward sign of their servitude under Roman law. There was no way to know how many of the people they passed were chattel to the Romans or even Judeans. She felt vaguely disappointed. Except for the lack of honking cars and radios blaring everywhere, she could be in modern Haifa.

She realized there was another difference; in modern Haifa you saw signs of the military everywhere. The IDF was a constant presence in a nation under perpetual threat from terrorists seeking its demise. It was a testament to how absolute Roman authority was here that there were so few soldiers in evidence and the port was left unguarded. A real challenge to the rule of the Caesars was centuries away.

This place and time had a feeling of the surreal. Bat had to remind herself that this was real, not a recreation. They were actually in the distant past. They were in so alien a period that they could openly speak English and not fear being overheard. Their language would not exist in anything like the form they used for over a thousand years or more. The Angles and Saxons were still far to the north in their deep forests. The British Isles were occupied by Picts and Celts and, for now, beyond the rule of Rome. And America was a place undreamed of beyond the waters of the Mare Incognita where the world ended. The thought of that made her a bit dizzy.

They drew some stares as they followed the streets eastward. It wasn't for their dress but for their height and the diverse mix of the group. Boats with his flowing red hair and beard, Chaz's ebony skin, and Jimbo's high cheekbones and striking profile. Lee stood out with the array of multi-colored tattoos running down his arms. Only Bat fit the place and time with her olive complexion and raven curls held back by a strip of cloth. No one challenged them, only watched and remarked. The odd caravan moved on through a gate and until the streets became dirt paths and they left the city behind.

In a lane between rows of date palms they decided to saddle up and make time. Before mounting, Jimbo had taken down a gear bag to remove his Winchester. He slid it into a leather boot and strapped it to the saddle where it would be ready at hand. The rest found their side arms and strapped on. Their holsters were concealed carry models. To anyone seeing them they would look like the kind of purses men wore on their belts to hold coins. They also retrieved CamelBaks, binoculars, boonie hats, and meal packs.

Bat added the snubbie in a thigh holster to her arsenal, securing it under the hem of her kilt.

"Sexy," Lee remarked.

"Me or the Colt? Don't answer that," she added quickly with a squint.

Jimbo and Bat mounted easily despite the lack of stirrups or pommel. It took Lee and Boats a few tries. The worst time of all was had by Chaz. He pulled his mount to a section of a low stone wall that he used as a step. The horse won three out of four falls before Chaz got firmly situated.

"I thought you spent summers on your Uncle Red's farm," Jimbo said.

"I didn't spend them playing cowboy," Chaz said, urging the horse forward with a slap of the reins.

"You always picked the fattest horse when we were in Helmand," Lee said.

"Fat horses are safer. They don't take off with you," Chaz answered. "This bitch has a gleam in her eye I don't like."

"I'll stay by you," Bat said and leaned from the saddle to run a hand down the neck of Chaz's mount. "Who's a good girl?" she cooed. The horse's ears came forward.

Jimbo rode ahead to scout. The rest followed at a trot leading the pack horses behind them. Before them they could see the land rising to the blue ridge of mountains. They knew from their maps that it fell away beyond those peaks to the deep Jordan Valley and the Sea of Galilee before ascending again to the Golan Heights. The orchards and farms would give way soon to the broken country of hills and defiles where they would need to be wary. While the Romans held the cities and surroundings, the land they rode for was without law of any kind.

Drive Curious

They were on the E-60 heading north and west for Auxerre. The highway was mostly sunken for long lengths between hills but would sometimes climb a rise. Then Caroline could see lights in farm houses and the dark shapes of trees. The moon cast shadows from set stone walls around farm fields making them appear to be outlined in black.

Stephen slept in her arms where she sat in the back seat of the Audi. She wanted to stop and buy a car seat but Samuel said that this was out of the question. She was in what she suspected was a stolen car driven by a man she knew next to nothing about toward a destination she wasn't certain of and away from a threat that had not been fully described to her. Child safety laws seemed low on the list of priorities to worry about. Still, it gave her something practical to focus her anxiety on.

Samuel drove without speaking, a French language pop station playing low on the radio. The traffic was light at this time of night. There seemed to be nothing ahead of them all the way into infinity. It was as if the world only became real as their headlights illuminated it and then receded again into nonexistence behind them.

The only stop they had made was at a roadside truck station. Samuel went into the brightly lit store alone. He returned with a paper sack of sandwiches, plastic bottles of milk, a tub of sanitizing wipes, and a small packet of diapers. Caroline noted a clean white bandage visible beneath the blood-caked tear in his coat. He must have done some first aid in the rest room. She also saw a dull metallic sheen about his wrist. Something like a wristwatch but with a broader band.

"Can you tell me where we're heading?" she asked.

"The White City."

"Chicago?" she said, confused. "We're going to fly?"

"Paris. I mean we're going to Paris."

"I've heard it called the City of Lights," she said. He did not reply and she left it at that.

They drove in silence for a while. Stephen slept, his breath a gentle current on the skin of Caroline's sheltering arm.

"You drive with gloves on," she said. "You do everything with gloves on."

"I try to avoid physical contact with my environment as much as possible," he said without turning, without even meeting her eyes in the rearview.

"That's a practical consideration, right? I notice you avoid touching anything. Is that a health concern? Are you being cautious about catching some illness?"

"Most people live in time," he said as if not hearing her questions. "They are born and live and die in a linear time line. A few, a very few, live through time."

"Like me," she said. "And the Rangers. And yourself."

"Yes. Except for me. I live without time."

She waited for him to explain further.

"What does that mean precisely?" Caroline asked at last.

"Because of the peculiarities of my birth I live outside of the normal constraints of time. I can more easily adjust to changes in my chronological location in that way. I do not live a life described in a linear fashion."

"You're unstuck in time," she said. "Like Billy Pilgrim."

"Who is that?"

"Nobody. A fictional character in a book I read a long time ago."

Samuel said nothing.

"When we met in Menton, on the beach, at the hotel?" she said.

Samuel said nothing. She glimpsed a flash of those extraordinary green eyes in the mirror.

"You were older then."

"Was I?" he said.

"A good twenty years older than you are now."

He said nothing at first. The fine hairs stood up on her arms.

"If you say so."

"Then this, this sudden urgent ride, has nothing to do with that?" she asked.

"No. This is about your son."

"Stephen? What does any of this have to do with my baby?"

"One of my parents was like you, a time traveler," Samuel said. "Your child is the product of two parents who visited a time period not their own. Several, in fact."

She put aside the surreal nature of their conversation. She locked down her emotional reaction to learning that her child was 'different' in an unanticipated and unwelcome way. The scientist emerged. Her intellectual curiosity took over.

"You mean traveling through the chronal field altered our genetics?"

"No. Not your gene structure. Something deeper. Something simpler yet more complex."

"Samuel, are we talking string theory here?"

"I'm not as familiar with the study of physics in your era as I should be. We may be talking about the same thing but I do not have your terminology for it. The scientific language is different."

"String is an area of theoretical science that seeks to explain how the basic particles of existence relate to one another," she said. "It can be used to theorize about everything from the causation of gravity to the existence of other dimensions."

"It sounds like Trivenchy's thesis called *Mica Prima*," Samuel said. "In it he explains that all matter comes from a single source and all relates back to the first piece of matter in creation; the remnant that holds the answer to the existence of everything."

"The God Particle."

"That is an evocative way of stating it."

"More romantic than Higgs boson, certainly," Caroline agreed. "You're saying that because one of your parents was displaced in time you are significantly affected on a sub-atomic level."

"Yes. That is the simplest way to phrase it."

"Which of your parents?'

"My father."

"Do I know him?" She already knew the answer before he said it.

"Yes. Richard Renzi."

Stephen was startled awake and began crying. Caroline cooed and rocked him as they rode through the night, holding him to her, absorbing his warmth into her to fight the sudden chill she knew had nothing to do with the cold outside the car.

A Stolen March

The cold desert sky was clear above them the night of their first camp.

Lee Hammond was able to take a reading from the position of the stars.

"We're late," he announced to the others. Except Jimbo who was on overwatch somewhere out in the dark.

They were cold camping. No fire. They didn't see a single human being once they passed out of the last orchard beyond the walls of Caesarea. A few wild goats were spotted but no sign of settlements or nomads. They'd mostly followed a rough eastward trail until the ground broke up. They settled on a ledge of rock scree in the lee of a hillside to rest the horses, eat, and catch some sleep.

"It's the tenth of September, AD 16," Lee said.

"That's a week past our target, right?" Chaz said.

"We're making good time," Bat said. "We're past the point we meant to make the first day."

"But we lost a day getting mounts and saddles. There's not a lot of wiggle room here," Lee said. "We need to be ahead of the convoy to set up an ambush. That means we really hump it from here on."

"So, we hump it." Chaz shrugged.

Boats, wrapped in a sheepskin and lying in the shelter of a scrub pine, snored on.

* * *

They broke camp and were back on the trail before dawn. Jimbo rode far ahead to scout the country. He made piles of rocks to mark where he changed directions. The ground was rising and breaking up. They counted on the fact that the topography had not changed too much in two millennia. There were more trees and brush than in The Now. The marsh-lands were larger than they would be one day. They left the wetlands behind as the elevation increased on the way to the high ground before the Dead Sea rift and the Golan Heights beyond. Jimbo would find the path of least resistance around the floor of hills and avoid settlements and caravans.

They were *in* time now, racing east to intersect a Roman army column they knew was marching north. Any more delays and they would miss the potential ambush points they'd pre-chosen. Jimmy Smalls was riding farther in advance than any of them were com-fortable with. They needed the knowledge of what lay ahead to make the best time. Besides, if the Pima ran into trouble there was none tougher. And the rest of the team would ride in if he let off a signal shot from his Winchester.

"With all the breaks and a day of hard riding we should reach the road by nightfall," Bat said riding even with Lee.

"Except we never get the breaks," Lee said.

"Those Romans have no reason to push," she said. "They're on foot and they stop at every twentieth mile post and spend hours making a fortified camp. Plus they have prisoners slowing them down."

"And we could get lost down a blind trail or run into weather or bad guys or just plain dumb luck."

"Who's chapping your ass?"

"This fucking horse," Lee said and levered forward to relieve the pain in his rear.

"You sound like Chaz. He hates horses."

"Everyone hates horses after two days in the saddle. Especially these saddles."

They rode on into a copse of cedar growing between the brows of two hills. They stayed off high ground where they might be visible for miles against the sky. Where it was possible they used wooded trails to reduce the dust raised by their passage. The shade provided some relief from the heat even though the mosquito population increased. They picked up the pace to a trot to leave the annoying clouds behind. The horses seemed grateful.

The team dismounted when they'd cleared the trees. They led the animals to follow a trail that curved away along the face of an escarpment. A small pyramid of stones was visible beneath a brokeback tree just beneath the ridge line. By it was an arrow of pebbles pointing off to their right through a narrow cleft. It was hard going and they'd need to move in single file. They were bathed in fresh sweat within minutes.

"I could buy us some time on the other end," Bat spoke up.

"How?" Lee said.

"I catch up with Jimbo. He and I can just go full out for the roadway without the packies to slow us. We can set up an OP and cover the road until you guys catch up."

"What if the bad guys show before we do?"

"We can hold them. I'm a sniper too, remember? Take down an officer and they'll either scatter or at least stop to think about it."

Lee looked at her, his eyes in shadow in the stark

sunlight.

"That's sweet," she said. "You're worried about me."

"I was weighing the tactical advantages. I was also thinking that only a dumbass volunteers for anything."

"Aren't Rangers all volunteers?"

"I wasn't casting stones."

"Good. The guy we're looking for doesn't approve of that kind of thing, right?"

"Okay," he said. "Go."

Bat swung up into the saddle and urged her horse into a gallop. She rode to the pyramid beneath the twisted tree, jerked her reins right and drove into the shadows of the constricted trail.

Jimbo slid from his horse at the sound of hoof falls behind him. He reined the mount athwart the trail and slid the Winchester from the leather boot. He trained it toward the rising haze of dust making a whirling smear against the yellow sky back the way he came.

Through the scope, Lee's girl leapt into view where she leaned back in the saddle of her gray mare and expertly picked her way down a rocky slope. She held the reins high and guided the mount along an angled path. Bat was a natural, moving as one with the horse. Jimbo raised the rifle and stood waiting for her.

"You got farther ahead than I thought," she said as she reined to a stop and dismounted.

"I kept a steady pace." He slid the rifle back in its scabbard.

She explained the change in tactics.

"It's a good option," Jimbo said. "I been reading up

on these Romans. Tacitus. The real stuff. He wrote that the legions were brave but could be easily spooked. A whole army ran, scared shitless in the Teutonburg once. Turned out it was acorns falling on their helmets."

"Let's go throw some acorns then," she said.

Her mount was blown and lathered with sweat. They would lead their horses at a trot for a few miles. It was a killing pace for them over the broken ground. For the horses it would serve as a rest, a cool down pace free of the weight of a rider. Jimbo led the way. He looked back a few times at the start to see Bat keeping pace, not falling behind. The girl was tough.

Lee had a keeper in her. Jimbo smiled. He hoped his friend realized this was not another girl to play with for a while and then leave without warning. This one would find Hammond and skin him alive if he strayed.

The Road

Exhausted, aching and thirsty, Jimbo and Bat reached the roadway as the last light was dying behind the hills at their back. The last ten miles had been spent following a game trail along a downward grade. Walking the mounts down the slope was a tiring chore as they watched for sure footing on a sliding shale surface beneath a thin layer of gray grit. The horses balked at the darkening skies until Jimbo covered their eyes with strips of cloth torn from their t-shirts.

"You look like a real Indian now," Bat said. The Pima was bare chested. She was down to a sports bra.

"The nose isn't enough?" He smiled back.

"Let's not compare noses," she said with mock huffiness.

The slope drew up level before a ledge beyond which the land fell away sharply. They could see the road surface down below following the floor of a natural gully that ran almost dead north/south for miles. Over the opposite side of the depression they could make out the shape of the Golan Heights rising dramatic and black against the stars.

The road was of crushed stone rather than the square-cut blocks typical of Roman construction. It was clearly man-made even in the uncertain light. There was a mile marker, an obelisk of white stone, visible along the verge. The road surface was of uniform width running dead center of the defile. That was the optimal path for a military road in this era. The engineers of the legions cut the grades for their roads to run below the skyline either laterally along the face of slopes or using natural cover like forests or the depression below them. A Roman army on the march could remain concealed from its enemy until it was too late to form an adequate defense, their approach concealed by the topography.

"Are we early or late?" Bat said.

"No way to tell." Jimbo glassed the road to the south through the scope of his rifle.

"And no one to ask," she said. The road was empty of traffic as far as they could see in either direction even using the powerful 30x lenses. No one would be abroad at this hour in a country where bandits roamed and evil spirits were very real.

Jimbo unstowed his nightvision gear and peered through it, sweeping it along the road and surrounding heights. No telltale signs of a settlement or even a campfire. No smoke against the sky.

"We take care of the horses and make a cold camp right here," he said. "I'll take first watch. In the morning we follow this south a little ways, see if anyone will talk to us. Give the others a chance to catch up."

The others caught up mid-morning the following day. They found the two scouts' horses tethered in a copse of trees midway up the stony slope. A collection of stubborn firs tucked into a cleft in the rocks. The three men decided the best option was to watch along the road for Jimbo and Bat's return. They rested their mounts and pack animals in the shade while eyeing the rocky ledge above the roadway for sign of their teammates.

Jimmy Smalls and Bathsheba returned by noon.

"What's your best guess?" Lee asked. He and Jimbo had taken a knee overlooking the road.

"We either missed them or they're not here yet. My money's on them being on the march to the south of us." Jimbo swept the country to the south with an open hand. "This is the only viable military road. They have to be along in the next few days."

"Any human intel?"

"We haven't seen any locals yet. Someone's sure to be along this afternoon."

"What's the water situation?"

"There's a spring about a mile and half to the north." Jimbo claimed he could smell water like a horse could. All Lee knew was that the Pima seldom missed when it came to looking for potable water even in country like this. *Especially* in country like this.

"Is it near a chokepoint like this one?"

"There's a twenty degree turn in the canyon nearby. We set up either side and we can stop them cold," Jimbo said.

"Let's take a look," Lee said, standing.

They found a caravan stopped at the spring when they arrived. Men and camels were watering there. The spring started high on the wall of the decline to trickle down a furrow in the rock worn smooth over the years. It gathered in a natural pool at the foot of the wall. The men were Arabs and dressed much the same way as the Rangers were familiar with back in The Now. The only notable absence was rifles. Each man wore a blade of some kind and one man leaned on a spear with a rusted point.

The camels were loaded down with sacks bound to wooden racks. The men gave them water from leather buckets filled from the pool. The group visibly tensed at the sight of two men walking toward them around the turn in the canyon. They kept a wary eye but did not reach for weapons. To their eyes, one of the men was an African dressed in some kind of armor. The other was a Macedonian perhaps and dressed in peculiar leggings and a black cloth singlet of one piece. Both men were tall. They led fine horses behind them.

Chaz and Lee stopped fifty feet from the men. Desert etiquette was eternal. You didn't just walk up to a bunch of nomads. You gave them time to make up their minds about you. Just in case they made up their minds the wrong way, the caravaneers were covered by Jimbo and Bat watching through scopes from concealment above. After a few moments the Arabs did a pantomime of pretending to have just noticed the pair of Rangers. One of them nodded and took a step forward. Probably their headman.

They let the guy speak first. He was first to the watering hole and held the conch. He spoke to them in a stream of slurred Arabic. Chaz picked a few words from the salad. Some kind of elaborate greeting. Chaz's Arabic was strong but the accent was hard to follow; a dialect lost to time.

"Best to you and your company and may fortune smile upon all here," Chaz bullshitted the guy along.

The headman squinted and pursed his lips at the tall black man's formal enunciation. He thought perhaps the African was a lord in his land or the slave of a lord. Perhaps owned by the silent Macedonian who he accompanied.

The blessings and well-wishes went on for a while and afforded Chaz a chance to accustom himself to the other guy's dialect. The headman was slowing down his speech like he was talking to an idiot. Chaz saw some of the others politely covering their mouths to hide smiles and stifle laughter. The small talk and gladhanding was over finally and they got down to business.

The Arab offered that they were packing salt for sale to merchants along the road.

Chaz lied and said that he and his companion were agents for a Roman merchant in Philippi. They were looking to make contact with a column of Romans from the XXIII with a company of slaves that were expected along this road. This caravan was coming from the south and may have seen the soldiers.

The headman rubbed his beard and narrowed his eyes before coming to a decision.

"There are Romans to the south. We saw them two days ago. They were not on the march," he said.

"What do you mean?" Chaz said.

"They do not march. They make a fort along the road."

"They make camp, you mean?"

"No! A fort. They pile stone. They dig a trench like Romans do. We sold them salt."

Chaz looked at Lee.

"Ask him about their aquilifer," Lee said.

Chaz did and the Arab described a horse affixed atop their banners.

"It's the Twenty-third Legion. But why are they stopped?" Chaz said in English.

"Fucking ask *him,*" Lee growled. They'd spent all their good luck at the start just as he'd predicted.

Chaz asked and the Arab shrugged.

"This Roman fort, where is this?" Chaz asked.

"Two days south by camel. More days on foot or by

horse." The headman nodded down the road the way he'd come.

"What is there? A town? A well?"

"A town of Jews. A quarry. A big quarry where they cut stone for the Herods."

"What of their company of slaves?" Chaz said.

"They cut rock," the Arab said and spat.

Chaz turned to Lee.

"A quarry. Fuck me," Lee said.

"History ain't what it used to be," Boats said.

Jimbo remained along the ledge watching the road. The others camped in the shade of wild fig trees to weigh options and share rations.

"Maybe they halted their march for a reason. Illness. Something like that," Bat offered.

"Or they got a heads-up," Lee said.

"How could that happen? How could they know we were here?" Chaz said.

"How the fuck should I know? This Harnesh figured it out and sent someone to warn them. Maybe they knew we'd be here even before *we* knew we'd be here. This shit messes with your mind," Lee said.

"We need eyes-on," Chaz said.

"We need a platoon, a company," Lee said. "This goes from a simple three point ambush to bad guys in a fortified position expecting trouble. And if they are encamped at a quarry that means the number of slaves is ramped up. Our guy is in a bigger mix now."

"Our guy." Boats chuckled through a mouthful of HooAH! bar.

"Yeah, well I wish he'd magic his own ass out of there and save us the trouble," Lee spat.

"That's not how it works," Chaz said.

"Spare me the Sunday school," Lee said with hand extended. "It is what it is. We ride up there and scope it out and hope that Tacitus wasn't full of shit."

"Tacitus?" Boats said.

"Roman historian Jimmy read. Says that the legions could turn pussy under the right circumstances," Bat said.

"I like that." Boats grinned. Sticky bits of protein bar dotted his teeth.

A series of high whistles brought them alert. Jimbo was waving them over from the lip of the canyon wall. Lee trotted down to him. Jimbo handed Lee his Winchester.

"Scope north. Below the dust cloud."

Lee could see small figures coming along the road toward them. A column of men four across with more behind lost in the heat haze and the rising cloud of dust.

"Those are soldiers," Lee said.

"Lots of 'em," Jimbo said. "And coming the wrong way."

A Change of Address

"How is your French?" Samuel asked.

Caroline had a French boyfriend for a while at college in London. They made frequent trips to Paris while they were going together and, after they broke up, she spent a summer touring Provence with some girlfriends. But Samuel didn't want to know any of that.

"It's fine. Better than tourist."

"Good," he said and pulled the Mercedes to a curb.

It was night and they were in an older part of the fifteenth arrondissement. The traffic was light on the two-lane street and the buildings loomed close on either side along narrow sidewalks. There was Sufi music dully booming from somewhere behind the dark faces of the apartment blocks. Samuel climbed from behind the wheel to come around and open the door for Caroline. He took the baby from her and closed the door behind her before handing the sleeping Stephen back.

"The bag," she said.

"You cannot bring it where we're going."

"You'll get towed here," she said.

"I left the keys in it. It will be stolen before the traffic wardens ever notice it." He took her under the arm and escorted her over the broken slabs of the sidewalk.

"Stolen again, you mean." She meant it as a joke.

"It does not matter. We will not be coming back

here." He guided them under an archway into a cramped lane between two buildings. The pounding music was reduced to a distant pulse behind them. Samuel put a hand to her back and they stopped in the dark passageway that smelled of sour wine, stale flowers, and piss.

"This isn't the best neighborhood, Samuel," she said and held the baby closer under her coat as a sudden chill fell over her.

"It will improve in a moment," he answered and raised his chin to point down the alleyway.

Caroline looked up to see a white mist building in the passage, growing more opaque by the second and climbing the walls to leave a white rime of ice on the ancient bricks.

"I don't know about this. You didn't say..." she began.

"Don't worry about Stephen. He's more suited to this sort of travel then you are," he said in an even tone.

"I've followed you without questions. Well, without many questions. But this—"

"It is the best place to hide. It is where you and your child will be safe. You live through time now, Caroline. There is no turning back." His hand pressed into her back gently.

She drew the coat tighter about Stephen to hoard their body heat together and stepped into the clinging fog. Her breath was visible now. She glanced upward and through the pale swirling haze caught a glimpse of rings above her—gleaming black rings dripping with frost. They were traveling through some version of the field generator created by her and her brother; a copy of their invention constructed by unknown hands in a time and place strange and foreign to her.

"How—" she began.

"No questions," Samuel said and took her hand to draw her through the field.

She emerged from the mist weak and disoriented and deeper in the alley. Samuel took the baby from her and cradled it in one arm while guiding her from the chilling cloud into a courtyard lit by a single gas lamp. Caroline gulped air and fought down the urge to vomit. She was still gasping as her head cleared. She gestured for her child. Stephen was placed in her arms and she saw that he breathed easily. His eyelids fluttered a bit but he was still restfully asleep.

"See, he is virtually unfazed by manifestation just as I promised," Samuel said and Caroline thought she saw a fleeting smile of reassurance.

"When is this?" she said, looking about. The courtyard was broad and lined about by dark buildings. But now she saw that empty flower beds lined the borders and a pair of bare fruit trees stood in an island at the center. The smell of wood smoke filled the cold air. Above the rooftops, smoke rose from flues into the starry sky. The persistent drum of recorded music was gone to be replaced by a dull rhythmic sound from an unseen source. It was the tramp of boots—many boots. She realized at once that the white noise of street traffic was absent. Looking up she saw that what she could see of the sky was not lined with the contrails of passenger jets.

"1871. Winter," Samuel said.

"We transited through time without a waystation step between," she said.

"I will explain more later. For now we must move to cover." He took her elbow and walked her across the courtyard, leaving the icy cloud to dissipate behind them.

He hurried her along cobbled streets empty of all

but a few high-wheeled carriages and small columns of marching men. She wore a cap pushed low on her head and he warned her to keep her face down as they moved swiftly from shadow to shadow.

"There is a curfew," Samuel said, holding her hand to guide her across the street.

"Is that usual?" she said and clutched the baby closer.

"Paris is under martial law. France is at war."

"And you thought this was a good place to bring Stephen and me?"

"War is the best place to hide," he said and drew her under the awning of a hotel. He placed his shoulder to the door and popped the lock with a sudden thrust to swing the doors open.

They hustled into the dim lobby of a middlebrow hostelry that brazenly called itself Hotel Exemplaire. She sat cradling Stephen in a shady corner while Samuel banged on the desktop to rouse the registrar. Caroline heard him explain in fluent French that they were traveling from Canada on business and their luggage had been stolen. There was an argument too swift for Caroline to follow that ended with Samuel producing a thick sheaf of bills. The registrar went silent at the sight of all the franc notes. Money exchanged hands and Samuel returned to the lobby to take her upstairs. At this late hour there was no bell staff to take them to their room. All as Samuel had planned, she imagined.

The room was a cramped suite with a sitting room and boudoir with a vestigial balcony over the street. There were no closets, as was the custom of the day, and no private bath or toilet, as was also the custom in bourgeois establishments such as this. There was a bowl of fruit on a table in the sitting room and wilting flowers from the day before drooped in a vase.

Caroline couldn't help but think what the furniture in this room would be worth back in The Now. Here they were common tat. One hundred and fifty years hence they were valuable antiques.

"What now?" she asked.

"What do you mean?" Samuel said.

"I have a baby, no diapers, no change of clothes for either of us and no clothes that are in period anyway," she said. "I need basic toiletry items for me and Stephen. And I'll tell you right now that I'm starving. And if I don't eat then Stephen goes hungry too. That's how that works."

"I am sorry you're hungry," he said. "I will pick up things in the morning if you make me a list."

"You'll steal? What if you're caught? We're stranded here, Samuel," she said with irritation. She was losing her patience with all this mystery and intrigue.

"I have enough currency to see us through for a long period," he said. "I can draw more from a bank account in Toronto should we need it."

"So, you knew we were coming here, to this place, and this time," she said.

"Yes."

"And you couldn't share that with me?"

"It was easier to convince you to cooperate closer to events."

"Bullshit. It was easier to manipulate me," she said and moved to the hallway door and turned the key in the lock. She removed the key and twirled it on her finger.

"I did what was best for you both and for Dwayne."

"Fine. Noted and appreciated. But now you're going to answer some questions even if it's only to take my mind off my growling tummy," she said, taking a seat at the table and gestured for him to do the same.

The scopes revealed that the column marching south toward them numbered around two hundred men. Two centuries. Using the NODs gear allowed for a digital view that cut through the veil of dust. The marching men in the front were dressed in belted tunics and wore hobnailed boots. They carried packs suspended from poles held over their shoulders. Most were bareheaded. Some wore broad brimmed reed hats or sweat cloths tied about their heads. A marcher in the lead walked with a cloth-covered object cradled in his arms; the aquilifer that identified their unit, commander, and legion number. They were Romans.

Following behind was a more ragged formation of men in longer, kaftan type garments belted at the waist. These men wore their hair in long braids and carried what looked like thin curved rods over their shoulders. These were unstrung bows.

"Assyrian archers," Jimbo said. "Auxiliary troops."

"They're coming the wrong way to be our guys," Lee said.

"A regular patrol? Maybe just a coincidence?"

"Or reinforcements for the fort the Twenty-third are building," Lee said, squinting at the approaching force through the scope atop Jimbo's rifle. They were three-quarters of a mile to the north and coming on at a steady mile-consuming pace.

"Not good news either way."

"What's that behind them?" Lee said, handing the

rifle back to its owner.

Jimbo fixed his eye to the scope cup. The rectangle of men four across and twenty deep came into sharp focus. He tilted his view and adjusted the range to take in shapes moving behind them. He wiped sweat from his eyes and fixed his eye on the shapes.

"Pack animals. Mules or donkeys," Jimbo said. "This is no patrol. They're mobilized. They're fully tactical for a long deployment."

"Shit," Lee hissed.

"What are our options?"

"We test Tacitus to see if he was right. Nail a few and see if they turn tail."

"From our perspective they've all been dead for two thousand years anyway, right?" Jimbo smiled.

Bat joined Jimbo on the ledge and both lay prone with rifles trained downrange at the slowly closing figures there. The rest of the team packed up and were ready to move depending on the initial outcome. Lee stood, aiming binoculars at the dust cloud.

"The aquilifer's mine," Jimbo said and swiftly adjusted his scope for the angle and drop.

"Show off," Bat said and settled in with the butt of her Winnie braced snug to her shoulder. She found a man in the second row of the column and sipped in a lungful of air. She was letting it out slow when Jimbo's rifle boomed beside her. She squeezed and rode the recoil of her own weapon then brought her scope down to check out the results. Her man was down and the men directly behind him were halting mid-step. The rest moved around the stalled group like a stream of water around a rock. She saw some of the men look up suddenly, eyes betraying alarm. The report of Jimbo's rifle reached them now like thunder from the hills. The men flinched again as the crack of her shot echoed the first. A few were trying to rouse their fallen comrade. Bat swung her aspect to take in a similar drama as men stood about the Pima's chosen target. One man stood holding up the cloth covered banner while others knelt by the fallen man.

"They're not stopping," Jimbo said and jacked a fresh cartridge home.

"Maybe they never read Tacitus," she said, driving her bolt back in place and sighting through the scope.

"How could they? He hasn't been born yet."

"Man, this shit does mess with your head," Bat said, laying the crosshairs on the head of a marching man. The drop, the descending arc of her bullet as it responded to gravity, would make for a center shot through the chest.

Boom. Jimbo's rifle.

Bat dropped her man. She jacked a new round and took a survey. The column was at a full stop now with knots of men gathered around the fresh victims sprawled on the road. There was no way to know what they thought was happening; men among them falling under an invisible weapon, the sharp roars reaching them off the surrounding rocks, no enemy in sight.

"They need further encouragement," Jimbo said and let out his wind to steady his eye. Bat did the same.

Their shots were nearly simultaneous. Two marchers were thrown to the road as if struck by the same hammer blow. That was enough for the rest of the legionnaires. They threw down their poles and packs and ran in a ragged mob back the way they came.

Jimbo stood and watched through the scope as the routed infantry raced back to mix in with the column of pack animals. Mules reared and broke from their handlers to join the retreat. Some of the cargo carried by the animals broke free of the racks and spilled to the ground from leather sheathes. There it was trampled by panicked men and beasts. All was soon lost in a thick pall of rising dust.

"You see what those mules were carrying?" Jimbo said.

"Arrows," Bat said, lowering her rifle. "Thousands of them."

"These guys are reinforcements," Jimbo said. "And those arrows are for us."

The third century of the XXX, the Boars, was in shambles. The fourth century had stalled on the road as the column on the march before them dissembled into a rabble. Centurion Marcus Rupilius Pulcher was enraged. His second optio and five others were dead, struck down by some invisible force. His men fled like women in a sudden rain. He strode among them striking them with his staff. Gaius, his first optio, screamed himself hoarse to get them to retrieve their dropped gear and form back into ranks. Adding to Pulcher's rage was the delight on the faces of the auxiliaries; the Assyrian bowmen. The black scum were amused to see a mighty Roman column turned to craven wretches at the sight of a bit of blood.

More than a bit, as it turned out.

The downed men showed wounds much like the lead projectile of a slinger might make: a neat round hole punched through the flesh. But in addition to the puckered blue puncture was a matching wound far more catastrophic where the projectile made violent egress. An insult the size of a man's fist betrayed the final destination of the pellet, gaping tears through which the white of bone gleamed. One of the men, the aquilifer named Albus, was missing half his head. The pellet entered just under his nose and sprayed the men closest with blood and brains.

The messenger had arrived by foot at their fortified castra three days before with orders from the prefect as relayed through Bachus of the XXIII. They were to send a force along the road into Judea to serve as adjunct to a cohort of the XXIII encamped at a nameless village fifty mile markers south. Their tribune decided a token force was all that was needed to meet the letter of the prefect's request and so sent two centuries and the auxiliary force of archers.

Pulcher dug with his fingers in the gravel beneath one man and found a misshapen lump of lead that was hot to the touch. It was like the pellets flung by slingers. But what man could send a simple ball of lead with such speed and force? And what was the sound of thunder that reached them from the slopes all around? It was unsettling indeed. He could understand but not forgive the cowardice of his men. There would be punishments. Not here. Not now. Later, when they reached the camp of the XXIII.

The centurion ordered the Assyrians to climb to the ledges above and give chase while he moved the centuries down the road in full kit.

In helm and armor with scutums gripped before them, the Boars trudged south. The bodies of their slain were left for the foxes, wolves, and buzzards. If prayers were to be sent to Zeus or Mars or Mithra in their names then those prayers would be muttered on the march. The hired boys cautiously led the mule train on in their dusty wake past the dead Romans already black with clouds of flies.

After two miles of fast marching, a pair of Assyrians slid down a rocky slope to report to Pulcher. They reached a place ahead where the ravine turned only to see a number of riders galloping south along the ledge.

"Was there sign of a machine of some sort?" Pulcher asked them.

"Machine?" One of them shrugged, nose wrinkled.

"A ballista!" Pulcher gritted his teeth. "Some devilish instrument of some kind!"

"No machine. Just men on horses," the little bowman said in his gutter Latin.

"Did you see them?"

"Only horses' asses and dust."

"Were they Jew rebels?"

"Did not see. Bandits maybe."

"What bandit has the balls to face a Roman army on the march?" Pulcher seethed.

The bowman thought of the Romans pissing themselves in fear and the six dead legionnaires lying in pools of their own blood. He said nothing.

Pulcher stood squinting into the glare off the roadway.

"You have orders, sir?" the bowman asked after a while.

"Go back to your own optio and tell him that he will divide your force into two units. You will move ahead of the infantry as a screen."

"They are on horse. We cannot catch them," the bowman said.

"If they stop, if they attempt to strike us again, you will engage," Pulcher said, red-faced.

The bowman thought again of the thunder and the

Romans struck down as though by the gods.

"Go!" Pulcher roared and sent the pair of Assyrians on their way with a kick.

The century, sweating under the weight of layers of leather armor, hefted their javelins and shields at the bark of the optio. They hove forward at a trot, eyes on the ledges above, searching for they knew not what.

Questions Beget Questions

Samuel left the hotel the following morning to purchase the list of items, or their nineteenth century equivalent, at the local shops. His clothing was odd but not so outrageous that it couldn't be explained away by his being a foreigner. Caroline's appearance would be scandalous with her denim maternity jeans and shoes that allowed her ankles to be seen.

Caroline was exhausted from hunger, stress, and the lack of sleep the night before. She'd given birth just two days before, relative to her anyway, and this was not any kind of recommended course of recuperation. Reminding herself that her female ancestors probably dropped babies and went right back to work in the fields, as the cliché goes, did little to comfort her.

She dozed on and off as she nursed Stephen with what had to be the last of her milk. She thought about what Samuel revealed to her the night before as she faded in and out of a restless sleep.

Her first questions were about the means of direct travel they made between the present and the past without an intermittent stop at a tube chamber of any kind. He explained that there were set places on the planet where through-field generators were in place and programmable by anyone with a calibrating device. The field openings could be pre-programmed but the target destination had to be chosen with a generous allowance for variations. Calibrations in the field were simply not as exact as those made in the more stable laboratory environment of a tube chamber. Locations for the field generators were chosen for the length of time their locales had remained unchanged. The alley they traveled through had remained virtually unchanged for centuries. They were safe as long as the target date was kept within the time frame in which the unnamed alley existed as they found it. If not safe then at least within an acceptable level of risk.

"That sounds like shooting blind," she said. "What if we came out in broad daylight in the middle of a garden party?"

"The mist helps to mask any sudden arrivals," he said with a bland expression.

"Then it's all fast talking and a hasty exit?"

"That is what it often comes to."

She coaxed him into showing her the calibration device. It was a smooth metal band that covered his right wrist below his bandaged forearm and above the leather gloves that he never removed. It was perhaps four inches at its longest point and fit snugly to the skin. Frankly, she found it a letdown. There were no details on the surface, no visible controls, no displays, no way to discern how it operated. He told it worked on touch and was directly keyed into his own physiognomy.

"Each calibrator is customized to the individual user," he said.

"How can you make such complex calculations by touch alone?"

"I did not say touch alone."

"Is there a telepathic component?" she said, aching to touch the mysterious metal wristlet. "You *think* about your temporal destination?"

"It is more complicated than that, more of a symbiosis. The device reads the chronal patterns created by my unique physical structure. There's really no language to articulate it. It just seems to *happen*."

She wasn't sure if he was humoring her because he thought she was out of her scientific depth or if she really *was* out of her scientific depth. Or perhaps the technology was so intuitive for him that there was simply no way to explain it to her. Like a five-year-old who can use a pad device but cannot convey how what does it to grandpa, who didn't grow up with such devices.

"The future you come from, the world you were raised in, is different from ours," she said.

"It doesn't do to talk about it," he said without expression. "If our work succeeds that world may not exist. Nothing is written in stone and nothing is inevitable."

"But what is it like? You can't blame me for my curiosity, Samuel."

He sat a moment regarding the baby cooing and squirming gently in her arms.

"It is a bleak place without choice. It is an anthill where each day and each year marches by without change, without love and with nothing to look forward to. Some are mollified by simple comforts and enforced stability. Others live out their lives as drudges, slaves—drones in a hive. It is a place where the flame in the human heart has been exchanged for a cold light."

"That's beautiful in its own way. Horrible words but well spoken," she said and fought the urge to reach for his hand.

"They're not mine. They belong to my mentor. He did not write them down. I committed them to memory. He was executed for his thoughts but they live on in all he met."

He stood up from the table. A bar of sun was reaching across the floor boards from the street windows.

"The shops will be open. I will take your list. Do not answer the door. I will be back with food then find the other items you will need to enable you to leave this room."

He left the suite without a farewell.

Caroline rested her head against the lace antimacassar draped over the high seat back. She closed her eyes. She was exhausted but her thoughts kept turning back again and again to Samuel's words. The man was a living paradox and, if what he said was true, her son shared the same qualities. And how those qualities would manifest themselves she had no idea. She feared for her child even as she realized that every parent fears for their child. Only their fears were more than unfocused worries of the unknown. Caroline felt her anxieties were sharpened to a degree by the scant amount of knowledge she had about Stephen's unique condition. The empty look in Samuel's eyes as he recited those words about his world frightened her. She could only hope that the Rangers' latest operation would alter conditions enough to prevent that eventual future from occurring. That by their actions they would spare her child the fate that Samuel Renzi suffered.

Here, alone in a Parisian hotel, she was overcome by a sense of isolation every bit as painful as what she suffered in a cave as a captive of man-eating primitives an epoch ago. At least, stranded though she was in prehistory, someone knew where she was; knew and cared and could come retrieve her or, failing that, mourn for her loss. But here her only lifeline was a man she barely knew, who was unknowable. If something happened, if he never returned to this room, she and her child would be trapped here with no one aware of where and when they were. They would left to lead their lives in a time that was not their own and die many years before their birthdates.

Merciful sleep overcame her at last. With the baby breathing softly in her arms, she slipped from consciousness into a dreamless void.

Samuel returned to the room with a sack of food. Bread, butter, cheese, a jug of milk, a slab of smoked meat, and a bottle of white wine. Also a bar of soap and a comb. He had three or four newspapers as well. One in English. Caroline awoke and set the sleeping baby at the center of the bed, surrounded by pillows. She sat at the table and ate like a truck driver. She even had a sip of the wine.

"I could find no fresh fruit or vegetables," he said. "The city is under siege. Food is expensive and in short supply."

"So, I shouldn't ask a lot of questions about this?" she said, poking the flank of meat with a fork.

"I am not certain I could provide more than a guess."

"You're not eating?" she said around a mouthful of Brie and bread.

"My needs are taken care of," Samuel said.

"Are you a vampire, Samuel?"

His bewildered expression in response to that made her laugh hard enough to spit food across the table. It was the first time she witnessed a wrinkle in his unflappable cool.

She munched a strip of the shoe-leather-tough meat while making him a list on a sheaf of foolscap she found in a desk. Stephen would need cloth diapers or muslin rags should commercially made diapers not be available. She was no expert on the history of infant care or an expert of any kind in the care of babies, for that matter.

"I'll need clothes and shoes. Find a dress I can wear outside. And a hat to match. It's winter here so I'll need a coat and a hat. A scarf or shawl as well. Another dress to wear inside. And something for Stephen. I guess a few of those pull-over dress things. They dressed boy and girl babies the same back then. I mean, here and now."

"What about sizes? I have never purchased clothes for a woman," Samuel said, taking the list.

"I wear a size seven shoe. That's roughly seven inches in length. Make it eight to give me some toe room. You can guesstimate the rest from my height. The clothing sizes probably won't be that standardized even in Paris. Buy some thread, scissors, and needles. I can tailor the clothes some. I have the excuse of having just given birth so that covers any frumpiness. It's not like we'll be doing anything social, right? Oh, and a bassinet or something like it for Stephen to sleep in." She handed him back the list after making her additions to it.

"I will."

"Do you have the money for this?" she asked.

"I have funds. Several millions in period francs."

"How is that possible?" she asked. "How long did you have to plan for this contingency?"

"My life is a series of contingencies," he said, heading for the door.

"Wait," she said.

He stopped and turned, his hand on the knob.

"What do I do if something happens—if you don't come back? Have you prepped for that contingency?"

"I have left funds in the desk drawer. They should

keep you indefinitely," he said.

"A lifetime?" she said.

"I will be back. If I cannot return then I have left word of where and when you can be found."

"With who, Samuel?"

"With myself," he said.

"I suppose that will have to do, right?" she said.

"There are worse alternatives."

Samuel departed without saying anything further.

She pulled the desk drawer open and found a thick pile of paper money decorated with images of a seated woman wearing a robe. By it was a cloth sack of coins. She spilled some on the table. Thick, shiny discs decorated with the profile of Napoleon the Third. There were several thousand francs here. She had no idea of their current worth. Back in the present they wouldn't get her far. In this time they might be worth a small fortune or be made nearly worthless by the inflation that comes inevitably with war. She spread the coins and found among them several hundred in American double eagles. What contingency did *they* serve?

Caroline replaced the bills and coins in the drawer and locked it. She placed the key in the pocket of her coat. She looked over the newspapers while she finished the heel of bread that remained. The papers were dominated by the news of war with Prussia. Otto von Bismarck was featured in cartoons and drawings. The Prussians and their allies were closing on Paris from the north and south, taking a new French fort almost daily. The stories mentioned Moltke and Prince Frederick as well as General Trochu and Wilhelm, the future Kaiser whose son would command Germany in the First World War. Napoleon III had been taken captive months earlier. She knew that Germany was not a nation at this time; just a collection of kingdoms, duchies, baronies and principalities. She recalled, from a required European history course years before, that this war was key in Bismarck's strategy of "blood and iron" to unite the German people under one flag.

She could remember bits and pieces of other facts but had no sense of the overall course of the war or details of its outcome. This troubled her and she searched her mind for what else she knew of this current conflict. At the moment she desperately wished she had five minutes with Google or even Wikipedia to check a simple timeline of events. She knew that France lost this war decisively. But what form did that take? She cursed herself for not paying more attention in required history courses or to the boring presentations of tour guides. Her area was physics. History wasn't terribly interesting to her unless it dealt with the sciences. Now that she needed the advantage of being from the future to inform her as to what to do next she was coming up ignorant. But she was as clueless of what the next few months held for Paris as anyone living their life out in these years.

The date at the top of the front page of *Le Figaro* was 4 January 1871.

The date troubled her. Searching her mind for the source of that unease was maddening. Caroline went into the bedroom and lay down by the sleeping baby and was soon asleep herself.

She awoke startled to the baby crying.

Caroline was not aware at first where she was. The room was dark and she fumbled for the switch of a lamp by the bed. Of course there was none there. She held Stephen to her and allowed her eyes to adjust to the gloom. She exposed her breast for Stephen to nurse and held the warmth of him against her. Her breath was visible in the cold room. She would see to the stove in the next room once the baby was fed.

Propped up against the headboard she listened to the sounds coming through the drapes. On the street she could hear the tramp of boots punctuated by shouted orders. The marching men would come and go with long silences between. It was after curfew and there was no movement outside. The stillness outside was near complete. It was hard to believe that Paris lay unseen all about her. It was more like a graveyard.

In the stretches of quiet the faint echoes of a rumbling cadence reached her ears. She thought at first it was thunder but it was too constant, too insistent. It was cannon fire. Was it the guns of the city's defensive forts at Saint-Denis and Vincennes or the answering batteries of the invading army? Or was it both? The booming reached her as a *leitmotif* through the glass; resonant enough to cause unease, not close enough to cause alarm. She decided instead to concentrate on the contented grunt of her son suckling at her breast. Caroline clung to this moment. This was all that mattered, all that was real to her. The rest was a surreal dream or half-recalled movie.

Stephen sated and burped, she found matches and lit an oil lamp. She held the baby to her shoulder and carried the oil lamp into the next room and lit some candles there. In the guttering glow she found piles of clothing for her and the baby along with more groceries and an open wicker basket large enough for the baby to sleep in. There was also a bundle of folded rags she could use for diapers.

All of the clothing was meant for her and the baby. There was nothing here for Samuel. She looked for a note of any kind but found none. Still, Caroline knew he had left them alone again and she had no idea for how long.

She folded a blanket to make a cushion in the basket and, after negotiating a change of diapers, laid Stephen inside and covered him with a second blanket to keep out the chill. She then got a fire going in the iron stove and fed it from a fresh pile of split wood set on the hearth. Samuel had thought of everything.

Soon the little room was comfortably warm, the baby snug in his new bed and the food that needed to be kept cold set on the sill against the icy-rimed pane of the window. Those simple chores completed, Caroline sat at the table and allowed herself the luxury of a good long cry.

Run and Gun

"I almost feel bad for them," Jimbo said, his eye near the cup on his scope.

"I don't," Bat said, lying prone by his side.

They were both sighting on the bowmen trotting over the crest of a stony hill. Long shadows stretched before the running men as the sun sank low in the sky behind. The shadows reached like fingers for a pool of darkness spreading over the land below. The road moved through more open country here. The walls of the ravine gave way to broken hills created by a massive flooding an epoch before. Perhaps the deluge of the Torah, Bat thought, the first of God's promises made good. The bowman followed doggedly, never seeming to need rest even as the day wore on to darkness.

The team could easily stay ahead of them on horseback. But the archers would eventually catch up and, following a few hours behind them, the infantry column. The slow motion chase was distracting from the search for the wayward slave caravan. The solution was clear to all: the Pima and the Israeli would provide a rearguard to slow pursuit and even halt it entirely. If these guys, as good as they were, took enough punishment they'd give up the game.

"Come on. You got to show respect. These guys are hard chargers. Covering twenty miles or more double-time," Jimbo said and moved his view to follow one archer hopping down the slope from one shelf of rock to another.

"They're Syrians. They're the oldest enemy of my people," Bat said.

"I thought that was the Philistines."

"Oldest living enemy. We killed all the Philistines." She let out a long sigh and the rifle kicked back into her shoulder. On the hillside four football fields away, a man was tumbling lifeless down the slope leaving a plume of rising dust behind him. A second dropped as Jimbo fired.

"So this is like what? Retro payback?"

"Like if you got to go back and be at the Little Big Horn."

"Not sure which side I'd take on that one." Jimbo narrowed his eyes.

"They're still coming," Bat hissed as she sighted on another. There were more than twenty in view.

"Let's stop subtracting and start dividing," Jimbo said. "Watch what I do."

Bathsheba Jaffe glassed the hill and heard the crack of the Ranger's rifle. A bowman fell to the ground near the base of the hill. He was clutching a leg. Bat could see that his mouth was open and howling in pantomime. Two archers stopped their descent to come to his aid and lift him between them.

Bat found her own target and put a round through the hip of one of the running men. She watched as he sprawled face first and began clawing at the ground, face pinched in agony. Again distance kept them from hearing the agonized screams. Through the scope she saw three archers carrying the man into the shadows at the base of the hill.

Jimbo fired again and took a man skylined against the ruddy sky at the crest of the ridge. A head shot.

The man collapsed lifeless. Those closest to him turned around and ran back to concealment on the other face of the hill. They now had one half of the pursuing force tending to two wounded men and the rest afraid to come into view over the hilltop. Two wounded men would take another four or more out of the fight as they saw to them. The bulk of the force was isolated and pinned down, terrorized by something they could not even see to strike back at.

"They'll wait till full dark to try and move again," Bat said.

"But we won't be here," Jimbo said, standing. "Let's get a few miles between us and set up again. We give them a false sense of a security, let them think the dark is hiding them, then nail a few more."

They trotted to where they left their horses in the shade of an outcropping, slid the rifles home in their scabbards, and mounted up.

"Giddyup," Jimbo said with a broad smile. They led the mounts with knees and reins to roughly follow the road snaking between the hummocks of rocky land.

"You're enjoying yourself," Bat said.

"Oh, hell, yeah," Jimbo said. "Like playing cowboys and Indians back on the rez."

"Who played the cowboys?"

"I was always on the cowboy side." Jimbo laughed. "Clint Eastwood is my main man."

"So, you really would be conflicted at Custer's Last Stand." Bat laughed.

"You think that's weird?" he said.

"Not as weird as this little princess riding out to make Christianity possible," she said.

They trotted into a dry wash and spurred the horses to a gallop toward their next hide.

* * *

"Clusterfuck," Lee Hammond said under his breath. "Mother of all clusterfucks."

He and Chaz Raleigh lay prone in a copse of junipers watching the construction of a watchtower and ring wall a thousand yards away. It was only the hour following full dawn and already nearly-naked guys were stacking pre-cut stones atop slathers of mortar mixed by others in a pit and passed forward in a bucket chain. Another crew was working on scaffolds to apply more mortar to seal the gaps. Still more were hauling stone forward on two-wheeled carts drawn by oxen. They worked at a steady pace and the ring wall was the height of two men already. The stout tower was growing as they watched. There was an encampment of nearly fifty tents laid out in neat rows within an earthwork constructed about the construction site. A deep ditch filled with sharpened stakes ran around the floor of the earth wall.

The fort sat at the foot of a steep slope that rose to a rocky summit. The summit was a kind of headland in a range of escarpments that stretched east. By the fort was a feeder road that led off the main highway and went into a gap in the escarpment toward something the Rangers could not see from their angle. Whatever was back there was the source for the building blocks the Romans were using to build the walls and tower. It had to be the quarry the Arab caravan driver had told them about.

"They're like goddamn beavers," Chaz said. He moved his binoculars to take in a knot of tile rooftops surrounded by a curtain wall a few hundred yards from where the fort was going up. It was a village they had no name for. It sat along the north/south road. It appeared to be the source of water for the fort. All day long camels led by boys made their way from the village carrying barrels of water that were drained into a stone-lined reservoir dug within the earthen wall. This water was used for mixing the mortar and for the legionnaires to use for drinking and bathing. Other villagers followed the camels hauling carts loaded with goods for sale to the Romans. Chaz couldn't see what they were selling. Considering the orchards stretching south from the village, probably dates.

"See their banner?" Lee said. "They have it set up in front of the largest tent."

Chaz swung his gaze back to the Roman camp. The sun gleamed off the polished brass aquilifer stuck in the ground before a bell-style tent. The figure of the trotting horse was visible atop it.

"That's our unit. The Twenty-third," Chaz said.

"I don't see any slaves," Lee said. "They're all wearing those sandals with socks like a bunch of German tourists in Miami. It's all soldiers building that place."

"They only want to use trained labor. These guys are engineer soldiers," Chaz said. "Remember what Dwayne told us about the guys rowing the galley he was on. All free men with mad rowing skills."

"Still seems like they could use a carpenter, right?"

Chaz laughed.

"Surprised you find that funny," Lee said, lowering his binoculars and eyeing his friend.

"It's funny. Nothing sacrilegious there, you atheist motherfucker." Chaz grinned. "The man was a carpenter."

"All the shit we've seen and you still believe."

"More than ever, bro."

"I respect that. I really do," Lee said and rose to his feet. Chaz followed him back through the trees to a clearing where Boats waited with the mounts and pack animals. The SEAL was on watch, and looking the part in his body armor and kilt with his crazy ginger whiskers and long hair completing the picture. The only conflicting image was the stainless steel Mossberg Mariner in his fists. The pump shotgun was not standard issue for gladiators.

"Did you see Jesus?" Boats asked in all seriousness.

"Wouldn't know him I saw him." Chaz shrugged.

"Man, I didn't think of that." Boats scratched his chin through the beard. "What do you think he looks like?"

"He won't have a halo over his head," Chaz said and took a seat on a rock. "He'll look like any other Jewish teenager, I guess. You could pass him at the mall and not notice him."

"Anyone interested in the plan?" Lee said. "We rest while we wait on Bat and Jimbo then recon that quarry."

"You jealous, Hammond?" Boats grinned.

"Of what?"

"The Indian and your girl sharing a kill together."

"You have one fucked up idea about romance, Boats." Lee smiled.

"So I have been told." Boats shook his head ruefully.

They took turns keeping watch and catching catnaps in the shade of the trees. The country here reminded them all of parts of the Helmand in Afghanistan: a rocky place with clumps of pine forest dotted around. And like that other place, the space between villages was unpopulated. Even if there were bandits wandering around they'd steer well clear of the Romans toiling away below. Like a remora on a shark, proximity to the legion fort was giving the Ranger camp cover. What troubled Lee and Chaz was, if bandits and rebels were no real threat to a large force, then what the hell were the Romans forting up for? Was it possible they were warned about the team's arrival? It was the only explanation. If Harnesh's influence could cause a change in the local imperial wonk's policy then it stood to reason Sir Neal had agents on the ground in this time and place.

There was no movement in the trees except for some spotted deer plucking berries off the juniper branches with their lips. Chaz was awake and watched them moving along silent as ghosts. It always amazed him how animals that big could move so noiselessly even over a floor of needles. That was what it was like to be prey. A big buck eyed Chaz while placidly munching the purple fruit. It raised its head at a crack of sudden thunder. A soft snort from its nostrils and it moved off with its coterie of does following.

That thunder was a gunshot. Chaz went to rouse the other two but Lee and Boats were already on their feet. They moved from the trees and spotted Jimbo and Bat walking their mounts along the floor of a gulch below them. They looked like something out of time, a mishmash of the Old West and a Hercules flick. Except it was Bat Jaffe cradling the rifle as she walked. No squaw she.

Chaz let out a low whistle and the riders found him in the tree line. They turned their reins and followed a trail up the slope toward the camp.

"Find water?" Jimbo asked as he slid the saddle from his mount.

"Not yet," Lee said. "You two slow down that other force?"

"We bought us some time," Bat said as she ran a brush over her mount's back. "But those are some tough monkeys. They'll keep coming on."

"You find the slave caravan?" Jimbo asked.

Lee filled them in on what they'd discovered at long range.

"We leave at sundown to recon in force to check out the quarry," he told them. "Both of you get some rest until then."

"Not until I find us water," Jimbo said. "These horses aren't going to be worth shit without it. And we might need them if we have to make a run for it."

He pulled his rifle from its boot and picked up some empty CamelBaks and walked into the trees.

"Speaking of tough monkeys," Bat said, watching the Pima recede into the gloom.

"You kept up with him," Lee said, cupping her chin.

"But I can't take one more step. I need sleep and badly," she said, shaking her head slowly and regarding him through heavy lids.

Lee took watch and sat with his M4 across his knees while the rest bedded down to recharge. Bat was as good as her word. Her head propped on her saddle at the head of a ground sheet, she was sound asleep in seconds. Jimbo returned within an hour with the CamelBaks bloated with fresh water. He insisted on watering the horses before lying down. Soon Lee Hammond was the only one awake. Even the horses dozed deeply where they stood on the running line strung between the trees.

Déjeuner Pour Un

Caroline Tauber grew restless after two days. After five she thought she'd go mad.

Staying to the two rooms for days on end, with her only human contact the two maids: one to bring her meals and another to take her laundry.

The rooms seemed to be getting smaller with each moment. How could she have thought this place was quaint? Or cozy? It was rundown and cramped and reeked of wood smoke and kerosene. There were no distractions but the newspapers and a few books. She could not even hold a conversation with the maids. She sensed it was her foreignness, her tortured French and a touch of class distinction. Though these rooms were modest and her clothing of middling quality, they were beyond the means of the girls who served the rooms in this hotel. And thus there was a societal divide that prevented all but the most mannered and inconsequential small talk.

It wasn't boredom driving her slowly mad. Who could be bored? The sounds of artillery rose louder every day as the Prussian batteries grew closer to the city. Shells were falling inside the outer defensive walls now. The papers, when there were papers, screamed of civilian casualties, hospitals and churches being bombarded and deeper shortages to come. There were more and more soldiers in the streets that she could see from her windows. They had been pulled from the outer forts and defensive positions to be in place should the Prussians and their allies breach the walls and enter Paris itself. Gun carriages rumbled by at one point and wagon after wagon of wounded passed beneath her windows at all hours. There were rumors of riots in the streets over politics and rationing. The troops could be fighting a war within and without soon.

She felt trapped. She sensed that was the mood of the entire city. But her plight was special. She was alone in a strange city in a time not her own, truly and utterly alone. And she had no idea when her self-imprisonment would end or if it would ever end.

Only Stephen kept her together. The care of a helpless infant was her only focus. She fed him and changed him and cuddled him and he helped her forget that the sounds outside the windows were not thunder but war. His presence was also a source of worry. Stephen was healthy and thriving and not terribly demanding. If he got sick she had no idea what she would do. She certainly could not trust the medicine of the day when even the basic concepts of cleanliness were in their earliest days. And with thousands of wounded crowded into every available hospital space, who would care for a single baby?

There were a few books in the room, novels mostly, and she tried read them, hoping to improve her grasp of French, only she couldn't seem to concentrate on the pages. She turned to using the sewing kit bought for her by Samuel. It occupied two days but she took in a rather nice dress in burgundy with black brocade. It didn't hang on her like a sack now. There was another bottle green dress that needed less work and a voluminous wool coat that she felt comfortable leaving at a fuller fit. And a pinafore-type dress that she could wear in the rooms over a starched blouse. There were undergarments as well that needed figuring out. A corset, bustier, pantaloons, and a bewildering selection of skirts that she knew were worn under the dress but their proper order eluded her. Also a tidy selection of gloves, scarves, and a carpetbag to keep it all in.

There were two hats and she favored a broad-brimmed black one with a veil. A fine pair of leather boots that buckled up the sides. They turned out to be a half-size too big but would accommodate the sweat socks she kept as her only modern garment. The rest of her 21st century clothes she tore into strips and burned in the stove.

She wondered at Samuel's knowledge of period dress. The wardrobe was reasonably complete. Caroline assumed he had help from an eager shopkeeper once that fat roll of francs came out of his pocket.

At the bottom of the carpetbag was an item she knew he probably needed no help selecting—a fat, ugly revolver with a box of shells. It served to remind her of the seriousness of it all, as if the sounds of the barrage outside would let her forget how dire her situation was.

The pistol looked peculiar, sort of like a cowboy's weapon but less elegant somehow. Caroline had no interest in firearms, but took the time to learn how to load it. It had a cylinder that held nine copper-jacketed rounds marked with .36 on the striking end. But it also had a larger barrel suspended below the first. After some jiggering she determined that this barrel held the paper-wrapped shells that looked to her inexpert eyes like they belonged in a shotgun.

She was never political in school or after and really had no opinion for or against guns. It was an issue that she never troubled to think about. And, as most of her education was in England, the subject seldom came up in conversations. The thought of having to use a firearm in her own defense never entered her mind. And she absolutely had never imagined she would be so often in the company of men to whom guns were a tool of their craft. But she'd been in a firefight now and even killed her share when the time came to choose between her own death and the death of another. She'd also been in a fight without a firearm at hand and knew which scenario she preferred. The brutal looking pistol would be her constant companion from here on.

On the sixth day she dressed in the bottle green dress and all its layers of underskirts. She balanced the veiled hat upon her head at what she thought was the proper angle using girlhood memories of Audrey Hepburn in *My Fair Lady* as a guide. She then slipped the cash and coins into a beaded purse, bundled up Stephen, and went downstairs to take a meal in the hotel's first floor dining room. She left the revolver hidden beneath layers of clothes in the carpetbag lying on the floor of an armoire which she locked. She did not anticipate a gunfight in the lobby of Le Hotel Exemplaire.

The dining room was a gloomy affair. The finely etched windows facing the street had been covered with boards to protect them from looters, vandals, and potential cannon shells. A layer of cigar smoke hung in the air where it wafted from a table where three gentlemen sat in hushed conversation. The only other diners were an older married couple who were just ordering as Caroline entered with the basket containing Stephen on her arm. An unescorted woman with a child was something to be remarked upon and her fellow diners made no secret that she was a fresh topic of conversation.

Caroline just didn't give a damn. She had to get out of the room or lose her mind. She sat demurely in a chair offered by a waiter and smiled as the same waiter filled a glass with some very doubtful looking water. He presented her with a hand-printed menu issuing slurred apologies for the scant bill of fare. She read the top two items, *consommé de cheval au millet* and *epaules et filets de chien braises,* and lost her appetite entirely. Her choice was of either horse or dog.

"I will have a cheese plate with bread, please," she said.

"We have only black bread today," the waiter said gravely.

"That will do. And wine."

The waiter plucked the menu from her fingers and vanished.

"Perhaps the lady would prefer a filet of Castor or Pollux," one of the cigar smokers said to the amusement of the others.

"Pardon?" Caroline said, confused.

"They are elephants," the married woman said with a disapproving glance at the table of guffawing men.

"*Were* elephants," the wit remarked to answering guffaws from his friends.

"The zookeeper at the Gardens shot them and sold the meat to a butcher," the woman informed her with an irritated glance at the table of jokers.

"He became a wealthy man over Christmas," the woman's husband added with a tinge of umbrage.

"Terrible," was all Caroline could say in reply.

"You are not French," the woman said.

"I'm certain that is obvious," Caroline said. It was an opening to a conversation and, as rusty as her French was, she was overcome with pleasure to speak to another human being. "I am Canadian but not French Canadian. I'm traveling with my husband and son."

"Your infant is so young," the woman said with a touch of disapproval. Caroline knew this was a *faux pas* on her part. It was not usual to bring newborns out into public so early.

"The room is so stuffy. I wanted Stephen to breathe some fresh air. I suppose I was mistaken," she said and produced what she hoped was an ironic smile as she waved away a strand of cigar smoke.

The woman looked doubtful. Her husband paid no mind to the conversation as plates of lumpy soup were set on the table before them.

"Your husband is not with you?" Apparently the woman was more curious than hungry.

"He's away on business," Caroline answered airily.

"Outside the city?"

"Yes."

"And when do you expect him to return?"

Caroline realized that the cigar smokers had ceased their own exchange and were listening to the conversation of the two women. The husband was slurping soup in a world of his own. She'd stepped in it good. How the hell could her "husband" be "away" on business with the entire German army surrounding the city.

"I'm not certain. I am worried though. I begged him not to go. The danger you know?" she said, feigning alarm. The woman's face softened. She probably thought Caroline was some kind of idiot. Let her think that.

The woman introduced herself and her husband and Caroline forgot the names as quickly as they were uttered.

"Caroline," she said. "Caroline Tauber."

The woman's face darkened. Her husband looked up from his soup with narrowed eyes. The cigar smokers frowned in their fragrant fog.

"Well, I will leave you to dine in peace," the woman sniffed and turned her back.

The waiter arrived then with a plate containing a wedge of runny cheese and a half loaf of coarse black bread. Caroline ate, grateful for the food as well as the silence, as bland as the former and uncomfortable as the latter was.

She finished her meal with two glasses of *vin ordinaire* and departed the dining room without any farewells from the married couple or the cigar trio. Their eyes followed her from the room.

Upstairs, an hour or so later, she was interrupted at nursing Stephen by a strident knock at the door.

She opened it to find the hotel registrar standing in the hallway regarding her with an arched eyebrow. Behind him stood a tall, broad man in a stained apron and the knobby nose of a heavy drinker. There was to be trouble and the little man had brought some kitchen help to back him up.

"May I help you, monsieur?" she said.

"Where is your husband?" the registrar demanded. The bitch in the dining room had run to the management.

"He is away on business."

"How can that be with war at the city's doorstep and the Germans days away from the heart of the city? I knew your husband was up to no good. He broke my lock. He arrived after curfew. Now he is departed leaving a woman and baby behind?"

"And paid you well for these inconveniences," she said, arms folded.

"What did you tell the other diners your name was?" His eyes gleamed.

Her reserve slipped a bit.

"Tauber, was it not?" He smiled, showing little yellow teeth.

"What of it?"

"Your *husband*—" he made the word sound like an obscenity "—signed my book as Monsieur P. Rivard. And Tauber... this is a German name, is it not?"

She began to protest. The obnoxious little man held up a hand and turned his face from her.

"You will remain in your room and I will go to the police or perhaps the guard. They will want to speak to you. Perhaps you will share the truth of this matter with them," he said, meeting her eyes. "Patrice will stand at your door until I return. We shall see what this business is that your man is about, German bitch."

With that he slammed her door shut and she heard the key turn in the lock and footfalls departing for the stairs. The giant kitchen servant, Patrice, would be left behind to make certain she did not leave this room.

Unforgiving Options

A low overcast turned the light of the moon into a pale glimmer that cast blue highlights on the rocks. The Roman fort lay in a pool of black shadow shed from the hill above. The glow of signal torches guttered and flared as the night wind stirred. The village beyond was dark and the road empty of traffic.

The Rangers saw no sign that the reinforcement column had arrived. They could expect them the following day for certain.

Through their NODs gear they could see sentries moving along the ramparts atop the earthen walls. Within the camp no one was visible but an aquilifer of the XXIII standing alone before the command tent.

Lee and Bat led the way over the open ground with Chaz and Jimbo following at intervals. Boats remained in camp with the horses. This would be a strictly infantry operation. They were in full battle rattle. All but Lee wore the period-modified body armor. In addition to that they were lumbered with side arms, CamelBaks, ammo, night gear, and their rifles. Bat and Jimbo sported their Winchesters. Jimbo had a cut-down twelve gauge in a scabbard on his back and a belt of buckshot and slugs around his waist. Lee and Chaz humped their M4s and ammo and had attached underslung grenade launchers to the rifles. Bandoliers of the fat 40mm rounds were slung over their shoulders.

"Render unto Caesar, my ass." Chaz chuckled drily

as they set out over the broken ground to skirt the fort.

They slipped easily past a widely spaced picket line set outside the ring of earthworks. They all wore their NODs and could see the sentries standing at their posts as clear as if under a noon sun. The Romans, struggling to remain awake, could see nothing beyond ten feet of their assigned positions in the muted moonlight.

Once past the fort, they climbed the slope at a punishing run. The thirty-degree grade leveled off to a table of land above the fort. The ground was rough but mostly level at a thousand foot elevation. The team leapt from surface to surface over the fragmented ground. They moved across the headland to look down at the feeder road snaking along between the slab-sided rock formations of a narrow gap. Following this led them along a curving ledge for a mile or more. They came to a spot where the plateau's tabletop summit fell away sharply into a bowl-shaped depression. Here lay the quarry.

It was a broad area bit from the rock in a half-circle formation a half-mile across. The land literally stepped up from the floor of the man-made hollow. Through the NODs they could plainly see where the rock had been cut in slabs by tools and then segmented to make blocks. Tall stacks of cut stone sat in orderly rows in the center of the pit. Along one wall of the quarry was a stone building with a roof of wooden planks. A wooden watch tower stood where the quarry opened up at one end to allow the feeder road access. They could see a pair of men in the open tower plainly lit by torches sputtering on poles. There was a fenced corral for oxen. Against the wall of the quarry yard directly beneath their vantage point were broad tarps slung between posts driven into the ground. These would be the slave quarters. Reclining figures could be seen in rough rows outside the shelter of the tarps. These were slaves who opted to sleep under the stars or were, more likely, an overflow from the unexpected arrival of the XXIII and their captive charges.

As tactical situations went, this one sucked about as bad as it was possible for anything to suck. The mission was to free the slaves from captivity or at least give them a running head start. But here they were all bottled up with one narrow route of escape and that route past a fortified position packed with soldiers from the baddest army on the planet. The Rangers' advantage of surprise had been blunted but they still had long range firepower unheard of in this period. Now they had to work out a way to create the leverage needed to give a mass escape a chance in hell of succeeding.

The moon was dropping to make the shadows longer and darker. The team sat away from the ledge to take a meal break.

"We can take out their guards easy," Jimbo said. "Bat and I put on suppressors and bring down the guys in that tower. There can't be more than twenty more in that hut. Slip down there and kakk them in their sleep."

"Then march a thousand prisoners past that fort?" Chaz said, "'cause that's the only way out."

"You can't even be certain the slaves will run for it," Bat said. "No one cooperates in a fluid situation. Some might just freeze and we need a one hundred percent evac, right? What do we do then?"

Lee sat sullenly skipping rocks.

"Could we get them to fight?" Jimbo said.

"And risk losing the target we came here to rescue?" Bat said. "Besides, that's no fighting force down there. They may be slaves but that's all they have in common. I'll bet most of them don't even share a language. They're not going to stand and fight together."

"They'll be too scared to bolt. Crucifixion is a bitch," Jimbo said. "As lousy as busting rocks is, at least they get to live."

"Clusterfuck," Lee said and tossed a spray of pebbles to bounce away over the rocky surface.

"You're the one who always has an angle, Hammond. These kind of shitty situations are your specialty," Chaz said.

Lee held up one finger.

"One. They're not going to move the slaves. Those poor assholes will die down there. So we're stuck with this scenario. But this part of scenario is static and that's good."

He raised a second finger.

"Two. The Romans can shut them in as easy as closing a door. Not good."

He raised a third finger.

"Three. We could lead the Romans away from the fort. Think of a way to draw them out. Risky."

A fourth finger.

"Four. Or lure them down the feeder road to the quarry and chop their asses up while they're in the gap. That has its risks too."

His thumb extended.

"Or..."

"Both," Chaz grinned.

"Or both," Lee said and closed his fist.

The horses heard them first.

Boats was in the trees well away from and a bit above the smoldering camp fire. He'd pissed in it to make it smolder. He didn't want a blaze that would take away his natural night vision. The smoky embers would serve as a lure for the curious should anyone come snooping around.

He was half-dozing, half-waking and wondering idly how a sailor like him always wound up so far from the sea. A horse snuffled softly. Another stamped a hoof. They smelled something on the cool wind whispering through the junipers. Boats watched the trees on the opposite side of the clearing. Shadows shifted between the boles. Shapes took form and parted from the dark to stalk across the clearing through the haze created by the dying fire.

A thrum like a swarm of angry bees cut the air. The bedroll Boats left as a decoy was pin cushioned with the trio of shafts. These were the fuckers who were dogging Jimbo and Bat. Boats rose silently to his feet and kept his eyes locked on the clearing where more dark shapes joined the others for a murmured exchange around the empty bundle of blankets. There were a dozen or more visible in the camp area and at least three times that number in the surrounding woods.

It was time to move on. That was it for the horses. No matter what happened Boats couldn't protect the remuda against these kind of odds. All he could do was lead the archers deeper into the trees and away from the rest of the team.

One of the bowmen was more pissed than the others and began cuffing some of his buddies. An officer. A real prick from the sound of it. The group began to break up to fan out for a search. Whistles and calls echoed through the forest. Boats could not have that shit happening. They were here in one bunch with their commander in range. The SEAL aimed to take advantage of that.

Boats raised the Mariner and let fly with three rounds of buck. The officer took the first load full in the chest and was flung back spraying blood. The next two rounds sent a spread of 9mm lead balls that struck three more of the archers. The officer was stone dead before he hit the ground. A second archer died gurgling. Two more thrashed and howled causing the horses to whinny in panic at the shrill animal sounds and the rank stink of blood.

The SEAL was moving as the third load left the shotgun. He jinked left to get out of the line of fire then hooked right to climb up the hill and deeper into the trees. He topped off the Mariner as he trotted, pulling more buck rounds from the loops on his belt. A cut-down M4 was slung on his back and a bag full of nasty goodies slapped his thigh as he ran.

A pulsing sound passed behind him followed by a clatter in the woods to his right. The little fuckers were firing arrows at him on the fly. He ran in a snake pattern, keeping the trees between him and pursuit as much as possible. More whistles, more clattering. There were voices calling off to his left. More answering behind and to his right. They were bracketing him. It was only a matter of time before they closed the arms of the pursuit and caught him between.

Boats threw himself into a shallow depression and dug in his goodie bag for his NODs. He was outnumbered and would be out-positioned in moments. His one advantage was the dark. He dropped the night-vision array before his eyes. The gloom of the woods vanished and all was in sudden stark monochromatic contrast. The SEAL could not have timed it better as a pair of archers stalked by where he lay recumbent in the shelter of the night. He let them move past him up the hill until they were closer to one another.

He rose to one knee, turning, and took them one after the other easy as shooting skeet. The buck loads slammed into their backs and lifted them off the ground to fall limp as dolls. They wore layers of leather plates that the buck cut through like slices of Wonderbread. Boats came to his feet slowly, noiselessly. Movement was not the key now. It was all about stealth. He was a fucking ghost, an all-seeing phantom among them, striking from every direction. He'd ninja their asses until they lost their mud and ran away. As he rose up an archer ran toward him up the hill with bow bent back.

Boats fired from the hip and the running archer stopped as though he'd rushed into an unseen wall. The arrow was loosed and skipped off the armor at Boat's shoulder. It felt like he'd been struck with a hammer even though he knew the shaft had been fired early. He felt a tingle down that arm. Another shaft whirred by just over his head and he dropped back to cover and rolled to a new position. When he rose again there was an archer just before him. They were closing about him like a noose. They used the flurry of arrows to drive him where they wanted him to be. Boats raised the shotgun and rushed forward to brain the man with the butt. The SEAL stumbled to the ground with the falling man and heard voices close by. He was on his feet and running laterally along the hillside. His best hope was that he'd broken out of the ring of pursuers. He'd make distance from them and use the Mike-Four to whittle their number further from a safe firing position.

A hammer blow to his right leg drove him to the ground. He slid down the slope, struggling to regain his feet. The leg was numb as though from blunt force trauma. Boats turned on his side and levered up on his elbows. He filled the air with buck at the sound of movement above him. A wet shriek rang out and the woods went silent.

Boats moved to stand and a lancing pain made him

gasp aloud. He looked down to see a long arrow shaft stuck through his upper leg at a wicked angle. The barbed point was through the front of his bare thigh, the shaft jutting from a ragged hole in the flesh. A good two feet of wood stuck from the back of his leg. A wide stream of blood ran down his leg from the exit wound. It looked black through the NODs lenses. The pain was growing and would get a lot worse and soon. If he was going to move it had to be now.

No option left to him but to follow the path of least resistance. The SEAL hobbled downhill. Voices called from all around. Boats could see the little fuckers moving fast through the trees around him. They were still blind to his location. One of them would run across the blood trail he was leaving and follow it right up his ass. He had seconds not minutes.

Below him he saw the tumble of a deadfall; rotting tree boles were piled up against the base of a line of stout oaks to create a natural defense position. Boats dropped to one knee and dug in his goody bag and pulled out a Claymore mine. He flipped down the metal legs and secured the mine to face uphill away from the deadfall before inserting the detonation wire lead into the plug atop it. Dragging his wounded leg, trying to keep it as straight as possible, he crawled/slid into a wedge between two fallen trees, playing the thin det wire out behind him.

He was invisible now but immobilized. Boats was making the best of a shitty situation. The plan was to hammer these fuckers hard enough to make them turn tail. They might leave him alone long enough to let him withdraw and find the rest of the team. He lay back, propped against the bark of a dead tree trunk with the plastic det clicker on his lap. He examined his wound. The leg wasn't broken but there was bone pain deep in his leg. There was a steady flow of blood from the exit wound but it wasn't pulsing. That would change if he was dumb enough to yank the shaft out. Better to let the flesh swell around the wound for now. But he couldn't have the wooden shaft sawing in his leg as he moved and he would *need* to move.

Boats slid his combat knife from the sheath on his chest and lifted himself enough to see the feathered end of the arrow protruding from his leg midway between the hip and knee. He used his fingers to secure it in place where it entered the muscle and sawed at the springy wood. It hurt like a bitch as the vibration traveled down the shaft into his leg and rocketed up into his groin. He bit down on a strip of belting clenched in his teeth and kept cutting until the shaft came away clean. The SEAL lay back panting and sweating, his mane of red hair sodden and matted to his head.

Voices came from above him. They were gathering together up there. Sure as shit one of them came across his blood trail and called the others. From his shelter under the apex of two fallen boles he watched them cautiously moving down toward him. They had arrows nocked and their bows curved back ready to fill the air with missiles. The little men glanced about, blindly scanning the dark ahead as the center man bent to follow the smear of crimson on the forest floor.

Four of them moved cautiously toward the deadfall with two more behind. All had bows raised and bent full back, moving the barbed points back and forth, sighting down the shaft for the target they knew to be here. Knew to be close.

The SEAL covered his eyes with one arm and flipped the cover off the clicker. He depressed the switch twice.

A charge of C-4 send hundreds of steel balls

rushing from the Claymore. In an instant the area before the mine was transformed into a ballistic hurricane of flesh, bone and blood as well as a cloud of dust and fragmented debris from the forest floor. The four archers closest to the blast were vaporized. The two behind were dismembered. A seventh archer unfortunate enough to wander into the kill zone lost both legs below the knee and collapsed with a high keening cry that died away as his blood sprayed from torn stumps. All in a fraction of a second thanks to the baddest anti-personnel weapon in the SEAL's arsenal.

Lying less than fifty feet behind the blast, Boats was deafened. His head felt like there was a clapper inside it striking off the inside of his skull. He fought to remain conscious.

He lost that fight.

At Madame's Pleasure

Caroline knew two things for certain. She could not be in this room when the registrar returned with either gendarmes or soldiers. And the single door to the hallway was the only way out of this room. The door was locked from the outside but the key was still in the slot. She knew this by crouching silently and peeping into the keyhole to see it was blocked by the barrel of the key.

Her room was on the third floor. The windows opened onto a narrow balcony that was mostly decorative. It was an escape route she'd hesitate to use if she were alone. With Stephen in her care it was beyond any consideration.

She swiftly packed the carpetbag with all it would hold then put on the woolen coat and hat and a pair of scarves. The baby was dozing in his basket but would not be for long if the plan she carried out was to work. Caroline retrieved the revolver from its hiding place and worked the hammer back with the heel of her hand. She then went to the door and pounded on it with her fist.

"My child! My child is ill! Mercy! You must have mercy!" she screamed in her tourist French and hoped she was selling her desperation. The drumming on the door and the shouts of his mother awoke Stephen with a start. His pitiable cries added to her performance.

She could see a shadow shift in the crack of light

under the door. Big, dumb, drunken Patrice heard her.

"Please, help me. Have mercy on a small child who has harmed no one. I beg you, sir!"

The key rattled in the lock and the door swung inward. Patrice entered the room with wide eyes void of suspicion. Caroline backed further into the room and raised the pistol in both hands.

"Please?" Patrice said once he realized what he was looking at.

"My baby and I are leaving," Caroline said, fighting to keep her voice steady. "Pick up that bag and I will not be forced to hurt you."

Patrice looked down at the packed carpetbag resting by the door.

"I am not certain..." he began.

"Well, I *am* certain, monsieur," she said and gestured at him with the revolver.

Reluctantly, he picked up the bag and turned his back on her as she indicated he should do with a twirl of the pistol barrel. She shifted to a one-handed grip and lifted the handle of the basket containing the squawling Stephen.

"We will use the back stairs and the servants' exit," she said, following the big man down the hall at three paces distance.

"Please do not shoot me, madame," he said with a small voice.

"Please do not make me," she said. The way was awkward in the narrow hallway with the weight of the basket in one hand and the heavy wool coat that fit like a tent over the brocaded dress and all the goddamned layers of petticoats. The boots had raised heels that she'd thought were so cute but now realized were impractical for getaways. This would have all gone so much easier in a pair of sweats and Nikes, she thought.

She turned at voices behind her. The three cigar smokers were coming to the top of the open stairway from the second floor. They'd seen her and were calling out in alarm. They looked as though they meant to catch up and subdue her.

Caroline raised the revolver, straightened her arm and jerked the trigger. The result was deafening. The big handgun threw her arm up like a pump handle. She felt the shock all the way to her shoulder. Through the smoke she saw an entire section of banister had been torn away at the top of the stairs. The three cigar smokers were descending the stairs three steps at a time, leaving top hats behind in a rush to be out of the line of her fire. She fired two more shots in quick succession to let them know the first was not a fluke. She could hear splintering furniture and the crash of from the floors below followed by the shouts of men and screams of women.

Through the clanging din in her ears the rising sound of a baby's wail. Her baby.

She looked down to see Stephen red-faced and howling in terror with hands held fisted to his face. Caroline cooed words of comfort even though she could not hear them herself. She was probably shouting and adding to the baby's fear. In a flash she recalled her predicament and swung the gun down the hallway toward where she fully expected to see Patrice rushing her.

The big man stood at the far end of the hall, frozen in mid-stride with his back to her and clutching the carpetbag. His shoulders were hunched in anticipation of a fresh fusillade. Smoke was still drifting from the weapon she aimed at him. Caroline used all her strength in her free hand to thumb back the heavy hammer and saw that the revolver cylinder rotated and clicked into place.

"Move on!" It sounded to her like it was coming from miles away through layers of cotton. She was shrieking though it sounded to her like a whisper. Patrice trotted toward the end of the hall and she followed with the pistol raised at the back of his skull.

They descended the tight back staircase and reached the servants' mudroom and the doorway to the alley that lay at the bottom. She urged Patrice to step outside and set the carpetbag on the cobbles. She ordered him away, out of her sight. A waggle of the weapon sent him running away down the alley toward the rear courtyard as fast as his big feet could carry him. Caroline dropped the revolver into a voluminous pocket of her coat and hefted the carpetbag. Struggling with her double burden she made for the street at the far end of the alley. She prayed that whoever the registrar went to for help capturing the mad German spy was too busy with the war to come back to the hotel with him.

Her hearing returned in the cold sting of the wind coming down the narrow passage between buildings. Stephen was still wailing in the basket. Beneath the sound of his cries she could hear the muffled rumble of cannon shells landing somewhere nearby.

"Goddamn you, Samuel," she whispered as she stepped out of the alley and onto a sidewalk crowded with foot traffic. They were all of them running in one direction. She turned to look at the way they came to see a dense tower of dirty gray smoke rising over the buildings to join the low shroud of winter clouds.

Caroline found shelter for herself and the baby in a restaurant set in the middle of a block of apartments. They were out of the wind and the cold and removed from the chaos on the streets. Soldiers were trying to keep order. They blocked entry to certain upscale streets, bayonets gleaming in the cold winter light. The mobs were encouraged to disperse, to go home and huddle in their basements and cellars. Some men, young men mostly, stood to engage the troops in argument or simply hurl abuse. Those were rewarded with rifle butts and boot heels and left to lie where they fell while their comrades fled calling back dire threats of the people's vengeance.

Within the dim confines of the restaurant the political discussions continued at tables crowded with refugees from the street. They were refugees of a certain class only. Two sturdy waiters stood at the door judging customers by their dress and deportment. Those who failed to meet the pair's standards were refused entry. Those who insisted on entry despite their appearance or manner of speech were discouraged with fists.

She took a booth at the rear and ordered a cup of tea, a glass of wine, and a plate of olives and hard cheese. It was understood that only paying customers would be tolerated. She selected enough from the scant menu to allow her a few moments to order her thoughts and dropped far more coins on the table than necessary to pay for her order. Stephen also needed to be fed and she nursed him using her shawl to conceal the suckling baby. There was little privacy here as the place filled up. Two men slid into the booth across from her, removing their hats and smiling greetings. They eyed the shifting shape beneath the shawl with openly lurid interest. They nudged one another like schoolboys. They made muttered remarks at the sounds Stephen was making on her breast. They giggled like children. Caroline pretended interest in a rather dreary landscape framed on the wall above the booth.

"A lady wishes to sit here," a man standing at the opening booth said in a deep rumble.

The two men protested. The man, a big man in a leather-trimmed wool coat, grabbed fistfuls of their clothing and dragged them from the bench. He cast them toward the crowd standing at the bar. He tipped his head at Caroline. He had the face of a boxer with a crushed nose and scarring along his brows. But his eyes were kind.

"Would you excuse the company of my mistress?" the man said.

Caroline nodded in gratitude.

The big man stood aside to make way for an older woman dressed in conservative clothes of magnificent quality. She wore a coat trimmed in ermine or mink over a high-collared dress of black silk embroidered with jade insets. On her hands were dove-colored gloves with a garnet ring worn on one finger. She walked with the aid of a gold-capped walking stick. Despite whatever infirmity she suffered she carried herself in a regal manner. The woman settled on the bench across from Caroline and removed her gloves, setting the ring on the table. The big man stood at the opening to the booth with his back to the ladies.

"Claude will make certain we maintain some degree of privacy," the woman said. "You should not have to suffer unwanted attentions while only seeking to see that your child is fed. War has made us all equally miserable but it is no cause to turn us to beasts."

"Um... thank you," Caroline said. "I was beginning to feel very uncomfortable."

"I am Madame Villeneuve," the woman said. "I assume from your charming version of French that you are foreign."

"Caroline Rivard. I'm Canadian though my husband is French. I am learning the language from him."

"The only place to learn any language is in bed," Mme. Villeneuve said and smiled when Caroline blushed. "Your husband has left you and your child alone?"

"We were separated by the fighting. I am trying to find him." Caroline resisted creating a more elaborate story than that. She opted for some partial truths. "Stephen, my baby, and I were evicted from our hotel. They did not believe I was married."

"These filthy Germans have made a tragedy of all our lives. Now they are outside our gates. They will not stop until they have made us all into Germans."

"Do you believe they will win? They will take the city?" Caroline wished she already knew the answer to that.

"I only know what I read in the papers which means I know nothing." Mme. Villeneuve sniffed. "It does not take a genius in military affairs to know that if their cannons are close enough to strike the Pantheon and the Sorbonne then we will soon see Prussians marching on our boulevards."

As if in emphasis to her remarks, the restaurant shook with a tremor of enough strength to set the chandeliers swinging. Dust streamed down from the ceiling. The clamor of conversation died across the dining room and bar for a few seconds then resumed as before.

"You say you lost your lodgings," Mme. Villeneuve continued. "Where will you and your child stay?"

"I will find a place," Caroline said. Beneath the concealment of the shawl she opened her dress further and shifted Stephen to her other breast.

"A woman alone? Don't be ridiculous. You will only face the same ignorance at any hotel worth staying at. The two of you will find yourself in some horrid pensioner where you will be robbed and worse."

"It's that dangerous?"

"Can you not feel it in the air? Unrest. Disobedience. The uncertainty of these days have given men license to act unlike they would in a time of security. No woman is safe even in as sophisticated an establishment as this once was. Those two pigs leering at you as they did! All decorum gone. Respect is a forgotten thing. It may become so anarchic that we will eventually *welcome* the Germans in to restore things to the way they should be."

"Then I have no desirable opportunities for shelter then?" Caroline was feeling as trapped as she felt back in her rooms at the Exemplaire.

"Nonsense," Mme. Villeneuve said, pursing her lips. "You will come to my home. I will not see a young lady, even a Canadian, cast upon the street with baby in arms."

Caroline's eyes welled with tears and the older woman held up a hand to quell any displays of emotion or gratitude.

"We will wait here until just before curfew. Then Claude will escort us past the army barricades to my home. You will be far more comfortable there and I will be far more comfortable with myself knowing I did not leave two innocents to a fate unknown."

"Thank you, Madame. Thank you for my baby more than for myself," Caroline said and dabbed at her eyes with a cloth.

"Now, let us see if they have any brandy of quality here. Would you care for a glass, my dear?" Mme. Villeneuve tapped a finger on Claude's broad back. The big man waved for a waiter.

"More than anything in the world, Madame," Caroline sighed.

The street before the Hotel Exemplaire was filled with a choking mix of wood smoke and brick dust. A twelve-inch Krupp shell had dropped through the roof of a theater a block away. It buried itself deep in the orchestra pit before detonating. The resulting blast caused the ceiling to collapse, leaving the one thousand seat emporium a flaming ruin and covering the surrounding streets with a thick fog driving pedestrians before it.

A man stood on the sidewalk across from the Exemplaire. The crowd moved past him in a rush. The man remained unmoving beneath the awning of a jeweler's as ash fell on them like snow. He watched as the hotelier returned with a gaggle of blue-jacketed soldiers and all rushed inside.

The watcher removed his Homburg hat, exposing a head of close-cropped white hair. With his elbow the dark man brushed ash from his hat before replacing it atop his head. He then turned up his collar and crossed the now empty street to enter the hotel.

A Wolf in the Fold

The Rangers atop the escarpment heard the sounds of battle from somewhere below. The multiple shotgun blasts reverberated to them through the still night air. They moved to the end of the headland at the top of the slope above the Roman fort. Bat and Jimbo watched the wooded hummock of land through their scopes but could see nothing, not even a muzzle flash, through the dense skein of trees.

Lee watched the fort beneath them. No alarm was raised. The sentries had to have heard the booms reaching them from the forest but paid them no mind. They hadn't yet had the experience of facing firearms so the blasts meant nothing to them but a curious noise of unknown origin.

An extended firefight meant that they probably lost the horses. There were too many shots fired. It wasn't a quick exchange with a small force. It was bandits perhaps but more probably the auxiliary archers showing up ahead of schedule. None of them were concerned about Boats. He knew to abandon the mounts and get the hell out.

The unmistakable sound of a Claymore erupting changed that assessment. That was a last-ditch, broken arrow move. The SEAL was in deep shit if he was playing his lethal trump card this early.

Down in the camp the Romans were rousing. They all heard it. It was loud enough and close enough to bring some of them out of their tents. The mine going off raised a visible cloud that rose above the treetops. They didn't make a move to mobilize but an officer was storming around in his undies, waving a staff and ordering men up onto the ramparts. That confirmed that they were warned to expect something even if they didn't know what form it would take.

"What about Boats?" Chaz said.

"Boats is fucked," Lee said. "That's the way it is."

"So, we leave him hanging?" Jimbo said.

"What would he want us to do? We don't know that he's been captured and if he's been killed then heading back over there is a pure bonehead play. Either way, we lost the horses."

"And the gear," Bat said. "We'll need to do something about that."

"Can't leave that shit back here when we leave," Chaz said.

"Yeah. Catastrophic anachronisms. Heard the lecture, bought the t-shirt," Lee snarled. "We have a new Priority Two. We stick here and watch the fort. If it is the Assyrians over there then they'll bring the horses and the gear to the fort. Once we confirm that we build a plan from there."

It was an unforgiving set of options but everyone on the team knew to move on. Mission creep is inevitable and shit happens. All the bitching in the world won't unscrew the pooch. They settled into positions to keep watch on the Roman fort and camp.

The sun rose behind them and the shadow of the headland receded revealing more and more of the land between the fort and the line of trees. As Lee predicted, men emerged from the forest leading a line of horses, their horses, with all the gear they left in camp back in place atop the packies.

As the column of men moved closer they could make out more details and saw something that Lee had not foreseen. Atop one of the horses rode a man. He was stripped naked. The man's hands were bound before him. A loop of rope ran under the girth of the horse attached to either ankle. A prisoner.

Boats.

Mettius Trivian Bachus ordered the barbarian brought to his tent. The man appeared to be a Celt. The flaming red hair and beard were common among those people but the man was exceptionally tall for that breed. Though his skin was marked with ink in patterns such as Bachus had seen before in Hispania. Some of the ink was artful but strange, including a quite realistic female figure wearing nothing but some strips of cloth marked with a pattern of stars and red bands. Another showed an eagle tearing at a snake and was very striking. If the man lived, Bachus would ask him about these grotesqueries.

Two soldiers threw the man roughly to the carpet. His body was covered with bruises received at the hands of the Assyrians. There was also the point of an arrow sticking obscenely from his leg.

"He's bleeding on my carpet," Bachus growled.

The Celt was lifted and tossed to a section of bare earth.

Also in attendance were Bachus's prime optio and the headman of the archer auxiliary, an oily brigand named Raman. The centurion also asked for Brulo, a brawny Sabine from his century.

Brulo was a dull-witted brute with a flair for creative cruelty. Titus, the prefect's lictor, was also with them in the tent. The man said little but Bachus had caught him time and again scratching with a stylus at a wax tablet. Scribbling notes for Valerius Gratus, no doubt.

Soldiers brought in some of the strange objects found amongst the prisoner's belongings. These were tossed in a pile before Bachus's camp chair where he sat warming his hands over a brazier to take the morning stiffness from them. He leaned forward to retrieve an object; a bottle of translucent blue glass made with impressive craftsmanship. Bachus fiddled with the top of the bottle and found the metal seal atop it turned in his hand until it came free. It was secured in place by a series of grooves worked into the thin metal in a manner most shrewd. He sniffed the contents and recoiled at the pungent chemical smell. Some sort of medicine, he imagined and set the bottle aside.

"He killed my men with this," Raman said in his atrocious Latin and held forth a long object of dull steel worked into some sort of wooden device.

Bachus took it in his hands but could make no sense of it. It was a machine of many moving parts but had no visible blade or manner of projecting missiles. He lifted it to his nose and found an oily smell along with the scent of sulfur. There was blood and hair matted on the broad wooden end of the weapon. Was it some sort of Celtic ceremonial club he was unfamiliar with? He tossed it aside. There were other objects in the growing heap but none of them meant anything to him.

The centurion stood and strode to where the naked man lay glowering up at him.

"Do you speak Latin?" Bacchus said in vain hope.

The man spat a string of words that meant nothing to anyone in the tent. His optio had spent much time in Gaul and could make no sense of it. It was certainly a language but not one known to anyone in attendance. Titus set aside his wax tablet. There was nothing in the prisoner's gibberish worth recording.

Raman, the archer headman, stamped on the man's wounded leg. The Celt bit off a cry of pain then spoke under his breath to the Assyrian who raised his eyebrows.

"What did he say to you? In what language?" Bachus demanded.

"It was Persian, sir. A most vulgar Persian spoken as a dog might utter it."

"And what did he say, Raman?"

The archer hesitated.

"He told me to have sexual congress with my mother," Raman said. Brulo brayed with laughter at that and clapped a hand to his mouth at a flash from the centurion's eyes.

"You will ask him only the questions I say to you," Bachus said and the Assyrian nodded.

Raman relayed question after question. How many are with you? Who has sent you? What is your interest in the slaves? Are you allied with the Jewish rebels? The Sanhedrin? How did you create the killing thunder?

The Celt gave no answer but to further insult the Assyrian. Bachus insisted that Raman repeat each outrage to him in full detail.

The prisoner had, in his responses to the questions, suggested that Raman touched himself in inappropriate ways, had carnal knowledge of a goat, was the issue of a camel and a backward monkey, consumed his own feces, and bathed in his own urine. Brulo bit his own hand to stifle laughter with enough force to draw blood. The two soldiers in attendance turned red in the face and studied the carpet beneath their feet with exaggerated interest.

"We shall take more expedient measures," Bachus said, unamused by any of this. He did not care for mysteries and this man was indeed a mystery.

"I want this man scourged but not so harmed as to prevent his speaking," Bachus said to Brulo.

"Branding, sir?" Brulo said, licking a fleck of his own blood from his lip.

"That will do." The centurion nodded and returned to his chair.

The fire in the brazier was re-stoked while Brulo departed to retrieve his tools. The Celt levered himself to a sitting position and sat gazing at Bachus with an open expression of bold appraisal. Was that animal cunning or true intelligence the centurion saw there? This man was dangerous, to be sure. And how many more like him were there out there on the desert even now? What was their purpose in being so close to a Roman encampment? Was this the vanguard of a larger army? Were they Celtic mercenaries hired by the Jews?

"Leave us," Bachus said to Titus. The chubby scribe goggled wide-eyed.

"But why, sir?" he wheedled.

"Because I do not care for you to report every military matter to your master," the centurion growled. "I am in command here not the prefect by proxy."

Titus, his face red and twisted with resentment, bowed and exited the tent.

Brulo returned shortly with iron brands, tools used to burn postholes for the assembly of wooden structures. He balanced four of them in the brazier and blew upon the coals there until they glowed red. After only a few moments the tips of the brands were an incandescent orange. The odor of hot metal permeated the tent. Brulo held the end of one of the irons with a swath of wool and plucked it from the brazier.

"Hold him still," Bachus instructed the two soldiers and leaned forward to watch with interest. Raman stood by smiling eagerly. The optio appeared to be bored by the tedium of it all and held a strip of scented linen to his nose in anticipation of the odor of singed flesh.

The soldiers moved to brace the Celt as Brulo closed on him with the brand. Before they could get a firm grip the bearded man bolted to his feet and launched himself forward to slam his forehead into the bridge of Brulo's nose. The Sabine went down hard with the Celt's weight atop him. Blood jetted from Brulo's nostrils in a crimson mist. The soldiers and Raman drew blades and advanced on the Celt who had rolled off the inert torturer to the pile of pillage that lay at Bachus's feet.

"No!" Bachus bawled. "He is only to be subdued."

The soldiers shoved Raman aside and beat on the naked man with the flat of their blades. The Celt rose on his knees with a roar and clumsily tossed a thick belt of some material at Bachus who fell backwards in his chair in surprise. The throw fell short and the belt landed in the coals of the brazier. The Celt dropped to the floor with the blades of the soldier's swords pummeling his back and shoulders.

Bachus rose to his feet, his face red with rage. He ordered the soldiers to stop their bludgeoning. Brulo appeared to be quite dead from the single blow to his face. The amount of blood was astonishing from so innocuous an injury. The centurion turned as a stink filled his nostrils. A most noxious smoke was rising from the thrown belt lying in the hot embers of the brazier. The belt was fashioned to hold lozenge-shaped objects of some unknown description.

He reached to remove the belt from the fire.

There was a deafening explosion.

Bachus was astounded to see his hand vanish in a spray of flesh, leaving only a ragged stump behind.

The beating hurt like a motherfucker but was worth it, Boats thought to himself as the twelve gauge rounds began to cook off in the fire. There were screams and oaths and the SEAL hugged the floor as the tent rocked to a firecracker stream of explosions. A lifeless body dropped on him in a sticky shower of hot blood. The rounds went off like mini grenades sending lead pellets everywhere. Boats felt the body atop him judder under the impact of one buck load after another.

The blasts died away and Boats slid from under the body. The guy was missing everything from the shoulders up. All around the tent men lay still or writhing. The big cheese who was asking all the questions was motionless in a pool of blood. His second-in-command sat on his ass crying like a baby at the bloody mess of jagged bone and ripped flesh that was all that was left of his legs. The little archer was crawling across the carpet using a hand to hold his guts in place and leaving a greasy loop trailing behind him leaking shit.

The SEAL stood and plucked a gladius from the hand of one of the dead soldiers. Then he picked up his bottle of Revolucion tequila. Standing balanced on one foot, he undid the cap and took a long pull from the blue bottle. Then he emptied the remaining contents on the little Assyrian bastard who was leaving a snail trail of gore across the carpet. Boats hobbled to the brazier and tipped it over. Embers reached the pool of hundred-proof agave and the archer was instantly engulfed in flames.

Boats tossed the empty aside and stepped through the flaps of the tent into the cool clean morning air.

All around, soldiers stopped in their tracks to see a naked giant emerge from the centurion's burning tent. The man was covered over every inch of his body in drying blood. He held a sword in his hand and eyed the ring of armed men as though mildly surprised to see them. Inside the tent, flames reached other combustibles among the heap of items pulled from the prisoner's camp. Muffled thunderclaps rumbled within and holes were rent in the cloth walls all around. A few legionnaires were struck down where they stood, blood gushing from wounds made by forces unseen. The soldiers withdrew, some taking cautious steps back while others threw down their weapons and ran for the partly completed walls of the fort. More fire erupted from inside the centurion's tent and running men were felled by blows from invisible blades that tore at their armor and flesh.

Through it all, the red-headed madman stood unflinching. He finally spoke in a guttural tongue none could understand.

"*Veni, vidi, vici,* huh? What a load of bullshit."

Passion and Procrastination

The Villeneuve home was in the center of a block along the Avenue Bosquet. It was technically a townhome, Caroline supposed. It felt more like a mansion with three expansive floors and large luxurious rooms topped with high sculpted ceilings. Mme. Villeneuve revealed that she was a widow of five years. Her husband had been a captain of industry who managed his family's holdings in land and shipping to build an even greater fortune. When the war broke out, the widow had been in Paris and chose to remain in the city rather than return to their country home in Versailles. Just as well, as it turned out, as the former imperial palace was now home to the Prussian general staff and, rumor had it, Wilhelm Friedrich Ludwig himself.

The cavernous house had more than enough rooms to house Caroline and Stephen. Mme. Villeneuve lived here with her son Jeannot, a student at university. There was also Claude, the tall man with the boxer's face, who served as a bodyguard as well as carriage driver and footman. His job was entirely the former now as they had sent their two carriage horses to the knacker's weeks before and had been living off steaks and soup made from their flesh. A chef named Anatole resided in the house as well as Inès and Corrine, the plump downstairs maid and the petite upstairs maid, respectively.

Caroline was shown into a sumptuous boudoir

straight out of a movie. A massive canopy bed dominated the center of the room. A fortune in finely carved furniture in black wood and accented in silver lined the walls beneath paintings—mostly traditional landscapes, still lifes and portraits—all hanging crookedly due to the recent tremors. A thick-pile Persian carpet trimmed in silk of Belgian blue lay at the foot of the bed. Corrine was running a cloth over a child's crib that had the most charming images of rabbits worked in the wood in bas relief with mother of pearl inlays.

"It was Jeannot's," Mme. Villeneuve said wistfully. "I could not bear to part with it."

"I am certain that Stephen will adore it as well," Caroline said.

"What do babies know or care of luxury?" The widow shrugged. "We indulge ourselves when we spoil them so."

"Still, it is all so generous of you." Caroline set Stephen in the crib on crisp clean sheets that Corrine had laid inside.

"It is my pleasure to have the sound of a child in the house once more," the widow said. "Now, you and your baby will rest. I will send Corrine in a few hours to let you know that the late meal is being served."

Caroline leaned back on the bed and watched the two women depart the room. When the door was closed she went to the window which afforded her a panorama of Paris that was still breathtaking even though marred with columns of smoke. She could see across the trees of a park to the silver band of the Seine. There was something wrong with this view. It took a moment for her to realize that the Eiffel Tower was absent. That structure would not rise to dominate the skyline for decades.

The sky below the low ceiling of clouds was

criss-crossed with the contrails of artillery fire. They formed loops and arcs that were marked by smears of smoke where they ended like evil and destructive rainbows.

She pulled the heavy drapes closed, throwing the room into comforting shadow. Caroline lay back, fully clothed on the bed and sank into its lush embrace. The canopy above was bare of curtains, allowing her to see the domed coffered ceiling. A fresco was painted there, an idyllic scene of shepherds and their flock crossing a pasture down to a winding river and a picturesque stone bridge. She smiled as she counted the sheep.

She drifted off before reaching the tenth sheep despite the occasional growl of the bombardment outside.

Dinner was served that evening in the formal dining room. Caroline suspected that the chunks of meat in the consommé were from the former carriage horses but she was too famished to care. There was fresh bread and even butter and the chef worked miracles with dried vegetables and beans to create a medley baked in a flaky crust. Dessert was a compote of figs and honey topped with clotted cream. It was hard to believe that she was in a city under siege by an enemy invader. But Jeannot, the Villeneuve son, served as reminder of that. It was all he could talk about.

"The generals are fools," he proclaimed. He was a tall, reedy young man of perhaps nineteen. His cheeks were covered with an angry blush of acne. "De Bellemare is the only one with nerve and they will punish him for his boldness. All they do is fall back and fall back. Fall back to what? They will soon be left with nowhere to stand yet they make no effort to break the ring of steel the Germans have constructed about us."

Mme. Villeneuve glanced at him occasionally but said nothing in reply. Caroline wondered who Jeannot was addressing then realized that it did not matter. The boy was an activist student. Back in college in London and Chicago, she'd seen her share. With his unruly hair and opinionated nature, Jeannot would be at home marching in organized protests and arguing in spirited debates on any campus she'd attended. It might be over immigrant rights, the environment or the injustice of fur used in fashion. For some it was a phase they grew out of. She sensed that perhaps Jeannot was not one of those. He liked to hear himself talk too much.

"Trochu petitioned Moltke for a ceasefire on humanitarian grounds. He sent word to the Prussian monster informing him that their cannon fire falls upon hospitals where wounded soldiers and citizens lay helpless. Do you know what Moltke said in reply?" Jeannot's eyes swept the table but the two ladies sat mutely dining.

"I will tell you!" As if any force on Earth might stop him. "He said that they use the red crosses on the flags atop the hospitals to sight their cannons! He said that! He said that he murders innocents with relish and looks forward to more murder! Enough to make the Seine run thick with blood!"

"Jeannot! Please!" his mother cried out. "Madame Rivard and I are dining and cannot do so in peace under the assault of your unspeakable analogies!"

"I only speak the vivid truth, Mother! While we enjoy our meals, Paris starves. And the generals do nothing to stop the potato-eating swine who come to bayonet us in our beds and rape our women!"

"Jeannot! For God's sake!" Mme. Villeneuve slammed her fork down on the table with enough force to slosh wine from their glasses.

"What would you propose that they do, monsieur?" Caroline said as much to break the current course of his colorful ramblings as to satisfy her curiosity.

"We are still many, we Parisians. How can so many be held prisoner by so few?" He seemed to notice her for the first time. "If every man, not just the soldiers, took up arms and stormed the Prussian batteries they would have no choice but to withdraw or be overwhelmed. It is simple mathematics."

"It is simple madness," his mother huffed.

"There is a movement afoot to make this a reality," he said, leaning eagerly toward Caroline and gesturing. "The students and the clubs are urging the city fathers toward this action; to allow Parisians to liberate Paris themselves! My club is the *Fraternité des Etudiants-Soldats* and we are prepared to fight! We could sweep over the bastards like a tide! Within hours the city would be free of them and their cannon!"

Caroline searched her mind once again, trying to recall if this event ever occurred. She remembered nothing. Certainly, if it had happened and succeeded it would have been memorialized. Something that foolhardy and heroic would be celebrated if it had resulted in victory. It would have been immortalized in the writings of Flaubert or Zola and been celebrated as a national holiday upon its anniversary each year. Caroline decided that it was only spoken of by idealistic young idiots like Jeannot.

"I think we all pray it does not come to that," Caroline said.

"Pray all you wish, Madame. But it is *man* who determines his fate," Jeannot said, grandly and stood to leave the table.

"Where are you off to?" Mme. Villeneuve protested. "It is past curfew, son."

"I have to meet with my fellow students. The patrols are too lazy or cowardly to act against violators." He bowed his farewells and left the dining room.

"A woman as beautiful as you for a dinner companion and he would rather go talk of war with his friends." The widow sighed.

"You embarrass me, Madame Villeneuve," Caroline said, looking longingly at Jeannot's untouched dessert.

"Nonsense, my dear. I do not recall having ever seen any woman with such a complexion or so lovely a smile."

Caroline sent a silent thank you to the sciences of dermatology and dentistry. If she learned nothing else in her trips to the past it was that skin and tooth care were uniformly neglected.

"I can only credit a healthy diet and plenty of fresh air." Caroline smiled.

"They must have an abundance of both in Canada then." Mme. Villeneuve smiled back with a hand before her mouth as was the custom to hide missing or blackened teeth.

"Your son is certainly passionate."

"About politics, absolutely," the widow sighed. "I sometimes despair for future generations."

Caroline reached for the remaining dessert plate still resting untouched at Jeannot's place.

"Shall we?" she said, placing a knife in the center of the sweet confection.

"It would be a sin not to," Mme. Villeneuve said with a solemn nod.

* * *

In the shuttered bar parlor of the Hotel Exemplaire, the registrar lifted his glass for a refill. The dark man with the fleece of white hair was paying and pouring and doing both generously. He did not even balk when the registrar suggest they turn to cognac—the fine aged bottle from the very top shelf. At prices made dear by the siege, the well-spoken stranger was paying through the nose and the francs were filling the registrar's pockets as the *Vieille Réserve* filled his head and warmed his insides.

The dark stranger was clearly not French but spoke the language like an educated patrician. He intimated, without tacitly saying so, that he was with the *Deuxième Bureau.* The registrar was flattered by the attention. The soldiers of the guard treated the registrar with scorn when he brought them back to the hotel to find the German woman was gone. Now all these questions from an important official were making the little man feel like a patriot.

The questions were all about the filthy German whore in room 22. What name did she call herself? Was there a man with her? When did he leave? Did she tell anyone what the name of the child was? Were any objects of an unusual nature found in her room?

"Unusual? Unusual in what way?" the registrar asked.

"Anything you may not have seen before. A device. A machine. An article of clothing of a design and fabric strange to you," the dark man said and tipped the fat cognac bottle to refresh his new friend's glass.

"An article of clothing?" The registrar was intrigued. "Was this woman known to wear clothing that was provocative?"

"Nothing like that. Something remarkable that she

may have left behind. Perhaps your maids saw something in the rooms that they would remember?"

"Shall we wake them?"

"Vigilance never sleeps," the stranger said in a hushed, conspiratorial tone that sent a thrill up the registrar's spine.

In the master boudoir at 33 Avenue Bosquet, Madame Villeneuve was prepared for bed with the help of Corrine. The widow dismissed the maid and sat at her vanity which also served as a writing desk.

From a drawer in the vanity she retrieved a journal and turned to the blank page that would be the entry for the day. She recorded the events of each day faithfully and had done so since she was a young woman, a school girl. The current journal, a fancy leather-bound book with vellum pages trimmed in gold leaf, was volume twenty and told the story of her life written simply, not artfully, as a list of each day's occurrences.

She wrote in the book more of habit than, as it was when she began the daily chore, as a way to divulge the secret passions of her heart. Earlier volumes were often scandalous and curiously made more so by her dry, matter-of-fact reportage of her dalliances. More flowery language would have made those trysts seem like romantic affairs of the heart indulged in by a young lady succumbing to the irresistible pull of infatuation. Told in her plain prose they read like an inventory of outrages described in the basest vernacular rather than the fond reminisces of an ingénue new to the ways of love. And that is how Mme. Villeneuve wished to recall them, honestly and without embellishment. These words were for no one else to read, only her.

Her youth was behind her now. In these days of the winter of her life she looked upon men with regret rather than hope. The last few volumes of her memoirs were taken up with luncheons or gallery exhibits or the events of her son's life rather than her own. She was a witness to, rather than a participant in, life in her dotage and was content with that.

But today was worthy of two pages or more in her diary. The charming young woman she had brought home filled the house with life once again. And to have an infant under her roof was something that Mme. Villeneuve thought never to see. Jeannot was an intellectual, a thinker rather than a lover, and his mother did not anticipate a wedding or grandchildren anytime soon, if ever.

The widow unstopped the ink bottle and dipped the quill inside to find the bottle contained only a gritty residue within. She had forgotten that she'd used the last of the ink on the previous night's entry. There was no real cause to call for Corrine to bring more. In any case, she was really much too tired to do today's events justice even in her flat prose.

Mme. Villeneuve set her pen aside and made for her bed. The heavy drapes were pulled closed, turning the continuing barrage without into a series of muted thumps.

She had no way to know the changes she wrought in her future by delaying her entry until the following evening. By doing so, she forestalled, for a day, the hell that her words would have called down upon her house. Upon her house and upon the heads of the young woman and infant peacefully sleeping two doors down from Mme. Villeneuve.

WITNESSES

The XXIII was in disarray.

Their centurion and his second were dead. The command tent was ablaze and sending forth projectiles from within, driven by some evil wind, to punish them all. Legionnaires lay dead or dying all about from grievous wounds. The soldiers stepped back from the maelstrom of noise and death, the ring of shields parting as it grew. The shields offered no protection as they saw them punctured through again and again; the thick oak staves riven and split and the flesh behind torn apart.

The prisoner brought in earlier by the Assyrians, the gore-splattered monster, was loping at them with a howl. He swung a sword over his head.

A soldier advanced to challenge the giant Celt with a raised shield. The madman was a long stride from him when the soldier collapsed as though struck by an unseen fist. A second soldier in the shrieking Celt's path dropped as well. Blood flew from between the fallen's teeth in a crimson spray. Some force was at work here, some powerful god or devil conjured by the chants of the naked berserker rushing at them. A dark god of vengeance from the cursed pantheon of the shrieking Celt was upon them all. Any who stood before him fell to a black curse as though to a scythe. The ring of soldiers about the tent opened further at the prisoner's approach. Rather than attack them, the

Celt dashed through the gap, making good progress despite dragging a wounded leg.

Boats limped on, cursing the agony in his leg and fighting to remain conscious. He waved the sword before him blindly as though to carve a path through the surrounding men. They made way for him and he hobbled into the ranks of tents at best speed.

Despite the arrow shaft in his leg, the thought of the flames reaching the plastic case of 40mm grenades drove him on. He saw the case among the other gear taken from the camp and dumped on the carpet in front of the head asshole. Boats had to make distance between himself and the coming blast. He emerged from between a row of tents to make for the interior of the earthwork ring wall. The steel point of a pilum plunged into the dirt before him. Boats looked up to see the thrower drop to his knees on the rampart above, clutching a fountaining chest wound. Someone was providing cover fire from above. The SEAL stood and pointed a finger at a clutch of soldiers on the ramparts. They held javelins up and back and ready to toss.

"Pow," he said.

One of the legionnaires staggered into his comrades with his lower jaw blown away. A second tumbled from the rampart with a hole punched though his gut. The rest threw down their pila and stumbled back, eyes wide with terror.

The concussive wave of the first blast was enough to lift Boats from his feet and send him flying. He tumbled to the ground, the air driven from his lungs. A scorching wind washed over him.

Behind him, thousands of bits of kinked wire shrapnel wicketed out in all directions, spilling men to the ground in whole and in parts. Mostly in parts. The pack of fleeing spearmen were swept from the ramparts in a red smear. More blasts followed in a rapid chain to collapse tents and pepper the surrounding ground in a lethal storm of liquefied metal rain. A section of fortress gateway, the mortar not fully set, tumbled down crushing the men seeking shelter within. Smoke and dust spread across the camp as the few who were able fled from the sound and fury. More of them were cut down as the secondary explosions continued to erupt from the center of the camp.

His head spinning and belly dragging, Boats pulled himself over the ground for the earthworks wall before him. His plan involved clambering up that wall somehow and getting on the other side. It all got hazy after that, something about a week or two in Florida and a lot of drinking. The world was so hot and noisy, he lowered his head to rest for just a minute before proceeding to Key West. Or was it Fort Myers?

Then he was gone, the gladius still firmly clutched in his fist.

Jimbo and Bat worked their Winchesters from atop the escarpment. They sighted and fired, sighted and fired, working the bolts as fast as they could to bring down any direct threats to Boats. The big SEAL seemed to have no real plan but flight. He was making his way from the burning tent using a peculiar crab-like gait. He was also bare-assed naked and gleaming red with blood from head to toe.

The Romans were looking to bolt as well. Jimbo could see it in their body language as they backed from the fire, gaps showing in their hedge of shields. Something was *pop, pop, popping* inside the burning tent—rounds cooking off. Strays were bringing down soldiers all around. Some of them stepped aside, creating an opening to let Boats through. Jimbo brought his crosshairs down on the soldier nearest the SEAL to widen the gap further and discourage any heroes.

Boats drew up when some guys in the wooden walkway along the earth wall began flinging spears his way. Bat took down one thrower then watched as the crazy SEAL stood pointing a finger at other soldiers on the boards above him. Jimbo sighted and made a messy head shot where Boats was pointing Dirty Harry style. Bat brought down another with a snapshot to the guts.

The Pima was lining up for a second shot when his view through the scope vanished in a white flash. The ground quaked beneath his feet. He and Bat backed away from the ledge as a series of explosions ripped a hole in the air. A pall of dust tinged with the sharp chemical stink of high explosives bloomed up from below. They recharged their rifles and watched the cloud creep over the top of the escarpment toward them. They dropped their NODs gear onto their heads and switched to digital. As the thunder died away they trotted to the ledge and swept the fort through their scopes.

The lenses revealed, in a monochromatic pixelated display, the figures of men stumbling, crawling and running from the fort and surrounding camp. Many more lay still on the ground and most of them in various states of dismemberment. This unit was all over, routed and running back to their Roman mamas. The horses followed the stream of men out through the gate made in the earthworks. Those that were left in any case. Among the men below lay three of their mounts. One was still alive despite having no rear legs below the haunch. She was whinnying in panic and trying to rise. Jimbo placed a shot through her head and she dropped to the dirt to remain still.

"Hate to see that," he said and jacked a new round.

Bat swung her view down the slope to find Lee and Chaz. Over the open sights she saw two figures moving down the field of scree toward the fort. She locked on them through the scope. They were already on the move before Boats emerged from the tent. The plan was for the two Rangers to move in close for a recon while she and the Pima provided overwatch. That all went to hell when the shotgun blasts started cracking off within the camp. Now they were humping toward the SEAL's twenty as fast as they could manage over the rough ground.

"I'm going down to back them up," Bat said and swung her rifle onto her shoulder.

"I'm staying here to make sure these bastards keep running," Jimbo said.

She started down the steeply angled slope to join her boyfriend for the endgame.

Bat caught up with the Rangers as they picked their way through the crop of sharpened stakes that lined the trench at the foot of the earthworks. Together they worked up the slope of packed soil to find the wooden planks of the ramparts empty of soldiers.

Through their NODs they pierced the spreading black smoke for signs of resistance. The repeated booms from Jimbo's rifle reached them from above. The Pima was picking off targets of opportunity to urge any Romans remaining to flee as fast as their sandals could carry them.

They quickly crossed the camp with guns up. Lee came across a man stumbling through the smoke. The man was no soldier and wore no weapon. He wore a finely trimmed beard and appeared soft. He dropped to his knees and held hands before him in mute surrender. His nails and fingertips were stained black.

Lee put a round through his head and moved on.

"That was cold, bro," Chaz said.

"Dude had ink on his hands. That means he was literate. You want to be in the history books?" Lee said.

The Rangers found the SEAL lying unconscious against the far wall. There were bodies all around him. Some were blasted to meat, cut down by the blizzard of shrapnel. Others lay drilled through with a single wound to head or center mass. These were victims of Jimbo's unerring eye. Bat helped them turn Boats over. He groaned and his eyes fluttered.

"Did we win?" he croaked.

"We kicked their ass, sailor." Chaz smiled.

"Hardly a fair fight," Bat said.

"If you wind up in a fair fight then your plan failed," Lee said.

"There was a plan?" Boats muttered before passing out again.

"Good news first," Lee asked the group.

Bat and Chaz worked on stabilizing Boats. Jimbo had come down from overwatch to join the others in the camp.

"The fort is ours. The captives are still in place. The enemy is severely hurting and on the run," Jimbo said.

"Bad news," Lee said.

"Our transport is scattered to hell and gone. A shitload of our ordnance went up in that fire. The enemy could regroup. And we know there's a relief force out there that could show up any minute," Chaz summarized.

"So, we're all on the same shitty page then," Lee said.

"And we have a man down, non-ambulatory with severe wounds in need of more and better treatment than we can provide here," Bat said.

"I can hack," Boats said feebly.

"The way I see it is we move on the quarry," Lee said. "If we don't use this momentum we have then we'll have to do this all over again when the reinforcements come down the road. And we're running low on ammo, no horses, and a man down."

"I said I can hack." The SEAL sounded pissed now.

"Sure you can, Boats," Chaz said as he stabbed the man's leg with a morphine dose followed by a cocktail of antibiotics and vitamin K. "We'll just roll your naked ass out there and you can do your wild thing."

"Fuck you," Boats murmured before surrendering to his weakened state and the painkillers.

"We come at the quarry from above or head on or both?" Jimbo asked.

"I say we take a cue from what Boats did earlier." Bat smiled.

The men in the quarry camp, slaves and keepers alike, were in fear.

They were already at work cutting and hauling stone from the walls of the cleft in the earth made by decades of labor. All work ceased as the ground shivered under their feet and the roar of thunder reached them. They dropped to the ground in expectation of further tremors that might drop the high walls above down upon their heads.

Yasak ben Zakai was chief among the masters here and the only one who remained standing. If his god meant to take him today then so it would be. He squinted up into the sky for a sign that this might be his time and saw only early morning sky with not a cloud in sight. It was not thunder then. He turned to the west, in the direction of the Roman camp, and saw a gray cloud rising above the top of the table of raised land. It rose thick and dark and brought an oily smell toward them on the wind.

The slaves and their guards and foremen rose to their feet and gazed at the cloud. They spoke low, trying to divine its meaning. Was this something the Romans caused? The cloud continued to climb into the sky even as the thunder died. More sounds reached them, sharper like the cracks of a whip. Then they too died away and all was silence.

Yasak ordered one of his cousins to run to the Roman camps and see what was happening. The man looked at him with whites all about his eyes. Yasak picked up a stone and flung it at his cousin who turned and ran to the quarry opening to the road. Yasak climbed the ladder to the watchtower where two more cousins stood guard. This vantage point offered him nothing but a view of the roadway where it turned away down the deep canyon to the exit where the foreigners' camp lay. He could see his cousin trotting reluctantly away and finally out of sight around the curve.

The slaves were driven back to work, the more experienced to use hammers and mauls to cut and shape the uniform blocks the Romans desired for their fortress. The less skilled, the new arrivals, to haul slabs for cutting and to fill baskets with gravel to clear the field of scree. It was dangerous and punishing labor and injuries were a daily occurrence. Many slaves were killed or crippled and had to be done away with. Thus the quarry needed new laborers constantly. Even with the high price of human flesh the Zakais made a healthy profit selling to the occupiers. These Romans seemed to be building constantly and consumed stone and brick and even gravel with an insatiable appetite.

The sun was rising and the shadows receding from the cut of the quarry. The full heat of the sun would bake the western rock face until later in the day when it moved to the eastern wall. Atop the open watchtower, Yasak took the full brunt of the sunlight on his face. He wiped his brow with a cloth to remove the sweat from his eyes. He blinked at the place where the road turned in toward the quarry. A figure moved there. To Yasak's astonishment it was a woman. She wore black armor and carried the banner of the Roman legion. The polished horse affixed to the top of the crosspiece caught the rays of the sun.

Behind the woman came two men. They walked easily, boldly. Each carried in his arms a black rod that was too short to be a spear. Yasak turned in the tower and called to his cousins and others to take up arms. They answered his call with swords and lances and rushed to the foot of the tower to defy the intruders standing where the canyon widened and well out of range of even their slings.

The woman, lewdly bare-legged and wearing her black hair free to her shoulders like a whore, stood with the Roman banner upright in her hand.

"We have come for your slaves," she called in stilted Hebrew. "We have slain the Romans. We will spare you only if you free the slaves you hold."

The overseers glanced at one another in

consternation. Who was this bitch and what was she saying to them? They were Jews but most of them spoke only the local dialect of Aramaic and only knew the old language from the words sung to them in the Holy Days.

Yasak's father was a man of god and letters and insisted that he and his brothers learn the old language.

"You are mad, woman!" Yasak called back in kind. "The Romans will see you nailed up for this intrusion!"

"The Romans are dead," she called back. "As you will die unless you free all within this place."

Yasak repeated her words for the others and, after a moment to consider the absurdity of it, all barked with laughter.

"You will die," the madwoman said when the men recovered from their mirth. "And I will choose the first to suffer my wrath."

With that the woman raised her empty hand and pointed a finger at the clutch of armed men gathered before the watch tower in a ragged line.

"This one!" she called.

A peal of thunder sounded and, simultaneously, one of the men, a second cousin to Yasak, stumbled backwards to fall to the ground. He lay there for a moment, his legs kicking and his life's blood pumping from a hole in his chest. Then he was still.

"Now this one," the woman called with hand raised.

A second sharp crack and another in the rank of armed men dropped as though struck with an axe, his arm near torn from his body and a spray of blood splashing over those close enough. The men parted in terror from their fallen cousins.

Yasak looked from the two still bodies bleeding out in the dust to stare at the three strangers still standing as they were on the roadway. The two men held their strange black rods to their shoulders. Wisps of white smoke rose from the rods as though they each contained a hidden flame.

"Release your captives!" the woman called. "Lay down your weapons and step aside and no more will die."

"It is a trick! She is a witch!" Yasak called to the men quailing below. "Take her, you cowards! Take them all! They are few and you are many."

Yasak's throat closed tight as he saw the brazen woman raise her hand to point a finger directly at him.

The Rangers and Bat walked forward into the open floor of the quarry.

After Chaz's shot took most of the head off the loud guy in the watchtower the rest of the tough guys threw down their weapons and fell to their knees. They were there, asses up and heads down and crying like schoolgirls. Lee and Chaz kicked a few to their feet and hustled them against a wall of the escarpment away from their weapons. The men kept their gazes on the ground, terrified of even looking into the faces of their tormentors.

"These fuckers were badasses when it came to pushing slaves around," Chaz said, slamming a boot into the back of a leg to bring a weeping man down to his knees.

"Down, pussies!" Lee said and motioned for the others to do the same. They dropped as one. The Rangers sniffed at an ammonia stink. These dudes were pissing themselves with fear.

Chaz walked beside Bat Jaffe into the heart of the quarry. The slaves, well over a thousand men, stood all about as though too riveted to react. All that could change in a heartbeat. Chaz had his M4 easy in his fists but his eyes were wary. It wouldn't be the first time he was attacked by someone he came to rescue. People reacted every which way but sane when there was blood being spilled.

Bat raised her arms. She didn't need to. She already had, for a variety of reasons, everyone's attention.

"You are free!" she called in the language she hoped at least some of them understood. From the look of them they were not all Jews. She saw black Africans and a few men with blond topknots. Certainly there were Greeks and Arabs and who-knew-what-all here too.

"The Romans are gone! Your masters are cowed! We have come to set you free!" She saw some of the men repeat her words to the others who in turn spoke to others.

"Who are you to free us? By whose authority do you do this?" A rail-thin man with a mane of white hair stepped forward.

Bat was unprepared for this. She didn't expect to have to answer questions. She turned to Chaz for help but he was standing transfixed and searching the faces of the men about them.

"They're your people, honey," Chaz said.

"What does it matter to you?" she said, turning to the old man. "You are free! Go and be free!"

"You give us a gift that is not yours to give. Only those that enslaved us may free us. We may not simply leave this place. Without their word that we are free we will be hunted like rabbits," the old man said and it was repeated around the men ringing them in.

Bat was losing ground here. This guy was reminding her of her Uncle Joel. And her Uncle Joel loved to argue.

"What's the hold up?" Lee said, striding to her side. "We're on the clock here, baby."

"They say we don't have the authority to free them," she said with a shrug.

Lee plucked the staff of the Roman banner from her hand and held it over his head.

"Who has the authority? I have the fucking authority!" Lee shouted. All stood around blinking at him uncomprehending.

He raised his M4 in the other fist and let rip with a long burst on automatic. The men flinched and wailed, eyes round in terrible wonder.

"I am the baddest son of a bitch in the valley!" he roared. "Now get your asses moving!"

The slaves ran now in a rush for the quarry opening. They eddied around the Rangers, eyes averted in fear.

"You just have to know how to talk to people," Lee said, turning to Bat.

"Can't get my head around this." Chaz watched the quarry slaves hare off down the roadway; some fell to their knees and bounced right back up to sprint away.

"All those Sundays in church singing and listening to the pastor," Chaz said mostly to himself. "And the guy that all that singing and preaching was about was standing right here in front of me. I mean I might have been looking right at the son of God."

Lee patted his brother Ranger on the back as Chaz let out a sigh.

"Let's hope it's a long time before you see him again."

The two men and the woman moved out at a trot to follow the fleeing mob, leaving behind the slaveholders to piss and moan.

The Fury of the Tetrarch

Valerius Gratus had his most plush couch brought into his office. His upright chair had become too uncomfortable over time so he now reclined as he officiated the duties of a provincial prefect.

That was not the only change in his palace. No longer was he attended by his staff of young slaves. Gratus had lost all interest in pretty boys and sold them to a slaver who took them away weeping in their new chains. The prefect's daily needs were now seen to by soldiers of the XXIII, giving his residence a martial air that he found comforting. And the prefect was concerned only with comfort these days.

He lay alone in his office except for the chinless wonder serving as his lictor in Titus's absence. The spotty clerk was pestering him for decisions on an endless list of tiresome demands and entreaties from local Roman officials and Jews alike. Merchants. Cheats. Pimps. Damn them all.

Gratus found it all too tedious. He wished only to lie in the dark and indulge in his own private Elysium. Was he a slave to be burdened? Were the troubles of his subjects his troubles to share? He lay wrapped in a thick woolen cloak despite the heat. He was always cold now it seemed. His skin was sallow and clung to his bones and shrinking muscles like damp paper. He ate nothing but honeyed sweets and drank nothing but leaded wine. His bowels troubled him and he struggled to void them. His teeth were loose in his gums and his mouth seeped as much blood as spittle.

Like all vices, there was a price to be paid for embracing the charms of the mysterious morphea. More like embracing a diseased whore, Gratus thought bitterly. Yet he drank a portion of the wine each night even as he despaired at his shrinking cock. As much as the white-haired stranger vexed him, he looked forward to the man's return with a fresh supply of what had become the single focus of his life.

The pimpled lictor droned on and on and the words made no sense to Gratus. To his ears it was like the mewling of an obstinate child or the cawing of a seabird. He lifted himself from the couch to tear the sheet of paper from the startled lictor's hand.

"Later for this!" he shouted. "Leave me! Leave me and stay away until I call!"

The lictor's lips quivered as he turned to go. Was the man going to cry?

"But pour me another draught of wine before you go!" Gratus called to his receding back.

The lictor sniffed as he tilted the jar to fill the prefect's cup.

"Shake it first, you horrible excrescence!" Gratus roared.

The lictor replaced the cork and gave the jar a vigorous jiggle to more thoroughly mix the lead powder with the potion.

"Now, away!" Gratus muttered once the cup was filled to the brim.

The lictor departed sullenly from the prefect's office. The supremely annoying man returned in what Gratus believed at first to be an instant.

"Honored Prefect, you have a guest!" the lictor brayed.

The prefect noted that his office was in shadow now; no sunlight showed through the gaps in the drawn curtains. He rose with some effort on one elbow to find the empty cup still in his hand. A broad red stain had dried on his robe. How long had he slumbered? He realized that the lictor was still speaking. Gratus looked up to see a second man entering the room. A Jew with a long braided beard and dressed in fine robes of black linen trimmed with yellow silk. He wore atop his oiled hair one of those peculiar hats that all the wealthier Jews favored. Gratus was so fascinated with how the contraption remained balanced atop his visitor's head that he only heard the last of his lictor's pronouncement.

"...envoy of the Herod Antipater, tetrarch of Galilee and Perea, the most honorable Channah Samarius."

The Jew strode boldly to the couch where Gratus was levering himself to a seated position with some difficulty. Two more Jews, hard men from the look of them, entered in the wake of the first and shoved the lictor aside. The prefect wondered idly where his personal guards were at the moment.

"Herod has received word of events within his kingdom of which he was not advised," this Channah said with eyes blazing from beneath dark beetled brows.

"Is this so?" Gratus said.

"His highness has learned that you are the author of this event. He has sent me as his envoy to receive your explanation for this flagrant violation of the trust between Tiberius Caesar and the ruler of these lands."

His highness. Gratus stifled a chuckle. This upstart Herod, as his brother and his father before him, ruled at the sufferance of Rome. And a brittle rule it was.

"Inform me of the details of this betrayal please," Gratus said and made an effort to stand before the man. He was gratified to find that he was a head taller than this upstart Jew.

"A Roman army has taken the young men from the city of Nazarea," this Channah huffed. "They have been marched north to be sold into bondage and the proceeds used to fill your coffers."

This damned Herod had spies everywhere. Was there a traitor in the prefect's palace? Or within the Syrian legate's command? More likely the Nazarenes sent word to Herod begging for his mercy.

"I acted within the bounds of my own aegis. I was under the belief that Herod had been informed of my actions." Was that true? Did the stranger ever mention the tetrarch Antipas by name? Gratus could not recall. In fact, he could not recall the white-haired foreigner ever mentioning by whose authority he acted.

"He was not informed," this Channah seethed. "He knew nothing of your actions. He wishes to know the cause of this. What gave the prefect cause for a reprisal such as this? Nazarea has been a peaceful place. It has raised no hand against Rome."

Gratus hesitated to answer. What reply would make sense? He had no actual cause for taking the captives. He sighed with visible relief that he had defied the stranger's wishes and not had them executed.

"Will you answer?" the Jew thundered up at him.

"It is a Roman affair and does not concern the tetrarch," Gratus sniffed.

"His highness enjoys a brotherly friendship with Caesar Tiberius. It is a simple thing to discover if your words are lies and find the truth behind the seizure of Herod's subjects."

That was true. Herod was known in Rome and, for a Jew, well thought of by many in the imperial house as well as in the Senate. And many powerful Romans were either in business with the wealthy bastard or indebted to him for loans. Though in theory the prefect of Judea was the reigning power in the province, Herod held the true power with the aid of influential friends in every corner of the Empire.

Gratus realized with a chill that owed nothing to the night air that he was in over his head in waters where predators glided. He had a sudden mad image of blood-smeared teeth clotted with raw flesh and shuddered at the thought.

"I have acted in error," Gratus said, forcing a smile that was more repellant than reassuring.

"And how may I tell his highness that you will make good this... error?" The Jew smiled most condescendingly.

"The captives are at a legion castra at a village belonging to the family of Sasson ben Zakai."

"Was it to he that you sold the Nazarene men?"

"Yes. They work cutting stone in his quarries. And are well cared for by all accounts."

"You will return the Nazarenes to their homes. You will surrender the gold you made from the sale of those slaves to Herod. Only then will his highness be satisfied. He will see no need to trouble Caesar with this... misunderstanding." The Jew's smile almost reached his coal black eyes.

"And how will I make repayment to the Zakais?" Gratus said, struggling to keep a wheedling tone from his reply.

"That is not the concern of the tetrarch."

"I will send a runner in the morning," Gratus said in a small, child's voice and sank back on his couch.

"You will send a runner now. Followed by soldiers to meet the returning caravan in order to escort them safely back to their families under the fullest protection of the Roman eagle that you can provide." This Channah turned then on his heel and, insolently, departed the prefect's office without a word of farewell.

Gratus lounged on his couch, bathed in sweat. He looked up to note that the envoy's two servants remained behind. They stood as silent witness to ensure that the prefect made good on his promise. His thoughts whirled as he struggled to retrieve the name of his acting lictor.

"Titus!" he bawled out at last.

"Tuccius, sir!" The lictor quavered as he appeared in the doorway between the glowering assassins.

"Call for a runner! A fast one! Two runners!"

The Human Storm

The House Villeneuve was in turmoil.

Young Jeannot did not return from his journey onto the streets the night before. By the early dawn hours there was no word of his whereabouts. Mme. Villeneuve would not normally have been concerned, the boy had spent many nights out drinking with his friends. But he left the house after curfew and may have been taken by the guard. They were not known for their gentle treatment of violators.

That was the least horrific of the possible fates her son may have suffered. The Prussian bombardment continued through the night with shells landing within the city, demolishing buildings and gouging craters in the streets. Jeannot could have been injured or even killed by a random explosive. Even now he could be lying dead in a gutter or dying on a filthy hospital cot.

"You cannot blame yourself," Caroline assured her. "He is a grown man. You could not forbid him from leaving."

"The feelings you have for your infant son will not abate as he grows older," Mme. Villeneuve said as she sipped a cup of chicory fortified with brandy.

"I do not presume. I only beg you to be easy on yourself. Jeannot was probably prevented from returning home by any number of innocuous reasons."

"Perhaps you are right." The widow smiled at the baby sleeping in her guest's arms. "I know that you are being kind. But a mother's worry cannot be assuaged."

Cause for her worry grew more urgent as the sound of shouts reached them from the street outside. They rose from a muffled grumble to a loud clamor of voices clearly heard even through the shutters and thick drapes covering the windows. Caroline parted the drapes to look out the windows facing Avenue Bosquet. Men were marching down the street in ragged ranks through the morning mist. There were uniformed soldiers dotted among them but the file was mostly men in civilian clothing. Some wore banners tied across their chests. Even more had ribbons pinned to their coats or knotted about their sleeves. There were flags being waved and most of the men were armed. Some shouldered rifles or shotguns. Even more carried pikes or axes or mallets. They shouted for more men to join them. They sang a cacophony of different songs with no real attempt to share a common key or tune. This was a boisterous crowd of men, most of whom appeared drunk, if not on spirits then with some sort of uniting fervor of purpose. The noise of the crowd drowned out even the insistent pounding of cannon fire from the streets beyond. The cobbles and walks were littered with sheets of paper. Some of the men waved them in their hands or threw them into the air to fall on the heads of the marching mob like confetti. All along the sidewalks and the median that ran down the center of the avenue, crowds stood and cheered encouragement. Some women waved hankies and wept while others laughed as they called out encouragement to the passing columns. Other women even walked with the men and a few were held upon the shoulders of marchers; a few bared their breasts to the cold air as though to officially stamp the procession as purely French in nature. Old men waved flags. Children stood in mute wonder. This was not a celebration or a parade or a protest. These men were marching to battle.

Caroline reported what she saw to her hostess who sent the man-servant Claude out onto the street to investigate. He returned a few moments later with one of the printed broadsheets in hand. The sleeve of his coat had been parted from his shoulder. He explained that some of the men had tried to draft him into their ranks. He assured his mistress that he had no intention of leaving her service and so forcibly resisted their invitations. Caroline wondered how many of those men were capable of continuing their march after their encounter with the imposing Claude.

Mme. Villeneuve read the printed notice with dismay. It was a call to arms for all able-bodied Frenchmen to join *le sortie torrentiale* to break the Prussian siege. In the most inflammatory language a fevered mind could imagine the handbill urged the men of Paris to take up weapons and join the fight. It promised that each man would be a hero eternal to the empire and any who did not heed the call would be thought cowards and worse. The seals of the city's most prominent clubs appeared at the bottom along with the embossed seal of the city itself and the bold signature of Jules Ferry, the mayor of Paris and commander of the National Guard.

Jeannot's words of the evening before were not idle musings. The government of the city and its citizens had been clamoring for an organized uprising for weeks. It became the cause of the day. In the student clubs, the Paris Commune, the bars and brothels, the idea that a half million Frenchmen could march out and spend their fury on the invaders took hold. First as an idle fantasy and then as an *idée fixe* that moved the men to action. In the end, the generals could not resist and agreed to lead a counter assault to lift the siege.

"There is not enough danger in the streets, my son marches to battle to die on a German bayonet." Mme. Villeneuve sat with a lace handkerchief to her cheek, eyes numb with shock.

"You don't know that Jeannot went with them," Caroline said with little conviction.

"I am not a fool!" the widow proclaimed and waved her visitor from the front drawing room. She wished to be alone to embrace her grief without interference.

"Can they succeed?" Caroline asked Claude as the big man gently shut the doors to the room, leaving his mistress to her sorrow.

"It is doubtful, Madame," he said solemnly. "The defeat and capture of the city is inevitable. The generals have tried to convince the populace of this with little result."

"You are a resolute people."

"We are a romantic people, Madame. And when romance is held too dear it becomes foolishness."

"But if this counterattack will fail then why have the generals agreed to lead it?"

"Perhaps because it is the only way to convince us that we have lost," Claude said and held the door to the kitchen open for Caroline and her bundle to enter.

"Excuse me for saying so, Claude, but for so formidable a man you are quite the philosopher," Caroline said.

"I am French." Claude shrugged. "What you call philosophy, I call seeing the world for what it is."

Anatole was within the kitchen. But rather than preparing their lunch he was pulling on his winter coat while Inès, the plump downstairs maid, stood weeping into the sleeve of her blouse.

"And where are you off to?" Claude demanded.

"I will fight!" Anatole declared. He jammed a hat

upon his head and snatched a broad-bladed chopping knife from a block.

Claude stepped close to him and batted the knife from the smaller man's hand with a flick of his fingers.

"You will not," Claude said and lifted the man from the floor by the front of his coat. A button went flying across the room from where Claude's big hands took twin fistfuls of the heavy cloth.

"You are needed here, you pompous little Breton," Claude said with no malice. "The Madame needs the comforts of her home and staff and you will not desert her only to be killed by some Bavarian whoreson."

"Only a coward refuses the clarion call," Anatole sniffed. He looked ridiculous suspended above the tiles, feet swinging and making belligerent challenges to the giant who held him.

"What good are you to anyone dead?" Claude set him down. "Now, back to your stove and make us breakfast."

Anatole slipped from his coat with the help of an openly blubbering Inès; only now her tears ran down a face transformed by joy. The little chef glared at Claude who took a seat on a stool. But the expression on the man's face was a front that did little to mask the relief in his eyes. He had made his display of courage for all to see and thus his manhood was secure.

Late that evening, either due to a widow's prayers or pure, stupid chance, Jeannot did return.

He came to the door well past midnight. Claude answered to a feeble patter from outside and drew the bolts open to admit the boy. Jeannot was covered in drying mud from his boots to his collar. His right hand was bandaged in dirty rags encrusted black with blood. He was drawn and exhausted. The young man looked as though he had aged a decade in a single day.

Claude ushered the boy into the dining room and sat him down before pouring a tumbler of brandy. Jeannot gulped the draught greedily. Claude ordered Inès to rush upstairs and alert Madame, who came down the steps with the help of Corrine and their Canadian guest. She was not so overcome with relief to prevent her from ordering Inès to sweep up the clumps of muck left on the floor by her son's passage. The widow sat in a chair close by her son and took his bandaged hand in hers.

"We came out of the fog within steps of their defenses at Gennevillers," Jeannot said from his seat at the head of the table. His mother sat by him holding his wounded hand, leaving his other free to hold the tumbler of brandy. He spoke huskily, drily, with no trace of emotion. His eyes looked pained as they focused inwardly while he told his tale.

"That surprised the swine. It really did. We swept over them, mobs of men rushing together to batter a single Prussian to the ground. There were children who joined us at the end. And women. I saw a woman fatter than Inès laughing like an asylum inmate as she drove a butcher knife into the face of a screaming soldier years younger than I. There was no rifle fire at first. It was man to man with bayonet and club. The trenches were packed with writhing men."

He took a long swallow of the brandy and Claude poured a new portion that reached the brim of the glass.

"I joined an attack on a gun position, a big twelve-pounder. I think our mad idea was to turn the gun and use it ourselves. Though I doubt one of us knew how to load or fire the damned thing. We slipped and slid up an icy earthworks hand over hand, climbing over one another to be the first. That is when the rifles sounded. The Germans recovered from their shock soon enough and trained their guns on us in ranks of three. It was like the old way, like Bonaparte's time. They stood in files loading and firing in terrible succession."

A single tear coursed through the dried filth on Jeannot's face.

"We died then in numbers. Our zeal to fight was washed away in blood. I ran. We all ran. We stumbled over the bodies of our own. Anything to escape that deadly noise. Somehow they came around our left. Our right? I cannot know. They came quietly with steel bared. They laughed as they caught us on the points of their blades. A big bastard with mustaches like a hair brush came at me and I grabbed his bayonet in my hand."

Jeannot held up the bandaged hand with a simpering sound.

"It was foolish but I believe it saved my life. I yanked the blade to one side and shot the man in the throat with father's pistol. I stole it from your room a few nights ago, Mama. The Prussian fell atop me. This blood is his." Jeannot touched fingers to his coat where it was stained black as ink.

"You need tell us no more," his mother pleaded.

"I lay beneath him. I felt his last breaths on my face. I lay still and listened to the dying all around me. I did not move as the *sortie en masse* was slaughtered to a man. I heard women scream and children make sounds like... like... there is no sound like that this side of Hell. I remained under my German feeling the warmth leave his body, covered with his blood, and acted as one dead. When the sun had gone down I crawled from beneath him... crawled..."

Jeannot turned and met his mother's eyes. His face was white, his skin like wax. Only his eyes, rimmed scarlet, betrayed the life inside the boy. He collapsed then sobbing on her breast while she patted his head and cooed comforting words the rest could not hear until he fell into a deep slumber there.

"I took the liberty of adding a tincture of laudanum to that last portion of brandy, Madame," Claude said and lifted the unconscious boy from the widow's arms.

"That was quite thoughtful, Claude," she said with a smile that might have been incongruous considering the tale of horror her son had told them. But her boy was alive and no one saw anything out of place in her joy.

Claude walked to the foot of the steps, carrying the boy like a child.

"May I help?" Caroline asked.

"Do you know of medicine?" the big man replied.

"I have had training," she said. Dwayne had shown her some combat medical procedures about treating wounds of all kinds. She was no expert but knew the rudiments. And, being from the 21st century she knew more basics about fighting infection than anyone alive in 1871. Hell, one mouthwash commercial on TV was worth more than a university education in this day and age.

Together, with the help of Corrine and Inès, they stripped the boy and washed him. He was bruised along the ribs and Claude checked for breaks while Caroline cut away the caked cloth tied around Jeannot's hand. The wound was deep across the palm of the hand but none of the fingers were threatened though she could see the white of bone through a gash at the base of the thumb. She cleaned the hand with hot soapy water. She picked tiny remnants of cloth left from his glove out of the sticky crevice of the wound with tweezers.

"What are the strongest spirits you have in the house, Claude?" she asked.

He left the room and returned with a dark bulbous bottle.

"Rum. From Antigua. No one could stand it but the master," he said and pulled the cork with his teeth.

He held a bowl under Jeannot's hand while Caroline poured a liberal splash over the wound. The boy winced audibly but did not awaken.

"It should be sewn closed," she said.

"I will do it if one of the maids will fetch the sewing box and thread the needle for me." Claude smiled gently and held up his scarred sausage fingers. The man was absolutely a boxer in his day.

"There is a sewing kit in my room," Caroline directed to Corrine. There were several unused needles in her case. They would be far more sterile than whatever was customary for use in this house.

The wound cleaned, closed and wrapped in fresh muslin, Jeannot was laid in the bed in a laundered night shirt. Claude would stay with him through the night. The crisis was over, for now.

Down in the dining room, Mme. Villeneuve accepted Caroline's prognosis with gratitude. The widow was dozy and confessed that she had helped herself to a cocktail of brandy and laudanum. Caroline helped her up the steps to her room. The maids worked together to see their mistress to bed as swiftly as they could manage.

And so Madame Villeneuve did not update her

journal for a second night, thus sparing them from the dark man with the head of ivory hair for one more day.

Strangers With Candy

Bat Jaffe never realized how exhausting talking could be.

She stood atop the earthworks of the Roman fort and addressed the clumps of freed slaves milling about the ruined camp. Her voice was hoarse from trying to explain that they were all free to go. No one was listening. She wasn't even sure most of them could understand her. They weren't running away as instructed or as expected. They were just poking around through the wreckage, helping themselves to whatever they found there. Others located the cook tent and were dragging out baskets of food that they gorged on. Bat called out to them but they ignored her. A few were wandering off over the rough ground in the general direction of wherever they thought home lay. But even those few didn't appear to be in a particular hurry.

"Give it a rest for a minute," Lee said and wet a bandana from his CamelBak. The big Ranger was carrying the banner of the XXIII.

"You taking that with us?"

"Bet your ass. This is gonna look great in my media room."

"What media room?"

"The one we're going to have," he said and handed her the dripping cloth.

"That almost sounds like a proposal," she said and

accepted the damp cloth which she held to the back of her neck.

"Way cooler than a stupid ring," Lee said and waggled the banner. The polished horse atop it caught the sunlight.

"We have to get them moving, Lee," Bat said, pointing her chin down at the men clumped below them.

"Remember, there's only one here that we're interested in," he said. "Some of them ran off. Maybe he was one of them. It's Jesus save yourself from here on. Our job is done here."

"Or maybe he died on the march or in the quarry. Maybe we came here for nothing."

"That's always a possibility."

"Then what?" she asked.

"Then the world we go back to is going to be a lot different than the one we left." He shrugged.

"*If* we get back. Mission failure would mean that the future changed from this point on, right? No Taubers. No time machine. No way back."

"I try not to think about things like that," Lee said.

"What if things *are* different? What will they be like? Rhetorically."

"Rhetorically?"

"Okay, theologically," Bat said. "If they're different, it's because Jesus's life was interrupted and the events he lived through were never recorded. What does that prove?"

"Maybe you and Chaz will be singing from the same hymn book."

"I don't think so, stupid. Jews recognize Christ as a philosopher just like Buddha or Plato. He lived and was influential on history. Subtracting him from the historical record would be a major shake-up to the status quo even if you don't believe."

"Like if there was no Elvis."

"Exactly."

"Maybe that should be our next mission," Lee said. "Go back and save the King."

"No one could save Elvis," Bat said, shaking her head sadly.

Down in the camp, Jimbo had lashed some tent cloth to a pair of poles to make a stretcher for Boats.

The wound on the SEAL's leg was turning ugly. It was swelling around where the shaft pierced the flesh. The skin already felt warm. The arrow needed to be pulled and the puncture wound cleaned end to end. Only there was no way to know if that might tear a vessel, leaving Boats to bleed out. The shaft pierced him at an angle where it could have struck any number of major vessels, including his femoral artery. They just weren't equipped for that kind of eventuality and the nearest surgery was a couple of millennia away. All he could do was stabilize Boats with antibiotics and try to keep the big guy from going into a fever. They'd all had dozens of prophylactic injections for whatever bugs they might run across. There was no way of knowing what brand of filth that arrow carried in with it. The sailor was a tough son of a bitch and could last a few days more. It would get sketchy after that.

Carrying the SEAL was a whole different set of problems. It was a four-man job minimum. While Jimbo had all the respect in the world for the former IDF wonder woman on the team, she just didn't have the size to keep up over the long haul under a load like that. Boats was well over two hundred pounds and they had a rough, days-long slog back to the coast with fifty pounds of gear each over bad country. It wouldn't work even if Dwayne was along and they had four Rangers on the job. They needed guns walking point and drag. They couldn't just be humping Boats like it was a marathon event through a city park.

Jimbo looked around him at the slaves they had freed. Instead of putting distance between them and their captors they were hanging around like it was a tailgate party. Two guys were fighting over a crock of wine while others cheered them on. The rest were either sitting idly on the ground or walking around listlessly. They all had lice. Their skin crawled with the critters. Some of the men were wasted physically, painfully malnourished and covered in sores. They looked like they'd never walk another step. There were plenty of others who still looked healthy enough; even a few who had some muscle on them. They were all of them little guys but they all looked as tough as old timber.

There were younger and healthier ones here, too. They had to be the recent captives from Nazareth. Among them was the man they came to save. Jimbo searched their faces, not sure of what he was looking for. He went to a Catholic elementary school on the reservation. The nuns had told him all about Jesus but none of them knew what he looked like. And no one here looked like the bearded rock star in his catechism books.

He walked up to a few seated on the ground chewing mouthfuls from a loaf of bread they were sharing.

"How about a hand, dude?" Jimbo said and kicked at the foot of the biggest one.

The man looked up at him sullenly and went back to chewing.

"We freed your ass, bro. How about doing a little work as a thank you?" Jimbo said and kicked the man's foot again.

The man spat a wad of bread at Jimbo. The Pima reached down and grabbed a fistful of the man's hair and yanked him upright. Jimbo planted a fist square in the man's face, sending him flying to lie unmoving in the dust.

"Up off your asses!" Jimbo roared.

The group understood the timeless language of aggression. They stood up as one and let Jimbo shove them into a line for an informal inspection. He picked the six stoutest examples, guys with good feet and sturdy calves and all their fingers. Years of quarry work had taken its share of digits off a lot of these guys. He pushed them from the line toward the stretcher. He gestured for them to pick the man up. Most looked at him blinking. One of them, a guy with a wild thatch of dirty blond hair and skin burnt bronze seemed to get it and was speaking rapidly to the others. The guy was covered in layers of work muscle and reminded Jimbo of a California surfer who'd been left in the dryer too long.

They rest got the idea from the surfer and lifted Boats off the ground as a team. Jimbo waved them to gently lower the SEAL. He dug in a pouch for the hard candies he always carried out of habit after Afghanistan. He unwrapped one and popped it into his mouth then handed a few to his stretcher team. They sniffed them then put them in their own mouths to chew the candies with the cellophane still on. Grins all around as the sweet fruit flavor melted in their teeth.

The surfer grinned broadly. His front teeth, uppers and lowers, were gone. He met Jimbo's eyes and tapped his chest with his fingertips. The dude was wearing a legionnaire skirt and sword girdle he'd looted off a Roman corpse. A gladius in a scabbard hung from the belt. Jimbo noticed the scars on his forearms. They were old and showed as pink lines against his mahogany skin. This guy had seen action as a soldier.

"Bris," the surfer said. Or maybe it was 'Brus.'

"Bruce?" Jimbo pointed and the man hesitated before nodding with enthusiasm.

"Jim," the Pima said, touching his own chest.

"Zim," Bruce said, brows knitted.

"Close enough." Jimbo nodded and held out a hand.

Bruce looked at it quizzically. Jimbo took the surfer's right wrist and drew it forward to take the hand in his own. Bruce smiled and laughed and pumped the Indian's hand with enthusiasm.

Happy as kids, the rest all hung around while Jimbo trimmed the cloth on the poles to allow for additional hand holds in the center of the stretcher. Then he had them lift again. Bruce took the job as team leader and directed the others to lift in unison with a series of cadenced commands. They bore the load well. Now they had a stretcher team. The Rangers and Bat would have hands and eyes free to cover the withdraw. These guys looked like they'd be able to keep up. He tossed them some more candies. They smiled and nodded. They had a deal.

"I thought we freed those motherfuckers," Chaz said, walking up.

"I'm not making them do anything, bro," Jimbo said. "They're doing it for the candy. It's the free market at work."

"Still don't seem right." Chaz shook his head at the men squatting on the ground sucking on lemon balls and butterscotch and grinning like kids. Some of their backs were thick with old scar tissue from where they'd been whipped. Their ankles and wrists showed signs of manacles worn for extended periods.

"You want to carry that big bastard all the way to the Med?" Jimbo nodded at the still form of the SEAL on the makeshift carrier.

"Hell, no," Chaz said. "But you better have a shitload of candy on you."

They turned at Lee running down off the earthworks toward them. Bat trotted behind. Lee held the legion banner in his fist as he ran.

"Dust cloud to the north," Lee called as he reached them.

"That column we bushwacked?" Jimbo said.

"Has to be," Lee said. "They strapped their balls back on and chances are they'll put whatever's left of the Twenty-third back together when they get here and then be right in our asses."

Bat waved her arms and shouted to the men in Hebrew. She warned them that there was an army marching on them. Most ignored her or looked at her dully. Others were stirred by her dire predictions that the approaching Romans would be looking to blame someone for the devastation of their camp. These men pointed at all the dead legionnaires lying about them and echoed Bat's alarm to the others. There was a babel of languages as the word was translated among them. The group was up on their feet, even the ones who looked to be at death's door, and began moving away from the camp at the base of the escarpment at best speed.

Jimbo made a lifting gesture with his hands and his team of candy-loving former slaves raised Boats from the ground and awaited further instructions. Lee nodded approval and laid the banner on the bier alongside the SEAL.

"I'll take drag for now," Chaz said and waved them on.

Lee trotted ahead to take point. Jimbo waved his stretcher team forward and the tiny column moved roughly west into the cloud of dust raised by the fleeing slaves. A couple of dozen other slaves followed after the stretcher team. Chaz noted that a number of them carried spears or swords picked off of the dead.

We have ourselves an army, Chaz thought, until the candy runs out.

Chaz climbed a corner of the earthworks and watched the haze riding into the sky off the road to the north. It was coming straight as an arrow for them. The pyres of burning tents were still sending up a thick column of dense smoke and the centuries bearing the boar banner would be unerringly drawn toward it like hounds to the scent of the fox.

He gave some time for the rest of the team to gain some lead on him. Chaz spent the time sending up a prayer for the Father to watch over His son.

"We done all we could," he said, squinting up into the noon sky.

Then he turned to follow his brothers across Galilee.

The Tally

The ground was covered in a blanket of black-winged vultures by the time the third and fourth centuries of the Boars reached the ruined fort. The kites circled in the sky above and descended through the mist of smoke to feed upon the carcasses that lay scattered singly and in heaps all about the ruined camp.

Enraged, centurion Marcus Pulcher strode into the camp swinging his staff and shouting. The carrion eaters were sent hopping from their meals and finally to flight as other soldiers joined in shouting and waving arms.

The camp was an abattoir. Everywhere lay soldiers in various stages of dismemberment. Some were burnt all over and folded into the fetal position peculiar to those who die engulfed by fire. Others were eviscerated or quartered as if by some unimaginably powerful beast. The sand was soaked with violet pools of blood covered over with clouds of black flies and crawling insects. The smell of cooking flesh rising from the inferno of the command tent was vomit inducing. Pulcher covered his mouth with the corner of his cloak and swallowed back bile.

All here were dead. That was something outside the experience of the centurion. Every battle resulted in approximately the same ratio of the dead to the wounded. But here there were no injured. Whoever created this slaughter saw to it that none survived. Gaius, his first optio, reported a rough count of over one hundred bodies.

"That is less than half of the company posted here," the centurion said.

"The rest were either taken prisoner or fled," Gaius said.

"Any enemy dead?"

"Not one, sir."

"Isn't that unusual, Gaius?" Pulcher said. "A battle this furious and the only corpses that remain are of Romans?"

Gaius offered no opinion.

"Sound the call. If any of our own have fled they will hear it," the centurion said, turning. "And bring to me any who return."

The cornicen of the third was ordered forward. The man removed the circular horn from its protective leather cover and climbed to a spot atop the earthworks to sound four flat blasts. Any legionnaire within hearing would answer the gathering call and return to the fort. And, indeed, the survivors of the XXIII straggled in from the surrounding desert all around. They entered with heads hung low and without meeting the eyes of their brother legionnaires. The highest ranking, an optio of the second of the sixth, was brought to Pulcher who waited in the shade of his command tent which had been constructed upwind a distance from the ruined camp.

The optio, a Lucani named Critus, told a tale that beggared belief. He related how the Assyrian archers came to the camp with a Celt prisoner who was revealed to be some manner of demon who called down upon their heads the fires of hell. Within moments this demon consigned their centurion and his staff to a storm of fire. He brought down the men of the XXIII with but a gesture from his empty hand. It was if this Celt had the power of death itself.

Pulcher might have counted the man mad if it were not for his own experiences on the road only two days prior. That and the condition of the dead visible everywhere he looked. What sort of weapon ripped a man to bloody shreds?

"And you broke, man? The Horses turned from stallions to geldings before this one man?" Pulcher sneered.

"Yes," Critus said and lowered his head in shame. He was an athletically built young man, too young to have made his position without the influence of a wealthy family.

"I should have you decimated," Pulcher said, his lip curled in disgust.

"Yes, centurion," Critus said, looking up now with a cold fire in his eye. "It is what we deserve and I—"

"But this Celt has already accomplished that and more!" Pulcher roared, rising from his chair.

"Honored centurion, I request that I be made an example of!" Critus said with defiance.

"I will have no useless displays of sacrifice," Pulcher said in a softer voice now. "You will bear this dishonor on your back as you pursue this Celt."

"Sir?"

"My men have force marched for two days to reach here. They are exhausted. Your centuries, on the other hand, have only suffered from the exercise of running out of sight of your attacker." Pulcher shot a dark glance about the tent to make certain that none of his officers responded to this unintended jest. He was not seeking to lighten the mood.

"I will—" Critus began.

"You will do only as I say. You will gather two score of your stoutest men. Tough bastards, you hear me? You will need runners, marathon runners if possible, do you understand me? Take only what you need. Weapons and water but no armor. And track down this mystery Celt and all who are with him."

Critus nodded.

"As you find and follow the trail left by these rebels you will leave sign. Once my men have fed and rested we will seek you out in force and engage this enemy. I don't care if they are devils or if they are men, I will have their heads. Do you understand and obey?"

"To the last of my blood," Critus said between clenched teeth.

"Then go. Leave strips of cloth as you run. We will follow with the combined force of four centuries."

Critus thumped his chest with his right fist and then departed the tent.

"Further orders, sir?" Gaius asked. Pulcher turned to regard them with a baleful eye. The second optio and the aquilifer snapped to attention.

"Have the men of the Twenty-third set to bury their dead. Our men are to stand down until the sun reaches the third quarter. We will then set out to pursue the Lucani optio and his heroes in search of these creatures who plague us." The centurion sat down in his chair, overcome by a deeper weariness than he had ever known.

"We will seek ribbons of cloth, sir? Like a children's game?" Gaius grinned.

"From our recent experience we know we will more likely follow a trail of the dead to our quarry," Pulcher said and held out a cup for his second optio to freshen with wine.

Under the Gaze of God

The Prussian guns started again before dawn. The shells flew from the mouths of the cannon to drop across the rooftops of the city like the tread of an angry giant. Mostly they spent themselves punching hollows in the cobbles of empty streets or shattering trees in the bands of fallow gardens that ran down the centers of the more fashionable boulevards. A few plummeted through rooftops and smashed through floorboards to find victims hidden deep in the hearts of houses. A two-hundred-pound bomb from a mortar detonated in the basement in Les Halles. It reduced a family of eight, including five children, their servants, and a visiting friend to vapor. The house remained standing by some miracle. The only visible damage was a hole drilled from top to bottom in its structure and cellar walls encrusted with an inches-thick layer of *papier peint* of clotted tissue, bone and clothing.

In the house of Mme. Villeneuve all was quiet but for the intrusion of the man-made thunderclaps coming through the bricks and plaster. Sometimes the quakes from the shelling seemed to be closing in on the house like a fist, only to recede into the distance bringing its deadly rain upon some other helpless souls.

The madame grieved as though her son had died in the mad assault of the day before. She mourned for the loss of his youthful spirit which she knew would be crushed by the sights he witnessed the day before.

Jeannot's hand would heal with only a scar and a story to recall its source. His real wound would be invisible; the dual shame of being a murderer and a coward. The young man was motivated by the peculiar brand of patriotism that only the French knew. It drove him to join the others in the forlorn and mad attack. The horrors of reality sent his brashness flying and he ran and hid and then killed not in defense of his homeland but only to save his own life. He struck at the enemy, not as a blow against those who had the gall to invade his beloved land, but in a frenzied, animal desire to survive.

His mother knew him as any loving mother knows her only son. He had a sensitive soul, unlike his father who never saw beauty or humor or wonder in anything. It was this same spirit that pulled him along with the rising tide of his fellows on their romantic crusade to lift the ring of fire from the city. The same frail spirit that wilted before the world of carnage he entered.

Time.

Time would bring him from his brooding funk and she would be there to see him through it. Oh, her boy would make it through, of that she was sure. He would no longer be the passionate, garrulous youth he had been. Those days were gone. That boy was gone. He would now be like so many other Frenchmen from so many other struggles: fatalistic, cynical and bitter. But he was alive and that was all she cared about. She would see him through these days unless a German bomb erased them all in the next instant.

She sat at the dining room table playing piquet with Caroline Rivard. It was Claude who suggested that they not play at the card table in the drawing room as that room faced the street and was vulnerable to debris thrown by the shells falling without. The formal dining room was at the stout heart of the house and protected by the surrounding rooms.

Her provincial guest picked up the thirty-two card game quickly and was playing well after only a few hands. They talked of trifles, the child asleep in a wheeled bassinet in the corner. The conversation and brisk play kept Mme. Villeneuve's mind from the tremors that shook the house from time to time as well as the suffering of her son still asleep in his room above. She was grateful for this unexpected company. Without Caroline's companionship she might have grown despondent and even been tempted to indulge further in wine fortified with laudanum. And what aid might she have been to her son then?

Caroline won the last trick on the last hand of this deal and wound up with the high score surpassing her host's cumulative score for the first time.

"You are remarkably skilled for a beginner," Mme. Villeneuve said and gathered the cards to shuffle them for a new hand.

"My brother won't play any games with me anymore. He thinks I cheat," Caroline said.

"Difficult to cheat in a game you have only become familiar with this afternoon. You have siblings?"

"Only one. An older brother. He's a watchmaker in Ottawa."

Mme. Villenueve caught the suggestion of a smile at the corner of Caroline's mouth. This young woman had more than a few secrets.

"Have we eggs, Mother?"

It was Jeannot standing in the archway to the foyer. He was dressed in a clean shirt and trousers and brocaded robe. He needed a shave and his eyes were red-rimmed with drooping lids as a result of the heavy dose he'd imbibed the night before. Mme. Villeneuve saw only the tousled-haired boy, bright-eyed and smiling, who had greeted her each morning during his earliest school years.

"We have not, my dear. But Anatole tells me he still has bacon, flour, and butter. I'm certain he can make you something to satisfy you," his mother said. "I am pleased to see you have an appetite."

"Famished. Good morning, Madame Rivard," Jeannot said with a bow of his head.

"Afternoon, I'm afraid." She smiled and nodded her head in return.

"Is it?" he said in an absent tone and left them for the kitchen.

Mme. Villeneuve riffled the cards together, allowed her guest to cut, and then expertly dealt the cards by twos to each of them for the start of play. She won the next two deals with scores that placed her well ahead of her opponent to take the game. The baby stirred then cooed in its bassinet. The widow made her apologies and left Mme. Rivard alone to feed her waking child while she repaired to the kitchen to watch her own son devour one of Anatole's creations made from the shrinking stock in their larder. Jeannot ate with relish and she was pleased.

That evening, by the light of an oil lamp, because the gas lines had been cut by Prussians weeks ago, Mme. Villeneuve sat for the first time that week to record the events of the past three days in her journal. She wrote of her concerns for her son, the anxieties of living in a city under siege and meeting Caroline Rivard and her infant Stephen and taking them into her home at 33 Avenue Bosquet.

By penning those words she invited into her home guests most unwelcome. The musings of the widow called down upon her house a terror from out of time.

* * *

The search program was named for Visvamitra, a Hindi demigod born of the thoughts of the god Brahma.

Visvamitra was a seer, a prophet of future events, so exacting in his predictions that his words of truth were feared by kings and commoner alike. The program attempted to live up to the mythology of its namesake for preciseness and exhaustiveness. It was powered by a vast global network of servers belonging to various embodiments of Sir Neal Harnesh's numberless holdings.

Its only task, and the purpose for which it was created, was to monitor Harnesh's enormous personal library of handwritten texts. It was not a security system. It was something far more complex than that. Visvamitra actually watched the physical copies of the texts in the library. Each and every page was scanned on a regular rotation to alert Sir Neal to any changes made to the pages themselves.

The nature of anomalies in time was not a constant as theoreticians would have us believe. The Butterfly Effect was, so to speak, *not* in effect in the main. So many alterations in the timeline were localized in nature. Though untold millions of copies of *Les Miserable,* to choose an example, were in print in hundreds of languages, none of these copies would be altered in the slightest if, by chance, M. Hugo were caused to spill ink upon a page of his manuscript while at the task of writing his novel and be forced to rewrite a few passages using slightly different wording than he intended. Those changes, those rewrites, would not be reflected in any modern print version of his classic. Only by observing the actual written page would one observe that change.

And so, by theft and purchase and other means, Sir Neal collected the world's most extensive collection of manuscripts that had only one thing in common: they were the very first iterations of their forms written in the hand of their creators and they were all non-fiction in nature. Histories, essays, biographies, treatises, and papers written by some of the most famous, and, in the majority, the most obscure, authors from the dawn of written language until the beginning of the 20th Century. There were journals and diaries penned by everyone from the most famous personalities in history to the least known and common. From the personal memoir of a certain Egyptian queen to the daily journal of a certain Mme. Villeneuve of Paris. Many of these volumes, like the former mentioned, were thought to be lost or never to have existed. But Sir Neal's fortune, combined with his unique mechanism to break the rules of time's inexorable forward passage, allowed him to send agents into the past to pluck literary treasures from libraries, schools and privates homes with impunity.

To the horror of any connoisseur of such things, each bound volume was unbound and its pages secured permanently within UV protected Lexan sheets to allow them to be seen from both sides. Ancient papyrus and vellum scrolls were unrolled and sealed within the clear plastic substance. These were carefully catalogued and stored in a zero-humidity environment kept just above freezing temperature and shielded from any direct light. Though they were stolen from history and the eyes of academia they were preserved for the ages with great care. Uniform sheets containing the handwritten works were in safekeeping within a protected subterranean warehouse carved from limestone rock. These sheets were fed from great cataloged stacks into a mechanized system that carried them along to banks of scanners where Visvamitra "read" each page of the millions of volumes once every twenty-four hour period. The sheets would flash by at dizzying speed under the lowlight lenses of the search program whose only purpose was to find differences, even the slightest alteration, from the previous scan. If changes to the written words were found, the volume would be separated from the rest and an alert sent to Gallant Informational Solutions Ltd in London where copies of the original text and new, altered, text would be brought to Sir Neal Harnesh personally. These would be examined by him and any actions taken based on his appraisal of their significance would be ordered by the man himself.

It is thus that an unknown widow writing of her relief at her son's survival and her gratitude for the comfort brought to her by a visiting Canadian was brought to the attention of man nearly two centuries later and deemed significant enough to require swift and bloody action.

Stone Soup

Jimbo kept the stretcher team at a steady walk-trot change up. Walk six paces and trot six. The terrain allowed for it. They were moving through the wooded hills to the west of the Roman road following the low ground. They were taking care not to skyline themselves against the falling sun. When one team would tire another would take up the burden of Boats. Bruce, the Dead Sea surfer dude, assumed leadership of the bearers. After the first few rotations, he took over calling the changes. But he never gave up his own place at the head of one of the poles. The compact dude was tireless and kept up a constant string of encouragement and directions to the other bearers that Jimbo assumed was rife with profanity.

The Ranger knew a hardass drill instructor when he heard one. Bruce was Army all the way.

It was a mile-consuming pace but they couldn't keep it up indefinitely. At some point they'd slow and then need a rest stop. Experience told the Pima that once it got dark a few of their volunteers would melt away. They were making good enough time to put distance between them and any pursuit by heavy infantry. If the Romans had cavalry they'd be fucked. Same result if the Romans let loose more of those little archers. Boats was slowing them down. They'd probably need a rearguard action. If they could just get through the night without any unexpected encounters or detours they had an even chance of slipping away.

The woods were rich with game. All around them Jimbo could hear hooves crashing away into the underbrush on their approach. A few times he spotted tiny deer in the second between their ears perking up and their rumps bounding away into the lattice of tree boles and tanglefoot. He heard the high yipping bark of foxes in the distance. Black squirrels leapt from branches overhead sending down a silent rain of needles.

A knot of partridges, with orange crests atop their heads, exploded out of a copse of scrub before them. Two of the freed slaves they'd picked up brought down a few birds with thrown stones. They grinned as they plucked the birds clean while they walked along. Jimbo was impressed. The two men downed five birds inside of a span of less than two seconds. No one back on the reservation could have done that well, not even Jimbo. And he'd brought home dinner stunned with thrown rocks many times growing up.

James Smalls was once again filled with the feeling of being truly alive in a place and time not his own. The men running with him were as different from him in culture as it was possible to be yet he felt an affinity with them. For all the miracles and comforts of the 21st century, he could never feel the freedom there that these men felt. Earlier today they were slaves. Here, only a few hours later, their separate fates were waiting to be discovered. A man could re-invent himself here if he had the nerve and the will.

Back in The Now, most men were on a path set for them before they were born. He'd left the rez and gone to war and survived. For what? To work a job where some shithead with a gun could take him out during a routine traffic stop? Or live to retire at fifty-five and wait until cancer took him? Even his missions into the past were only brief respites from a life that felt like it was already planned for him. Coming back from prehistoric Nevada and the ancient Aegean left him with a longing for a world that no longer existed; a world where a man was challenged every day by forces beyond his control. There was no conserving risk in the places he'd seen. You went balls out every minute and fuck the consequences.

Maybe he was crazy. Most men would be reduced to PTSD cases by the shit he'd been through since Dwayne asked him to join Team Tauber. Jimbo found that instead it gave him peace. It made everything seem more real; every breath he took was like an invigorating drug washing his lungs and heart and brain clean. It wasn't just thrill-junkie euphoria either. That was the kind of thing Lee Hammond lived for. Maybe, he thought, it's like I belong here in the past. Maybe it was in his blood. He was just a red-skinned savage deep down inside and little more than a century from the last time his people lived the old way. Well, if that was it then he could get behind that. There might be one of these times he'd just stay behind to make his own history.

Bat, trotting behind him, said something.

Jimmy Smalls came out of his own thoughts.

"Yeah?" he said, stopping.

"We need to think about resting these guys," Bat said again.

"Past time we took a look at Boats' condition, too," he said.

The sun had sunk low over the hills now. They'd moved out of the tree line to a lower elevation of broken country of ridgelines marching in descending order to the coastal plain. Jimbo waved the stretcher bearers to halt and lower their passenger. The other tagalongs stopped as well.

"I'm going to run ahead to Lee and let him know," Jimbo said and pointed up a slope to a grassy peak atop a hillock. "How about you move the unit up to where we can keep watch on our six from that high ground?"

Bat nodded and spoke to the few men she knew understood Hebrew.

They made camp on the slope of the hillside below the peak. Hammond took a prone position at the crest to watch the ground around them. It was a nasty badlands that terraced away down to the coast three days hard march from their current position. The land here was riven with shallow gullies that could hide an army in its shadows. These furrows could also hide their unit from sight so long as they found ones they could follow westerly. They'd take a short break and move on to increase their lead on any pursuing force.

Bat and Chaz tended to Boats. The SEAL's skin was hot to the touch. The wound area was inflated and looking angry. Boats was in and out of consciousness. Bat managed to get some water into him while Chaz strapped a Mylar blanket over him. They shot him up with a new infusion of antibiotics and antipyretics close to the wound site. Now it was up to time, the power of prayer and the sailor's dogged will to live.

Jimmy Smalls was handing out protein bars after showing the tagalongs how to peel off the wrappers. He rationed out water from their shrinking supply. He shot a half-second stream from his CamelBak into the open mouths of the men around him. They'd need to find water soon. He'd take over point from Hammond when they resumed their march and sniff out a tank or an open spring.

The little militia began gathering kindling for a fire

until Jimbo waved them off. He kicked the pile of sticks aside. The two men with the game birds protested. They held up the stripped and gutted birds and shook them in Jimbo's face until he held up a hand to them. Bruce interceded and grumbled something that made the men stand down. The Pima undid his pack and pulled out a chemical heat stick. He unfolded a PVC half gallon camp pot and filled it with three inches of water from his reservoir system. He gestured to the hunters to hand him a game bird. Jimbo tore the legs and wings from it and dropped it in the water. He split the breast and added that as well, followed by a liberal splash from his trusty Tabasco bottle and a dash of salt. The gang of men gathered around and watched in rapt fascination. Jimbo activated the heat stick and inserted it in the folding pot. Within thirty seconds there was steam rising from the pot. Bruce clapped his hands on his thighs and babbled to the others who simply stared at this everyday wonder in dumb amazement.

Jimbo left them watching the pot. Bat was sitting by Boats, dribbling water on his lips from the straw of her CamelBak.

"Can you make sure they give that bird at least thirty minutes?" he asked.

"Sure. Where are you heading?" she said.

"I'm going to go back the way we came aways. I want to make sure no one's closing the gap on us."

"You know, those guys think you're a miracle worker." Bat nodded toward the ring of men staring at the steaming pot with mouths open.

"That's how rumors get started," Jimbo said and slung his Winchester over his shoulder. Bruce rose to follow but Jimbo waved him back down with a smile. He descended the slope after a high sign to Lee Hammond lying invisible in the dark at the top of the hill.

Bat turned back to Boats and used her fingers to moisten his dry, cracked lips. In addition to the wound to his leg he had a lump to the back of his head that was swollen with fluid. One of his eyes was puffed shut and a dark purple bruise was spreading from his jaw to his right ear. The man had taken an epic beating but was still hanging in. She took a thumb and pulled up one of his eyelids and was startled when he spoke to her.

"We in the clear?" His voice was a wet rasping sound.

"Not yet, Boats," she said, keeping her voice level and calm.

"What's the situation?"

"We're making good time. We're three days, maybe four from extract."

"I'm holding you up."

"We're managing. It's good."

"No bullshit." He locked hot, red-rimmed eyes on hers.

"No bullshit, sailor," she said levelly.

Then he was gone again.

Jimbo was downslope and nearing the tree line they'd left at twilight. The temps were dropping. His sweat-soaked tank top felt chilly against his skin under the armor. The woods were quiet but for the distant sounds of a high, truncated yelping. Bat Jaffe had told him it was jackals that made those sounds. She said they were a common sight outside the kibbutz she'd lived on when she was younger.

He stopped dead on the slope and scanned the trees. He raised the rifle to his shoulder and scanned the shadows through the scope, the night vision on and wide open for maximum contrast. The eidetic memory that he honed as part of his tracking skills was telling him to look closer.

Something was wrong.

Something was different.

Something was here that was not here when they passed earlier.

A fluttering shape at the edge of the wood, moving in the breeze.

The Pima crept down the hill. The rifle traversing back and forth. The eyes looking for movement in the shadows.

He approached and took the shape in his hand.

A bit of tattered red cloth tied with a knot to the end of a scrub branch.

Jimbo turn and ran, full out, back to the camp.

Bruce's name was actually Byrus.

Bat learned this by questioning him through one of their Jewish tagalongs who also spoke Greek. Byrus was a Macedonian. He'd been a slave as long as he could remember. "Born in chains," as he colorfully put it. He spent years as a pit fighter before being sold by his owner into the quarry. How many seasons ago he was not sure.

She asked what he would do now that he was free. The man only shrugged and returned to watching the mystically boiling pot.

"Some of us will return home," Iyov, the translator told her. "Many, like Byrus, have no home. They have always been slaves. Or they would not be welcome there."

"How will you survive then?" she asked.

"Become thieves or bandits. Maybe join the rebels. There's little difference in the end. If we are caught we'll wind up on a cross."

"Then we have done you no favor by freeing you."

"You have not freed us. We are still slaves. A dog unleashed is still a dog."

"I am sorry. We had to do what we did," she said.

"None of us is free, are we? Not for long anyway." Iyov made a spitting noise.

Byrus said something in his basso voice that sounded like he once gargled razor blades.

"He asks why you used your power to release us from the quarry. What makes you kill Romans with such zeal?" Iyov said.

Bat wasn't sure how to answer that.

"There was one among you of great renown," she said after a moment's thought.

"A man important to your people?" Iyov said after relaying her answer to the Macedonian.

Bat was considering how to answer that thorny question when Iyov fell forward, gagging on the iron tip of the spear blade that suddenly appeared from his throat.

The Intruders

It was night once again in Paris and the few newspapers that saw print were filled with rumors of peace. Artillery fire had become more sporadic throughout the day until finally abating altogether as the low winter sun sank behind clouds of smoke from fires still raging in Clichy.

The streets were empty. The populace was spent. They retreated to their homes and their churches in exhaustion. They were past celebration or shame or resentment. Tomorrow they would mourn. Tomorrow they would think again of the future. Tomorrow they would face the terms of surrender.

The House of Villeneuve had taken to bed mostly. Only Claude wandered the lower floors making certain that the candles they'd lit were damped for the night. The sound of voices from the street caused him to halt on the stairs. He turned to step to the foyer and listen closer. Men were directly before the house and coming closer. They were in hushed argument, not wishing to be heard. The empty streets echoed their utterances in the cold night air, amplifying them so that Claude could catch the tone if not the words. One voice rose above the others and, after a moment of silence, something hard struck the door of the outer portico.

A crash of splintering wood and glass informed him that, whoever this was, they were through the street door and into the entryway of the house. Claude moved to the stout front entrance door and made certain all the bolts were shot. Seconds later the hammering began on the other side. From the noise of them, two heavy iron mallets were striking the door in tandem like lumbermen felling a tree.

Claude was confident that the door would hold against such an assault. The street-facing windows of the house were heavily barred and entry through them near impossible. Even so, he reached into a stand by the door and retrieved, from among the umbrellas, a heavy cavalry saber that had rested there unnoticed by visitors for decades. He unsheathed the curving blade with no difficulty. One of his self-assigned duties was to keep this relic of his days in the Hussars cleaned and oiled in its scabbard. Now that ritual chore rewarded him with a ready weapon to face these intruders.

He glanced up to see fresh orbs of reflected light upon the ceiling at the top of the stairs. The cacophony had awakened the house.

"Remain upstairs, mesdames!" he called.

A new sound, deeper in the house, reached him. Metal upon metal rang. Glass tinkled musically. The kitchen and pantry at the alley rear.

"Merde," he hissed to himself then shouted, "Anatole! Get out here!"

A flutter of women's voices from above. Claude raced down the back hall for the kitchen. Anatole appeared before him in a nightshirt, sputtering questions.

"The front door, you fool!" Claude thundered as he raced past the man. "Get the girls and shove furniture before the door! Quickly, man!"

Claude was in the kitchen and through the pantry to find men in dark clothing outside the rear portico and prying the wrought iron bars free from the gate there. He backed toward the doorway to the house to secure the copper-clad service door. The men tore away the ladder of bars to shoulder through the alley gate for him. They were armed with the tools of tradesmen: hammers, adzes and knives. There were five that he could see.

And one more man with them who stood at the back with hands in the pockets of a fine woolen coat in starkest contrast to the rest of the grubby crew clothed in layers of ragged garb. The man had skin of mahogany made all the darker by the fringe of snow-white hair visible beneath his tall silk topper. The man snapped orders to the others. These were no common looters and this was no random assault.

The big footman lunged and speared the most eager attacker through the guts. Claude twisted the blade and pulled it free. The man shrieked. Blood jetted from between fingers laced over the wound. The others hesitated. The dark man growled a fresh order in high-mannered French and the gang pressed forward over the kicking body of their comrade. Claude drove the hilt of the saber into the face of one man and felt the crackle of breaking bone through the steel. He booted another in the knee, hearing the joint snap with a report that could be heard over the grunts of his assailants and the shouts of the dark man. The attackers renewed their efforts, emboldened by rage, and carried Claude backwards through the door and into the house by the weight of their numbers.

Caroline was still awake thanks to Stephen.

He was fussing. Perhaps it was the silence of the night after so many days of constant rumblings from outside. She had the baby back to sleep after rocking him in her arms and pacing for what seemed like hours. The hammering on the front door reached her as she was laying the infant back in the crib. She stepped to the hall to see Claude shouting for the chef, surprised to see a sword in his fist. The front door was shuddering in its frame under steady impacts striking it from the other side. Mme. Villeneuve joined Caroline, a candelabra held aloft in her hand. Jeannot brushed past them and charged down the steps to help Anatole and the maids haul a large chest and then a spinet piano from the drawing room and against the door.

"Who is it? Have they identified themselves?" the widow called down the stairs.

"Looters, Mother!" Jeannot shouted back. "Come to rob the house!"

"Why have they chosen us?" Mme. Villeneuve said with more irritation than apprehension.

Caroline did not know who they were but she knew they were not robbers. She knew why they were here and why they chose this house.

"Where has Claude gone?" Mme. Villeneuve called down.

The sharp crack of an explosion sounded from below, followed by another and another.

Caroline backed toward her room where her child was now crying, startled by the sudden noise rising even above the rhythmic hammering. She swept up the squalling, wriggling bundle and held it close to her with one arm. Her hand searched beneath the mattress. There were shouts and then screams from below. A crash of furniture and heavy footfalls pounded up the stairs. Caroline backed into the far corner of the room which seemed to grow smaller with each step.

A man in clothes made filthy with soot and ash threw the door wide and strode for her and Stephen with a leer on his face. A younger man with a gaunt face and hungry yellow eyes came in behind and spoke a warning.

"It is the child. He said the child must not be harmed."

A chill rose up Caroline's neck like an icy fist encircling her throat.

She raised the LeMat and squeezed the trigger as her child's father had shown her.

The slug struck the sooty man dead center in the chest. He barked a cough and collapsed lifeless. The gaunt man's ochre eyes opened wide as he backed for the door. He held up a hand in a gesture of surrender or pleading. Caroline thumbed the hammer and squeezed again. Three of the gaunt man's fingers vanished in a spray of bone and blood. The bullet continued on to take the man just above the eye. His body was lifted and thrown spinning against the doorframe. Bits of his skull and scalp stuck to the flocked wallpaper.

The baby screamed in the dying din as her hearing returned. Stephen was red-faced, his little chin furrowed and quivering with unreasoning fear. She renewed her grip on the infant, holding him tight to her side and held the smoking pistol trained on the empty doorway. Her aim and her arm was steady and unwavering.

"Mademoiselle Tauber? Or is it Rivard here?" came a cultured and maddeningly calm voice speaking impeccable French from somewhere out in the dark of the hallway.

"Speak English, motherfucker," she snapped.

"We only want the child. I suppose you know why."

Caroline remained silent. She would not engage this man on his level.

"He is very special. Very unique. A gift to science and mankind. You must appreciate that. You must know he would be treated as a treasure by—"

She squeezed the trigger and put a hole through the wall by the door where she supposed the speaker was standing on the other side.

"I see. A mother's love, then," the voice resumed after a moment. "I fully appreciate your position. You could come along, if you wished. You could be the boy's guardian. You could see that we mean him no harm."

Another shot. This one further left. It drilled through a cameo portrait hanging on the wall. She fired again lower and to the left. A cry went up in the hallway and something heavy struck the floor hard enough to make the boards beneath her feet quake. More cries from without and feet retreating down the stairs.

"Ah," came the voice, still irritatingly serene and reasonable. "You have disposed of one of my hired men with the added benefit of the rest fleeing."

She said nothing. Stephen's face was frozen in a silent shriek of terror. The voice from the hallway resumed.

"I suppose that is what comes of paying in advance, eh?" The voice had a patrician English accent with a touch of something foreign. He was baiting her into speaking. She would not rise to his taunts.

"You know who I come from. You know who sent me. The man is like a father to you. He would be the same to your son."

"He's a lying bastard," she said and then slid to her right on bare feet. Dwayne always told her to shoot and move, shoot and move.

"Sir Neal wishes only to welcome you back, to share his confidences with you and the rewards of all your research. Your brother as well."

She squeezed again. This time through the doorjamb, splitting it top to bottom.

The silence was long this time and she watched over the smoking barrel of the revolver, quavering now under its weight and from the effort to hold her arm straight for such an extended time. The door swung slowly inward. A dark man with ivory hair stepped into the doorway holding Mme. Villeneuve in a chokehold before him. In his other hand was a handgun of flat back metal—a modern automatic of some kind. He held it easily, pointed from his hip at her midriff.

"Neither one of us can miss, Caroline," he said with an easy smile showing teeth that gleamed in the haze of gunsmoke that hung in the air. The widow clutched at his arm in a feeble effort to release the grip that was asphyxiating her. Mme. Villeneuve's face was turning crimson, her lips parted to draw in air that would not come. Caroline kept the pistol trained on the man who continued speaking in measured tones.

"Spare the child any more of this. Think of what is best for Stephen's interests," he said, stepping into the room over the bodies of the two hired men. The toes of Mme. Villeneuve's slippers brushed the floorboards in involuntary spasms.

She thumbed the hammer back and trained it once again on the stranger. She squeezed the trigger. Only a metallic click rewarded her effort.

The ivory-haired man dropped the widow choking and gasping to the floor. He reached out a hand to Caroline. His smile beamed wider even as his eyes turned to glittering black stones.

"And so we are done," he said.

She drew back the hammer again.

"Mademoiselle, please," he said, the fixed smile

collapsing a bit at the corners.

Her thumb pushed forward a lever recessed into the curve of the hammer and she applied a steady pressure to the trigger.

At this close range the buckshot from the underslung shotgun barrel had no air time to spread into a wider pattern. The buckshot took the man from the future like an iron fist traveling at ballistic velocity high in the chest and neck. He was flung from his feet and through the open doorway. A fountain of blood sprang from his torn gullet. His body struck the far wall and dropped in a heap to the floor. His legs pumped in some instinctual animal response from his dying brain telling him that he must flee. Too late, too late. He lay still.

Setting the gasping Stephen on the blood sticky floor by her, Caroline knelt to Mme. Villeneuve. She loosened the widow's collar and supported her neck. Natural color began to return to the older woman's face. Her eyes searched Caroline's. Her lips formed words but no sound. Caroline leaned close to hear the woman over her child's panicked shrieks.

"Jeannot," the woman whispered against the pain in her throat.

Eye to Eye

From atop the hill, Lee Hammond saw the figures appear from the grass as if by magic. They converged on the loose gathering of men down at the camp on the slope below his position. He was sighting on one of the attackers when he heard a whisper of movement in the grass behind him. Spinning around he saw three naked men, smeared head-to-toe with mud, racing toward him with raised swords.

* * *

The men rushed in from the dark all around the camp. They were among the escaped slaves and their liberators inside of a heartbeat. The attackers were naked but for skirts and singlets. They made Bat think of the cheap Hercules movies her dad still liked from when he was a kid. The men wore short-cropped hair that identified them as Romans. Within seconds half of their party was on the ground dead or wounded and the rest fighting for their lives. Gunfire exploded close. Chaz was in the fight somewhere behind her.

Bat drew her Sig Sauer and brought down a man who thrust at her with a spear point gleaming with fresh blood. She turned and sighted on another man hacking at a fallen slave with a short sword. A double tap lifted that man off his feet.

A hammer blow between her shoulder blades drove her stumbling. She turned, dropping to one knee and sent a three-round burst into a swordsman rearing back for a second strike. A dull ache turned to lancing agony as she fought to regain her feet. The armor caught the sword blow. She wasn't cut but she took all the blunt force between the shoulder blades. Gasping, she dropped to her knee again. A wet gasp sounded close behind her. She threw herself on her side and swung the Sig's foresights toward the source. Byrus was there drawing the blade of his gladius from the back of a Roman's head. The man buckled to the dirt, his blood streaming from a mortal wound to shower over Byrus.

The Macedonian wore a face of pure feral menace. Gone was the genial grin she'd grown accustomed to over the course of the march. This was the pit fighter she was seeing; an animal spirit that survived God alone knew what horrors to survive to this day.

He rushed to stand astride her, catching the blade of a new attacker on his. She rolled on her back and fired two rounds point blank into the attacker's crotch. The man fell back howling with Byrus riding him to the ground, chopping furiously. Bat struggled to her feet and made for where Boats lay unprotected. Her feet tangled in something. She fell hard. A Roman had used the pole of his spear to trip her up. He stood over her chuckling darkly.

Bat whipped the Sig to line up on him but the man was fast and struck her wrist with the butt of the spear. Her fingers went numb. The automatic spun from her hand. The man bent to grip the bodice of her armor. She drove the heel of her hand into his face with all her force. The blow smeared his nose across his face with a liquid crunching sound. Blood jetted from his nostrils.

He kept his hold on her and drove her back down on the ground. The back of her head struck the hard earth. She saw white speckles at the edges of her vision. The Roman spat a gobbet of hot blood in her face before setting to tearing the armor from her. The buckles frustrated his efforts. He sat hard atop her to draw a knife from his girdle to begin sawing at the straps.

One hand feebly slapped at her attacker while the other sought the Colt snubby from the concealed carry holster on her belt. His weight was bearing down on her midriff and she couldn't get her fingers to it. The man took a handful of her hair and banged her head off the ground once again. The speckles covered her narrowing field of vision for an instant. She fought back the darkness long enough to drive fingers up toward the man's ruined nose. She got two fingers into the mess of fractured gristle and hooked them both hard. The man roared in pain and swatted at her blindly, his hands striking glancing blows off her face and shoulders. He shifted his weight trying to release himself from her two-fingered grip buried deep in the soft flesh of his septum. She rose up with him, fingers locked into twin hooks. Her other hand dove under her pinned thigh and found the rubber grip of the .38. He was shrieking now and clasping her arm in both his hands trying to force her to release her hold. Bat twisted her wrist upward and jerked the trigger of the holstered Colt.

A searing heat washed down her leg. The weight of the man came off her waist. Her fingers were jerked free of his face in a gush of blood. She freed the snubby and fired three more rounds center mass, spilling the man back. Rising to a sitting position against a crushing tide of nausea she could see Jimmy Smalls swinging his Winchester like a club against a pair of brawny Romans with short swords.

From behind her she heard a heavy chopping sound. A man's body fell beside her, spasming as the blood left it, gushing, around the blade of a gladius stuck to the hilt through his chest. She put the last round from the Colt through the man's skull and watched it come apart like a melon. A high keening shriek reached her and she realized that it was coming from her. It only stopped when she felt a hand grip her arm. She whirled to aim the revolver up into the face of Boats crouching over her. The hammer dropped again and again on a spent round until the SEAL gently plucked the weapon from her fingers and tossed it aside.

"That's goddamned unfriendly, girl," Boats said with a sloppy grin before sagging to his knees.

She crawled to him gasping as he collapsed on his back. He was spattered with blood but there were no fresh wounds. The blood was not his own. It ran off him in rivulets carried on a lather of greasy sweat. The big sailor was breathing regularly. His fever was broken.

Bat reached over him and took the revolver from his limp fingers and reloaded it. She turned then, training it around the camp. The slope was lit intermittently by flashes of gunfire. Chaz was firing three-round bursts into the dark at targets she couldn't see. Jimmy was walking across the camp putting rounds from a handgun into writhing figures on the ground. The action was over for now. This was the mop up. Byrus strode up to her smiling like a shy child; his joy ghastly in contrast with his gore-smeared face and body. He dropped a severed head to the dirt by her. It reminded Bat of a cat her mom had back in Cleveland—always leaving dead mice and birds on the bathroom floor.

She laughed at the memory and Byrus nodded at what he thought was her approval.

"Good kitty," she said and gave in at last to a

blizzard of speckles that joined in a wall of white to wash away the world.

Bat came around to someone speaking her name. It was the tail end of a senseless dream and her name was being called again and again in an endless loop.

Lee was over her and she squinted to see him clearly. The sky was alight with the watery glow of a gray dawn. She'd either slept or been passed out for hours.

"Sit up, baby," he said and supported her to a seated position. He undid a leather bota and held the spout to her lips.

"Take a sip. A small one."

She did as she was told. Her mouth filled with a bitter draught. She spat it out in a spray and sat forward coughing.

"It's watered vinegar," Lee said. "Our visitors left it. Good for you. Electrolytes."

"Shit," she said and shoved him away. He made a grunting sound and she saw for the first time that his shoulder was wrapped in a stained dressing.

"Oh my God, Lee."

"It's all right. Asshole got a piece of me. We're all hurting, including you," he said and offered her the bota again. "But we need to move now and bitch later."

He helped her to her feet. She felt last night's fight over every inch of her body. Each muscle was stiff in its own way and her headache was fierce. Her fingers explored a tender spot on the back of her head. There was a burn down her leg where the skin was scorched by the muzzle blast from the snubbie. The worst was the pain between her shoulder blades where the sword had struck her at the beginning of the exchange. It hurt to lift her arms. The soreness pulsed with her heartbeat and radiated to the back of her neck making it agony to turn her head. She was ambulatory and it wasn't going to get any better laying here. She'd pop some Tylenols and soldier on.

Jimbo stood further up the hill toward the crest, glassing toward the east with binoculars. He stood with the Winchester rifle cradled in his arm. Bat never really thought of him as a Native American. But right now he looked every inch the warrior brave. He would be at home in Apacheria or the Black Hills. The streaks of dried blood on his face even mimicked war paint.

The slope of the hill was a slaughterhouse. The grass was greasy with drying offal and the flies were challenging the morning chill to begin gathering over the bodies scattered all around. There were a lot fewer of the tagalongs than there'd been the day before. Some already lay under hummocks of fresh dirt; graves dug and filled by a burial party directed by Byrus. The stocky Macedonian was caked with blood not his own. He noticed her and smiled broadly, his few teeth showing white against the mask of carnage that painted his face.

She counted six graves. There were eight in the burial party excluding Byrus. Two more of their volunteers sat by where Boats lay on the stretcher. Chaz was there treating them for what looked like serious wounds. One man hummed to himself while holding an arm fractured in two places. The other was having his leg bound by the Ranger and was biting down on a twig, eyes wide, pellets of sweat standing on his skin.

There should be more of their militia members. They probably ran off during or shortly after the fight. They still had enough to act as bearers for the SEAL. But the two additional wounded would hold them up further. The equation was getting worse. Bat found her Sig and Colt had both been returned to their holsters while she was out. Her Winchester lay next to her pack. She picked up both and walked over to where Boats lay.

The SEAL raised himself on one elbow and smiled at her. He looked better than he had the day before but that wasn't saying much. There was color back in his skin but his eyes were still red-rimmed. She crouched by him and touched his forehead with her wrist. He wasn't warm anymore but his skin was paper dry.

"You need this more than me," she said and offered the bota of diluted vinegar.

"I had a dream. You were in it," he said and took a long slug.

"Did you get any shots today?"

"Chaz stuck me a few times."

"Need any pain meds?"

"I don't want to sleep through what comes next," he said, tossing aside the empty skin and lying back again.

"You sure? I'd like to fast forward through it," she said.

"Listen up," Lee Hammond said, addressing the group. "Bat, can you translate for the locals?"

"We need to move now," he continued with Bat alongside him repeating in Hebrew and both allowing time for the relayed translations.

"These bastards last night were an advance scouting party. They fucked up by letting us know they were here. Jim found where they marked their trail. That means there's a force following on after. We're going to have to keep up the pace to stay ahead of them."

"They might have called up some cavalry by now," Jimbo spoke up. "Or maybe sent runners to alert a legion that's marching right now to cut us off."

"You're giving these fuckers a lot of credit, Smalls," Lee said. It was always last names when he didn't want to hear any more.

"I sure as shit am giving them a lot of credit, Hammond," Jimbo said, low and even, biting back his annoyance. "They conquered most of their world and held it for centuries. These aren't some pack of clenched assholes. This is the Roman fucking legion and they will march right up your ass."

"What's your suggestion?" Lee said.

"I hold back as a rearguard. I use some strips of cloth like the scouts did. Lead the Romans away from your route of march to some ground where I can slow their asses to a crawl. I can buy you a day, maybe two. Enough to reach the coast."

"It's not a great plan," Lee said.

"It sucks cock. But any plan is better than no plan. Just running isn't going to work," Jimbo said.

"Lee..." Bat started.

"What do you need?" Lee said, cutting her off.

Jimbo traded rifles with Chaz Raleigh. The Pima would take the M4 with grenade launcher and all the remaining 40mm projectiles. He'd hold onto his cut-down pump shotgun as well. Lee stripped the M203 off his own rifle and handed it to Jimbo as an extra. They left him with ten thirty-round magazines for the rifle, a half bandolier for the pump and some baseball frags Lee had squirreled away. It would have been awesome to have some of the Claymores but they all went up back in the Roman camp. They left him a half-dozen self-heating meals and a few protein bars. Jimbo emptied his pockets of all the hard candies and Tootsie Rolls he had for the stretcher crew.

"I'll find water on my own. You're going to need

every drop without me to find it for you," he said.

"You just make to that pier in Caesarea," Chaz said. "If we're not there you wait. We'll be along, right?"

"Yeah. What's time mean to us?" The Pima shrugged.

"And give these fuckers hell, you Apache," Lee said and held his hand out.

"You know that," Jimbo shook first Lee's hand then Chaz's. Bat stood on tiptoes to kiss his cheek.

"We shall meet again at Philippi," Chaz pronounced with a touch of gravity when Bat had stepped away.

"What the hell does that mean?" Jimbo said.

"Julius Caesar's ghost says it to Brutus. It's Shakespeare," Chaz said. "I told you before the place sounded familiar."

"Well, day-um," Lee said.

"Fuck you, you don't read books with no pictures in them," Boats called from his stretcher.

"You know what? I think I can't wait until you dumbasses leave me alone here," Jimbo said. "Really. Get going."

Lee turned to the remaining tagalongs and raised a hand palm upward. The stretcher team lifted Boats. The remaining two ambulatory locals helped the man with the broken leg along. The sad procession made their way along the brow of the hill away toward the west. Only Byrus remained behind leaning on a bundle of Roman spears. They were pila, the deadly javelin carried by regular troops. They were six feet long with an iron shaft ending in a pyramid point making up half their length. The iron shaft was set in a wooden handle. They were designed for throwing and as a close-quarters jabbing weapon.

"Get your ass moving, Bruce," Jimbo said.

Byrus stood shaking his head with vigor, a smile fixed on his face.

"I mean it, dude. Go with them." Jimbo pointed after the group. Only Bat turned back to give him a last look before they were out of sight around the slope.

Byrus stamped the spears on the ground and scowled.

"Yeah. I know that look," Jimbo said.

He drew his knife and crouched to cut a number of strips of cloth from the skirt of a Roman corpse. Jimbo stuck the lengths of red wool under this belt and lifted his pack to slide into the straps. A bandolier of grenades went over one arm and he held out the other to the grinning Byrus.

"If you're going to be in my army then you hump your share of gear, Bruce."

Byrus took the bandolier and settled it over his broad shoulders with an expression of consuming pride. The Ranger hung his rifle in the combat sling, the Macedonian hefted his bundle of spears, and together they set off back east at a trot into the trees.

Farewells

The toll at House Villeneuve was great but could have been far worse.

Claude was dead. He died in the kitchen of the house but was not alone. The corpses of three of the intruders lay in the kitchen, pantry, and rear entryway in the wake of his retreat. A broad smear of blood led away from the pantry and into the alley where a fourth man lay dead with the blade of the saber still lodged in his chest.

Jeannot had been struck unconscious in the melee at the foot of the stairs but recovered by morning with nothing more than a headache and blurred vision. A concussion, certainly.

Anatole, the chef, had a face swollen with bruises from where he was beaten near senseless by the invaders. But he was far more concerned that the Madame had seen him clad only in his nightshirt. Inès and Corrine were reduced to tears and shivers and only recovered somewhat after several draughts of cognac.

Mme. Villeneuve took to her room where she remained in bed succumbing, Caroline suspected, to draughts of wine mixed with laudanum to dispel her pain and shock.

In addition to the wreckage caused by the home invaders, the house was a slaughterhouse of bloody corpses. Including the four men shot dead by Caroline—three hired villains and the man who hired them—there were four more victims of Claude and Claude himself to be disposed of. Anatole left the house when the sun came up and brought back some rough and silent men. Corrine assured Caroline that these men would be discreet. They were frequently hired to do work about the house and garden and could be trusted to keep their secrets especially when paid with the gold coins found in the pockets of the slain intruders.

All would be taken to the mass gravesites set about the city for those unnamed dead who were found in the rubble or who fell on the day of the forlorn counterattack against the Prussian lines. The winter ground was frozen too hard for burial. The corpses would wait until the thaw before being tipped into trenches and covered.

Only Claude remained behind. Anatole, with the help of Corrine, the less squeamish of the maids, sewed the big man in sacking and placed him in a shed in the alley where the cold air would freeze him solid until a proper funeral could be had.

A few young men came to visit Jeannot. They were fellow students from his university. They were appalled that Jeannot himself answered the door. Where was that dour footman who usually greeted them? Jeannot told them that Claude was dead. They shrugged at this. So many dead in Paris these days. They made a few remarks about the state of the house and their host mumbled a few remarks that did little to assuage their curiosity.

Caroline gave them their privacy by withdrawing to the small library room with Stephen. Through the closed doors to the adjoining room she could hear them talking as young men will in dramatic and lofty terms. She assumed from their bluster and Jeannot's relative silence that none of them had participated in *le sortie torrentiale.* Not one of them had seen or experienced what had turned Jeannot from fervent firebrand to sullen automaton in a single morning. There seemed to be more life in the young man after the previous night's events. It was as if they served as a tonic to restore some of his resolution. The look of one who is lost was gone from his eyes despite the occasional vertigo brought on by the head injury. The repulsion of the intruders, though it was mostly Claude and Caroline's actions that routed them, gave him a renewed strength, a restoration of his manhood.

Despite this, Caroline overheard only brief contributions from him in response to the heated discussion of his friends. They spoke of capitulation and surrender. They would probably have spat in the floor were they not in a house as well regarded as that of the Villeneuves. Rumors were rife that Prussian troops would soon occupy the city and that the upstart Wilhelm had been proclaimed Emperor of the Germans at Versailles. It was a deep insult to all Frenchmen. A halfwit puppet of the Krupp family and this Bismarck crowned him at the winter residence of the kings of France. A bloody Prussian dressed up as a Napoleon from a comic opera. What were Prussians, after all? Only damned Poles who spoke German. It would be absurd were it not so profoundly loathsome.

Inès brought a tray with a bottle of wine and the few mismatched glasses that had not been broken in the previous night's siege. Jeannot apologized both for the glassware and the vintage, the Villeneuve cellar was rather depleted. This set the students off on politics again, damning the mayor and the generals and the enemy. There would be no vintage this year. The Germans had seen to that.

Caroline lost interest in the conversation.

Translating the words in her head was tiring and the speakers were bores; like the young anywhere and at any time who see the world only through the passions of their own personal politics. She dozed, the comforting warmth of the baby radiating in her arms. She could feel Stephen's gentle breath on her breast.

A muted clanging noise awoke her, sounding once, twice. The dinner gong rung by Inès. The library was dense in shadow. The early evening of winter was on the city. The young men were still talking in the next room and their voices rose excitedly at the prospect of dining. Caroline suspected that this was the purpose of their visit all along—to mooch a meal from a friend's kitchen. There would not be much left in the Villeneuve larder but she doubted this would matter to the uninvited guests.

She waited until she heard them depart from the drawing room before emerging from the library. Stephen was stirring and would want to nurse again soon. Caroline was surprised at the bottom of the stairs to see Mme. Villeneuve descending. The widow's eyes were glassy and she required a hand to the banister rail to keep her steady. Despite that there was a hard look to her eyes and the set of her mouth.

"My dear, whoever you may be," she began. Her voice was thin but resolute. "I must ask you to leave my house. At once."

"I understand, Madame," Caroline said.

"I do not understand all that was said last night. I understand that they came for you and they came for the child. Claude was murdered and my son very nearly so."

"I will get my bags and we will depart this evening," Caroline said with lowered head.

"It sickens me that I brought you into my house

assuming you to be but another innocent victim of this horrid war. Instead I invited the horror to act out within my own walls."

Caroline had no reply to this but to stand aside to allow Mme. Villeneuve to pass and make her way to the dining room and the male conversation booming from there.

"Immediately, Mademoiselle," she said, without turning. A final insult.

Eyes stinging, Caroline hurried up the steps to her borrowed room and flung all her belongings into the carpetbag. The revolver she left behind. She had no idea how to reload the awful thing and was frankly relieved to be shed of it. She bundled Stephen into layers of blankets and herself into her brocaded coat and broad-brimmed hat to return to the ground floor and slip quietly from the house. Uncaring laughter pursued Caroline as, unseen by her, the young boors around the dining table made idle jests and consumed the last of their hosts' hoarded victuals. She stood in the biting cold and pushed the door closed behind her. The mallet-scarred surface was rough under her gloved fingers.

She stood upon the walkway before the house deciding which way to turn; a decision that seemed entirely inconsequential as she had no idea where she might find shelter in this city in spiritual as well as physical ruin. Tears started in her eyes and ran in chilled streams down her cheeks. She was afraid. For her baby and for herself. The illusion of security provided by Mme. Villeneuve's household was shattered—an illusion. Caroline and, now she knew, her child were hunted. Her enemies knew where to find them and had, literally, all the time in existence to locate them and...

"Caroline."

Caroline looked away, dropping the carpetbag

and clutching Stephen tighter. She was moving to bolt away when the voice spoke again.

"It's me."

She turned to see a man in the tattered livery of a coachman stepping from the street toward her, a hand held before him and a smile creasing his face.

It was Dwayne.

The Arbor Path

The children's game that first optio Gaius referred to was being played in earnest.

Two centuries of the XXX and an additional two centuries made up of survivors of the XXIII began their march before dawn. They moved into the woods following strips of red cloth left at intervals along a narrow game trail through the trees. They were forced by the confines of the pathway into marching in a rank two men in width. The line of men snaked through the woods in a column over a mile long. Men in lighter armor and without shields trotted through the dark forest on either flank. More men ran ahead as scouts to find the sign left by Critus and his advance party.

Centurion Pulcher secured horses for himself and his optios and aquilifier from the local village. They paid a dear price for them, made dearer when Pulcher was informed that these were the same mounts captured earlier from the rebels they were pursuing.

Pulcher rode at the head of the column, ramrod straight in the saddle, to give the men an example to follow. The legionnaires of Caesar and the Senate were courageous to a fault but their faults were many. They did not like surprises and they did not like marching through close terrain like this damned wooded country. Pulcher had seen men under his command sleep through the night even though knowing they faced a pitched battle the following day. Their bravery was not in question and, in combat, they would die before yielding an inch of ground. He also knew, from bitter experience, that they could be routed like sheep by a sudden change in fortune. Each man was valiant with a code of personal conduct that was inviolate. But often, as a unit, they would succumb to a kind of contagious terror—a hysteria. And so the centurion rode high in the saddle, head erect and looking neither left nor right. His aquilifier rode behind to his right with the banner of the XXX held uncovered and aloft for all to see. The men following would take strength from that.

A scout returned down the path ahead with another man in his company. The man was soiled and bathed in sweat. His hair was matted black with dried blood.

Pulcher motioned for the column to halt and dismounted to meet the scout and his bloodied companion on foot and out of sight of the men. He did not need omens and portents to weaken the will of the soldiers.

"Is this one of the man who accompanied Critus?" he asked.

"He is, sir," the scout replied. "We found him on the trail ahead. He says he was coming to meet us."

"Is this true?" Pulcher asked directly. The man was missing an ear that had quite recently been sliced or torn away. His eyes were wide and shifting. His hands shook as though palsied. There was the stink of piss about him.

"I was sent back, sir. To warn you, sir," the man stammered.

"Warn me?" Pulcher sniffed. "Of what?"

"We encountered the rebels last night. There was battle and many were slain. The enemy fled to the west."

"And you did not pursue?"

"They were many in number, sir. Hundreds or

maybe more, sir. Critus continues on after them even now, sir. He leaves the strips of cloth for you to follow as you ordered, sir."

"And this is true?"

"Every word, sir." The man bit his lip. By the gods, he was close to weeping. The display repulsed Marcus Pulcher.

"Where is your sword?" the centurion asked.

The man looked to his empty scabbard but offered no answer.

"You may have the temporary loan of mine," Pulcher said and withdrew his own gladius from the sheath on his girdle.

He grabbed the coward's proffered hand by the wrist and jerked the man toward him at the same time driving the flat tip of the sword up under the man's ribs to rip open his lungs and heart. The man sank lifeless to his knees. Pulcher twisted the blade hard and pulled it out with an obscene sucking sound. There was no blood. The man died where he stood.

"Drag this trash from the trail," he said, stooping to wipe the blade of his sword with fallen leaves. "I won't have my men offended by the sight of him."

"What orders follow, sir?" the scout said.

"We continue on. We see if this dog was telling the truth that we might expect the way to our enemy marked with ribbons." Pulcher turned then and walked back to where the aquilifier stood holding the reins of his horse.

The lead scout, an Umbrian named Nasum by his comrades for his prominent nose, came upon two bands of crimson cloth dangling from a branch that hung above the trail. Two ribbons meant a change in direction. The men they hunted had left the trail. Nasum placed his fingers in his mouth and whistled for the other scouts to join him. When they appeared he pointed left and right of the trail and the men hared into the bracken to find the new pathway.

A call drew Nasum and the others to the north where a scout stood pointing at a ribbon hanging from the low branch of a cedar. Nasum ordered one of his scouts back to where the two ribbons hung. This man would wait for the column and direct them onto the new track and to the rebels they sought.

The rest of the scouts, led by Nasum, continued on at a trot following the red ribbon trail deeper and deeper into the woods under the midnight shadows cast by the canopy of trees overhead. They could not see the sky but for the occasional beam of sunlight piercing the roof of boughs. And so they could not see the wheeling rings of buzzards high in the sky to the west and growing ever further south of them as they ran after their intended prey.

The ground became too rough and the trees too narrowly spaced for the combined centuries of the two legions to continue in column. They broke into disparate straggling lines urged on by the curses of their optios. Their pila and shields snagged on branches and they swam in sweat under their armor. The men at the front used mattocks to clear a path through the undergrowth for the rest to follow. They attended to the whistles and a calls of the scouts rushing ahead.

Pulcher took to foot. His aquilifier led both their mounts up a steep incline thick with trees and bracken.

All around him was the din of hob-nailed boots crashing over the forest floor thick with twigs and needles fallen from the crown of nature above them. They marched like the boar from whom they took their name, unmindful of the noise they made and scornful of any who would oppose them. They were good men, tough men, and eager to redeem the courage lost to the damnable Jew magic that slew so many of their brothers. No one was more eager than the men of the XXIII. Pulcher was pleased to see that they had taken the lead on the march. They rushed up the hillside, pulling themselves up using handholds of scrub and pushing off from the boles of trees. They moved like men with a purpose in which they had invested their hearts. Their faces were grim and hard. He could see in their eyes an overwhelming hunger to spill the blood of the rebels who slew their officers and their comrades and shamed them all.

A series of high whistles came from the left of the ragged line of march. A scout came stumbling along the slope to where Pulcher stood.

"Nasum found a better way up, sir!" the man said, gasping for breath.

"Is there sign there? Are we still following the trail left by Critus?" the centurion asked.

"Like a dog in heat, sir. A dry stream, sir. Runs straight to the top. It's the way the rebels fled, sir," the man said with head bowed.

The optios were called and the cornicen sent for. The soldiers followed the blasts from the trumpet and moved to the left, eastward, across the gradient following the calls of the scouts. There lay a deep cut in the hillside, a remnant of a seasonal waterway now dry in the late summer months. Broad and floored with river stones, it was as near to a road as the soldiers had seen since leaving camp. They reformed into columns by century and started up the wash at a trot.

Pulcher watched the men moving by in order once again and was gratified. Most pleasing was the sight of the XXX, his own boar-topped banner bobbing overhead, taking the lead now for the crest of the hill.

Nasum knelt on one knee on the scorching gravel and looked about him with narrowed eyes.

He held in his hand a stone rounded by millennia of waters passing over it. Tied about it with a stout knot was a length of red wool cut from a soldier's skirt. The trail followed up the dry wash to level ground at the top of a mesa. Here the earth had been deeply scored with steep banks above which the thick cedar forest formed a hedge either side.

Buca, a half-Greek, trotted up to him ahead of the first legionnaires reaching the crest far behind.

"I don't like it, Buca," Nasum said.

"What is there to like or not like? It is sign. Our quarry lies ahead." Buca shrugged.

"The coward we found—" Nasum scanned the trees as he spoke "—he said there had been a battle. We've seen no sign of it."

"Perhaps he lied."

"And perhaps he cut off his own ear?"

Buca tilted his head as a curious dog might.

"And there were wounded he said. We've seen no blood," Nasum said. "Where is the blood? Some of the men following the rebels would be bleeding, no?"

Buca nodded slowly then looked back at the dust cloud rising above the ranks of the approaching centuries.

"And this knot," Nasum said, holding the ribbon-wrapped stone up for the half-Greek to examine. "It's not the same as the other knots. I noticed it back when the trail turned north. Different knots."

"You will tell this to old man Pulcher?" Buca blinked. "You will tell him you are worried about a change in knots?'

"Mithra's tits, I'm not mad, you pederast," Nasum said and tossed the stone aside. "Come on. We'll keep moving ahead to the next red marker."

The Hares and the Tortoise

Jimmy Smalls recalled what Lee said about how being in a fair fight meant your plan failed.

He watched the army tramping up the gully toward him over the open sights of his M4. He was back in the trees away from the ledge and sheltered by the gloom that blanketed the ground between the big cedars. Byrus crouched by Jimbo, leaning his weight on the bundle of javelins held in his hands and watching the approaching centuries without the slightest sign of unease.

There were no bowman among them and for that Jimbo was supremely grateful.

Some skirmishers double-timed ahead of the first column. Jimbo let them pass. They gave him a bad moment there when two of them stopped at the last ribbon he left and took a look around. Then they just moved on. If they suspected something they weren't letting on.

He drew a bead on a rider in the lead of the ranks of marching men; an officious looking bastard in what Jimbo recognized as a centurion's helmet with its sideways plume. The guy looked eyes front like they were in a parade.

A dude with a trumpet trotted to keep up with the officer. A rider holding the banner with the boar on top of it rode behind and to the centurion's right. These were the guys he and Bat stood off on the road two days ago, Jimbo realized. And those horses they were riding looked awfully familiar. Those were the saddles they bought back in that market in Caesarea. Jimbo sincerely hoped that none of their gear got left behind intact. Boats swore it was all stacked in and around that tent back in the camp when things went ka-blam. Morris Tauber would have a fit if he found out they left any working ordnance for the locals to find. As it was, the ruins of that fort, if they were even still visible back in The Now, would be a chronal toxic waste dump of anachronistic bits and pieces.

Time for that later. Time for everything later. Right now it was Thermopylae with the odds flipped in his favor.

The Pima slid the grenade tube forward where it was slung from a rail under the fore end of his rifle. He slid a fat 40mm HE round into the tube and snapped it back in place to the trigger action. He made a motion to Bruce to cover his ears then held the rifle up at a sixty degree angle and eyeballed the three rectangular formations of men moving steadily closer, crowding the dry wash from wall to wall.

He'd never seen a prettier ambush in his life.

"We call this Kentucky windage, Bruce," Jimbo said and noted that the smaller man was dutifully holding his hands clapped to his ears. A grin split the Macedonian's face as he anticipated what was to come next.

Jimbo depressed the trigger and the rifle kicked back in his hands with a loud *pop*. The grenade rocketed skyward on a cloud of gas and looped back down at a steep angle to strike near dead center atop the rear block of men. He didn't wait to see the results and fed a second round into the launcher and let it fly at a sharper angle. This one dropped to the left of the century in the lead and ripped a gash across the massed men that bisected the unit into two halves along a bloody tear.

Through the drifting smoke and dust he could see that the whole line of march came to a dead halt. The officer was fighting to stay on board his panicked mount. The horse fell finally, hooves kicking wildly. The guy with the banner was down on his ass, his horse going full out away down the gully at a gallop. Orders were being shouted and Jimbo watched in astonishment as the broken units closed ranks and continued the march. The centurion was on his feet now with helmet gone. The three formations continued on, shields raised, and left a trail of their dead behind them.

Jimbo stood now and directly aimed at the first block of men to send a third round into them. This one skipped off the rocks just before the front wall of shields and tumbled under the feet before detonating. A bloody geyser of men and parts of men sprayed up, collapsing the center of the first five ranks. The screaming rose from the wash as Jimbo watched the block of men part then coalesce to close the awful wound as they marched on.

The centurion called again and the formations morphed in one smooth motion. Shields were raised and held aloft to be locked in place to form a roof atop each unit.

"The tortoise," Jimbo whispered. He'd just witnessed one of the legion's signature moves with his own eyes. But it wasn't going to do a thing for them. He fired a fresh grenade from the hip and bounced it off the shield roof of the lead century to hit the ground rolling toward the second. The blast caved in the front ranks of that formation as if they had collectively run into an invisible object in their path. They halted for only a few seconds then stepped over their own dead to close the gap with the block of men before them.

"Crazy bastards," Jimbo said to himself and then to

Byrus, "Time to move, dude!"

The Ranger had his pack shouldered and rifle slung. He looked back to make sure Byrus was following. That's when he saw the men rushing toward them along the lip of the ledge. There were a half dozen stripped to tunics and girdles and sprinting with swords in their hands. They were close enough for Jimbo to see the fierce look in their eyes. He knew that look. The killing look.

He sighted and fired past Byrus, knocking down the lead runner. Byrus turned in time to see a second man drop into the wash, spilling entrails as he fell from a double tap to the abdomen. The little man freed one of the javelins and flung it in an overhanded throw with the athletic ease of an Olympian. The point of the spear took a swordsman high in the chest. The other three were closing the gap, swords held low for the jabbing motion that made the gladius feared the world over.

"Get the fuck out of the way, Bruce!" Jimbo ran forward and shouldered Byrus aside. He sprayed the three remaining Romans with a burst of automatic fire and brought them down in a stumbling heap.

"Fuck me!" Jimbo muttered and yanked Bryce along with him into a run. He let the M4 drop onto its sling and pulled the pump shotgun clear of the sheath on his back. He could hear more movement through the trees above them. Jimbo trained the shotgun toward the sound as he ran and pumped double-ought and flechette rounds into the brush. A shriek rose from the foliage.

Caesar's boys may have not known anything about non-linear warfare but they damned sure understood the value of throwing out a screen of flankers. The bastard down there leading them was no dumbass. He hissed to Byrus and they both turned sharply to move into the woods and away from the gully where they could be trapped against the ledge.

Jimbo gave Byrus a shove to send the man ahead then turned and sent some suppression fire uphill at his invisible pursuers. He knew it wouldn't stop them but it might make the Romans half-step it and that's all the edge he was looking for. He made to follow Byrus, running flat out and expecting a slinger's stone to the skull or an Assyrian arrow in the back at any second. Nothing came after them but shouts. The fuckers were moving to ring them in, drive them toward the wash and close the noose.

The Pima re-sheathed the shotgun and brought up the M4 to load a fresh round into the grenade launcher on the run. He snapped it closed and spun just long enough to loose a lateral trajectory shot back through the trees. It was a pure bonehead, backyard Rambo bullshit move. The grenade could strike a tree and bounce back at him. He heard the clonk, clonk, clonk of the steel round striking wood as it rebounded through the woods behind him. He collided with Byrus throwing them both flat. The ground shook under them. A storm of wood shards flew overhead in a ballistic sleet of deadly daggers. A black cloud of vaporized earth bloomed behind them. Clots of dirt rained down. Jimbo saw a length of timber taller than himself fly into the woods end over end. He pulled Byrus to his feet and they ran at an angle up the incline and away from the animal screams rising at their backs.

He'd hurt them. That was the plan. He set the Romans back on their ass and took them away from the direction his friends were traveling.

Now for the second part of the plan: get himself clear and not wind up on a cross. He was not Spartacus and had no plans to be. He ran easy, leaping fallen trees and ducking low branches. The little surfer dude kept up with him step for step carrying that bundle of javelins on his shoulder like it was weightless. Jimbo's burden seemed lightened as well. The heavy bandoliers of grenades swinging from his shoulder. The scabbard of the scrounged gladius slapping his thigh as he ran. They were nothing at all. He just went *mano a mano* with the baddest motherfuckers of the ancient world and came out on top.

He knew that it was an adrenalin high and he'd pay for this elation when the crash came on him and the ammo started to feel like it weighed a ton. But he was in the moment and he never wanted it to end. Running with a good buddy after a good fight and nobody in the world would ever know they were here or ever care about this nameless battleground. It was all he wanted. It made his life up until this day seem small even though he knew he'd done some pretty awesome stuff in his life. But this just seemed so goddamned real. It was all about right here and right now.

God help him, he was loving it.

A crashing sound in the brush before him and two beefy legionnaires appeared sweating before him. He and Byrus had let themselves get ringed in. Cherryass mistake. Jimbo raised his M-4 high to take the downward stroke from a gladius. Sparks flew. The second Roman rushed in with a pilum held low in his fists. The wicked point was aimed for his guts.

Jimbo stomped a booted foot down into the knee of the swordsman and heard a popping sound before the guy dropped screaming to the ground. He turned to the spearman too late. The squared-off business end of the javelin took him hard in the lower ribs. The armor spread the impact. The point glided over the Kevlar and the spearman followed the momentum of his attack, colliding with the Pima. Both fell to the ground together.

Byrus reached them to drive his gladius hard onto the back of the spearman. Jimbo threw the shuddering man off him, wiping the man's blood from his eyes in time to see Byrus chop down to split the swordsman's skull where the man lay grasping his twisted knee in his hands.

Shouts behind them growing closer. Footfalls sounded behind them, sandals cracking through the undergrowth and coming nearer. Jimbo went to stand and the pain in his side from the spear point sent an almost electric thrill of pain through his chest. He went to one knee. Byrus grabbed the bigger man's elbow to haul him up. Jimbo clenched his teeth and manned up to get through the agony that threatened to take his breath away. That fucker cracked some ribs, the Ranger thought, and went to spit at the now inert corpse lying at the head of a stream of blood. His mouth was too dry.

The little Macedonian shoved Jimbo against a tree and left him. He struggled to stay on his feet, dizzy with pain, his back to the stout cedar trunk. He saw Byrus leaping toward a gang of Romans exploding from the forest shadows for them. The surfer dude that time forgot was slashing with his short sword like some wild thing, growling and snapping as he burst in among the attackers. Men screamed and howled. A soldier jabbed with a pilum and Byrus cut the wooden shaft from the long spear point with a single stroke and booted the man in the nuts. He then turned to a swordsman, batted the man's blade aside and pulled the man onto his steel until the gladius's blade exploded from between the man's back ribs.

Jimbo raised his rifle to help Byrus out. He aimed at

a sweating swordsman and depressed the trigger with no result. He looked down at the M-4 to see that the sword strike from that first legionnaire had dented the receiver on the weapon. The rifle was eighty-sixed. The dude with the broken pilum had gotten past Byrus and was racing with the severed end of the wooden shaft held in his fist like a club. Jimbo clawed for the Colt 1911 he had holstered on his sword belt.

He cleared the holster and was raising the weapon when his arm went numb and the pistol dropped from his numb fingers. The spearman had brought the hard wooden haft down on his forearm and was swinging it back for a blow to Jimbo's head.

That's the last the Pima saw before the sky, and all around him, turned a starless black and he was adrift in the Big Fuck-all.

When Are You?

Dwayne took her in his arms. Mindful of the baby, he pressed her to him gently.

His coat was gritty against her cheek and stank of wood smoke. She didn't care. Stephen wriggled in protest between them. Dwayne took her shoulders and stepped back, eyes on the child. There were equal parts joy and regret in those eyes.

"Dwayne," she began.

"I want to hold him," Dwayne said and scooped the baby from her and held him close.

She studied his face then in the hazed moonlight. Black soil highlighted the lines Dwayne's face. There were more there than she recalled. What she thought was weariness in his expression she now recognized as age. Cold spiked up her spine with the realization. This man was older than the man she said goodbye to in Berne, considerably older. The gray at the temples was not discoloration from ash. The hard lines about the mouth and eyes, the sag of the lids. Twenty years had passed since their last meeting. She touched his sleeve and he lifted his gaze from the cooing infant.

"Dwayne," she began again.

"I wish I could explain, Caroline. There was no other way. You need to leave here now. Tonight."

"For where? For when?"

"Don't worry," he said, his expression softening. "No time will have passed for you. Or for me. You'll see me again just like you left me."

She was speechless, not something she could ever recall being.

"I can't tell you anything else. Don't ask me, Caroline. Samuel would be here but it didn't work out that way. One thing I've learned is that you can make almost any mistake right if you try hard enough. But you can never make up lost time."

He handed the baby back into her arms and embraced her once again.

"We're in no rush. Harnesh's people can't open a window until sometime tomorrow local time. Still, it's a good idea you two leave now."

"Aren't you leaving too? I mean. With us?" she said, swallowing tears. She wanted to cry like a child and could not focus on one single cause for it.

"I'm good. I'm safe here for now. Invisible to them." He pulled back a ragged sleeve and showed her a gleaming steel wristlet like Samuel wore. He smiled that wolfish grin of his. "Besides, I'm kind of looking forward to seeing their faces."

She smiled back. Her mind was swirling with questions that he forbade her to ask. The questions themselves terrified her. This was a man who shared a life with her that she had yet to live. His memories were her future—hers and Stephen's. She fought down her anxiety and a crushing sadness that would overwhelm her if she gave it a second's consideration.

"Then we'd better move along. There's still a curfew in effect," she said and was surprised when he picked up the carpetbag and took her arm in his.

"We always said we'd do a real tour of Paris someday," he said casually.

"Not like this," she said and they moved through the gloom, the city silent but for the ring of tramping boots moving away along the cobbles of an adjacent street. After a bit she recognized the route they were on.

"You're taking me back to the place where Samuel and I came through the field," she said.

"It's still in place and programmed to open. We have some wiggle room. Like I said, no crazy need to rush but we're still on a timetable." He gripped her arm closer. She looked up at him but his eyes were fixed on the path ahead.

She had questions but they were all about events to come.

"Harnesh's man, the one with the white hair, he's dead," she said.

"Madeline Villeneuve wrote about it. You were quite the woman of mystery for a while there, babe," he said and turned to smile at her. "You did good."

"It was for Stephen. I'd die for him, you know that."

He said nothing. His smile faded and he looked away. The chill from earlier returned deeper than before.

They stayed to the shadowed side of a broad boulevard. Tramping feet echoed toward them and Dwayne pulled them into the deeper darkness under a tattered storefront awning. They watched a troop of soldiers tread by in formation, an officer striding before them with a sword on his shoulder. They wore Uhlan style helmets and trousers with the stripe down the leg; cavalry who'd been reduced to infantry after their horses went to the butcher. Dwayne and Caroline waited until they were out of sight around a turn in the avenue before continuing on. A building in their pathway had collapsed in the recent shelling to block a street. Dwayne took the baby and helped her climb over the hill of rubble. They came down the slope of bricks and broken mortar to the garden area and the alley where she and Samuel had entered only a bit more than week ago. They stopped at the mouth of the narrow passage and he gently returned Stephen to her arms.

He took a slim black case from his pocket and placed it in the carpetbag.

"Everything you need is in here. A throwaway cell phone, an American Express black card, passports, visas, and driver's license."

"Who am I now?"

"Mrs. Sydney Jean Hochheiser of Calgary, Alberta," he said and smiled at her wince.

"Well, I've been pretending to be Canadian anyway. What about the clothes?" she said, glancing down at her voluminous brocaded skirts.

"There's plenty of period re-enactors walking around Paris these days. No Frenchman is going to risk losing his cool by reacting to you. Use the card to buy some casual clothes and whatever else you need and take the train to London. There's already a suite there in your name at the Marleybone. It's a four-star. When you get there call me."

"And say what exactly?"

"That you and the baby are fine unless..."

"What?"

"You might get there a little sooner than anticipated."

"Like our six-month vacation from the world?" she said.

"It shouldn't be that far off."

"I hope not. I wouldn't want Stephen to be walking the next time you see him."

Dwayne laughed then started to say something. He bit off the words as well as the laughter. He looked past her with hard eyes. She turned to see the first tendrils of white mist forming.

"Wait until it fills the alley," he said.

"Once more," she said and stepped to him. He took her and their child to him and held them as though they contained a healing power to make his world right again. Her tears came then and he crushed her closer.

"One thing," he said, no louder than a breath in her ear. "Tell Hammond, 'the oracle at Joppa.' Just that. He'll know what it means."

"The oracle at Joppa," she whispered back against his neck.

"You have to go. Now," he said, releasing her.

The baby in her arm and the carpetbag in hand, she walked away from him into the engulfing mist.

"Don't look back," she heard him say. It sounded like a warning he'd often repeated or even a statement of philosophy rather than a timely thought of the moment.

Caroline did not look back. She only walked into the alley back toward her own present and his past.

Caesarea Redux

"We're exposed here. We can't keep waiting," Bat Jaffe said.

Lee Hammond said nothing in reply. They were hiding in plain sight on a terrace above the walled harbor. It was the oldest part of the city. The pillars were green with age, the tiles cracked and weed-choked. For three days they'd been living like the rest of the town's homeless in whatever nook or niche they could find to get out of the weather. They were starting to draw attention from the locals. Lee stood with a foot on a curtain wall, watching the boats coming and going over the sun-dappled water.

"Boats needs real medical care. Antibiotics. Surgery," she said.

Lee spat. His eyes were locked on the broad stone pier where their raft lay concealed in ten feet of water.

"We can come back, Lee."

He turned to her then back to where Chaz sat by the wounded SEAL in the shade of a tattered awning. Boats was conscious but in pain even if he'd never admit it. They were keeping him hydrated and doing their best to drain the pus from the swollen wound in his thigh. There was nothing they could do to stop the fevers he was spiking more and more frequently.

"We can come back," Chaz said.

"And where do we look?" Lee said.

"Jimbo will make it to the exfil point. He might

have to take his time but he'll make it. He'll leave a sign. You know he will," Chaz said.

Lee scanned the pier again.

"Are we in range of the field?" he said.

"For a text message," Chaz said.

"Text Mo Tauber," Lee said. "Give him the date. We leave tonight."

Chaz retrieved the transponder from his pack and booted it up.

Lee walked away down the terrace. Seabirds parked there fluttered and skittered from his path. Bat followed.

"It's the only option," she said.

"It's still fucked up."

"No argument there."

"Jimbo will make it. That Indian can make it out of any tight spot. He made it out of one carrying me on his back once." Lee looked away from her.

"We get Boats away safely and come back," Bat said.

"And sit and watch this shithole? For how long?"

"Maybe we can get a timeline. Some kind of fix on when Jimmy might make it here."

"How's that work?"

"I have to think that the contact we had with the Romans will wind up in their history somewhere," she said. "That's what happens? You guys rewrite history, right? That's what we came back to do, am I right?"

"You think we can rely on retro-intelligence. That's never as reliable as you make it sound," Lee said.

"It's something, isn't it?" she said.

As it turned out, Marcus Rupilius Pulcher was an illiterate.

He would never have written an accurate report of the events leading to the destruction of five centuries in any case. The optio who served as his scribe was dead, his head ripped off by one of the killing bolts of lightning that fell upon them in that draw.

The centurion knelt in his tent draining his second skin of wine. It did not improve his mood. It did nothing to quell the screams of the wounded lying outside in the rough camp laid by the few survivors. The remaining men of his formation, those who had not already run away, were so small in number that a proper sentry could not be posted. There was no relief for those who suffered from injuries. They could only shriek until their throats were raw. They would lose consciousness and bleed away until they were lifeless, still and pale.

Pulcher's own wounds were painful but he would live. His right arm and leg were scored with gashes made by tiny bits of wire that had appeared there instantly with the clap of thunder that reduced his forward century by half The same scraps of metal gutted the horse he was riding. He'd fallen hard from the saddle, narrowly missing being brained by the kicking hooves of the dying animal.

Here in solitude, he removed his armor and tore his clothing into strips to bind his arm and leg. His body broke out in a chilled sweat from the pain. The binding cloths were swiftly soaked black with his blood.

For all the sacrifice of his men there was nothing to show for it. They never even saw their attackers. It was as if they were struck down by a force of nature. They had drawn the ire of some dark and vengeful god. There was no opportunity to draw blood, to sink their blades into the flesh of their enemy, to hear his cries for mercy.

It was his command. All fault would be his. All shame would be upon his name.

He regarded the gladius that lay before him in its scabbard. The sword was purchased by him in Damascus. The blade was the finest steel. The hilt and tang were polished brass worked with a clever skein of oak leaves. The grip was red oak stained dark with his sweat over the years. The pommel was the head of a roaring lion, its mane worn smooth by his resting palm. It cost him nearly a year's pay and he never once regretted its purchase. He unsheathed it and admired the gleam along its razor edge. There was a nick in the blade back near the hilt where it had once caught the blow from a Parthian axe-head. One of the many times it saved his life. One of the many times it drank deep of the blood of the enemies of Rome.

Pulcher set the lion-head pommel in the loose dirt before him and rested the tip of the blade against the soft bone where his ribs joined. He wondered idly who might own this blade after this day. It did not matter now. With a violent exhalation to empty his lungs he drove himself forward onto the sword with all his weight and force.

He was dead within seconds with little pain but for bitter memories fleeting past.

With him died history.

The Ocean Raj

"Caroline? What's this number? It's not the Berne exchange or the burner I gave you."

"I changed phones after you left, Dwayne. I thought it was safer."

"You're probably right."

"Miss me?"

"I've hardly had time to, babe. Been busy as hell since I got back. Your brother just got the guys through the field. I was gonna call you."

"You would have missed me anyway. I'm not in Berne anymore."

"What are you saying? Why not? I just left you there yesterday. Is it the baby?"

"Stephen's fine. It's kind of a long story and I can't go into it now."

"Is that him I hear?"

"Yes. We're both safe. Samuel came and got us. Something came up."

"Samuel? What was it, Carrie? What came up?"

She sighed.

"All right, I'll come get you and Stephen."

"No, Dwayne. We're good here. We really are. Morris needs you there."

"All right. I'll come get you when this op is over. You can tell me all about it then."

"Listen, Dwayne, when Lee gets back you need to tell him something."

"What?"

"Tell him, 'the oracle at Joppa.' He'll know what it means."

"That's it? What's it mean?"

"I wish I knew. I wish to God I knew."

"You sound tired, babe."

"So do you. We should both get some sleep, right? Love you."

And the connection was broken.

Dwayne Roenbach pocketed the sat phone. That was his infant son he heard in the background. He readily admitted he knew jack shit about babies but he was damn sure three-day-olds couldn't say ma-ma.

He had a lot of questions but could tell by the tone in Caroline's voice that she didn't want to hear any of them right now. It wasn't irritation he heard at the edges of her answers. It was more like a despondency. She was probably just tired as she said. Both she and Stephen were safe. That was enough for now.

Dwayne thought about leaving the bridge area to look for Morris Tauber to update him on his sister. But he didn't feel like a lot of questions either, especially ones he had no answers for.

It was two days later during a routine opening of the field that the text message came through.

PREPRED TO EXFIL—SND CRRNT
POS AND EST WINDOW
MEDEVAC NEEDED SRGRY
RESPND—RESPND—
SPRRW

A detailed star fix was attached setting the time of transmission at 20 September 16 at 02:56:17:01.

SPARROW was their personal code for any kind of urgent request. It was from the Rangers' days in Iraq and Afghanistan. It was taken from one of Chaz Raleigh's frequent quotes from scriptures. "His eye is on the sparrow." To Chaz it meant that whatever happened next was God's will. The others took it up as a more poetic way of saying "fuck it." It translated into their unit distress code.

Dwayne figured it was Lee sending the text. If Hammond thought they were in deep shit then they were. He called down to Mo to come up and join him on the aft deck where there would be no distractions. The scientist came out of the hold blinking like a mole in the sunlight. The resemblance was made even more accurate with the fuzzy ginger beard Tauber had grown either out of neglect or intent. Maybe he thought he looked piratical. The horn-rimmed glasses spoiled the effect. He looked more like near-sighted haystack.

"I'll get with Parviz and Quebat. See if I can get them to goose us to a forty-eight hour opening," Tauber said after Dwayne filled him in.

"Tap the brakes, Mo. Us going into panic mode doesn't help them. Take your time and fine tune the Tube to make the through field open as close to the window we give them as possible. And to hell with a medevac. They need a surgeon. Let's take a week before the next opening and bring a doctor here."

"You're right. You're right. But we still need to make a brief manifestation to send our return text. A minute or two at the most. The guys can get that up in twelve hours."

"I'll get the response together."

"After that, the best we can do is create a field

opening twenty-four hours or more relative from their last text even if we waited a year. I can dial it close but not that close, Dwayne. They'll have some hang time on the water waiting."

"The waiting on this end is a bitch too," Dwayne said.

"Welcome to my world," Morris said, turning to climb back down into his universe beneath the waterline.

Dwayne met with Geteye, the *Ocean Raj's* first mate and acting skipper in Boats' absence. They went up to the bridge where there was privacy. With the *Raj* at anchor in calm seas there was no need for anything but a skeleton watch.

This guy certainly knew how to grow a beard, Dwayne thought. It was thick as carpeting from his eyes to the base of his neck and complemented by a bushy untamed afro atop his head. The only revealing feature on the man was his eyes. They were deep brown with scarred lids. The man had seen his share of fights in his time. There was a keen intelligence there and an easy grace to his movements that someone ignorant would mistake for idleness. Dwayne knew a professional soldier when he saw one. Geteye was the perfect complement to his blustering and garrulous captain.

They talked about the risks and advantages of pulling the *Raj* closer to shore to shorten the row time for the team when they made for the field opening.

"I follow the news on the wireless, Baas," Geteye said, eyes on the charts spread on the scarred metal table between them.

"Yeah?" Dwayne knew to wait for the man to get

to his point.

"The Gaza is burning up, Baas. Closer we get to the coast the more Israeli patrol boats we see."

"You think we'll get boarded?"

"I *know* we get boarded, Baas. I know we get shitload questions and we don' have shitload answers."

"How much do you know about what goes on below deck, Geteye?"

The man smiled. A rare show of tobacco-stained teeth.

"I know enough, Baas. I know we don' wan' no boarding party. More than that I am just another dumb kaffir earning my pay." He lifted the bottle of Egyptian beer he'd been using to weigh down a corner of the chart and took a long pull.

"We'll maintain our current position then." Dwayne returned his smile. "I don't want my team adrift in shipping lanes where they can run into trouble."

"Whenever the hell that is, Baas."

Dwayne searched the other man's gaze for a sign of what he meant by that. The eyes betrayed nothing. But that told the Ranger what Geteye wanted him to know: I'm *nobody's* dumb kaffir, Baas.

There was no more to discuss. They finished their beers and returned to their stations.

A week later the motor powered inflatable puttered from the icy mist and into the modified hold deep below the *Ocean Raj's* main deck.

The team was suffering from exposure to salt and sun. They had remained at the pre-arranged coordinates for nearly three days, taking turns paddling against the current to remain within the projected field area. All were exhausted and Boats was aflame with fever. Chaz and Lee carried him from the Tube chamber. Bat stepped from the raft holding the banner of the XXIII in her fists. The Rangers, carrying the SEAL, followed Dwayne into a fully equipped surgery where a doctor and surgical nurse hired in Cyprus waited.

Both the doc and nurse had been paid cash in euros, with the promise of more, to be brought here by seaplane in the dead of night. They assumed it was something to do with the drug trade. Terrorists would not pay an advance. Six hundred thousand in untaxed euros would buy their confidence.

After checking vitals to make certain Boats could stand going under the knife they cleaned and prepped the wound site. They began work on the surgery to remove the arrow shaft from the SEAL's leg. They shooed the Rangers from the room, promising to have word in an hour or more.

"You're minus one," Dwayne said. He sat on a bench speaking to Chaz and Lee while they showered. Their gear lay in a filthy heap on the shower cabin deck.

"He stayed behind, covered for us," Lee said from under the steaming needle spray.

"We couldn't wait. Boats was in a bad way." Chaz was seated on the floor of his stall letting the hot stream pound him, an open bottle of Jack in his fist. He was taking long swallows.

"I know the situation. I just wish you'd told me in your text," Dwayne said.

"Why?" Lee said, reaching around the stall wall for the bottle of Tennessee whiskey.

"Joppa? Yeah I know Joppa," Bat Jaffe said, toweling off her hair in her private cabin.

"How well?" Dwayne asked.

"I've been there," she said. "It's the namesake for my family. It's called 'Jaffa' now. Why?"

"Because we're catching about two days sleep and we're going back," Lee said.

What the Blind Woman Saw

It was a shrine to Ceres, the goddess of fertility.

The construction was recent and Roman and contrasted with its surroundings with its fluted columns of purple-veined marble and gleaming roof of polished copper. It sat in the shade of young trees at the center of an open square surrounded by sagging dwellings taken over as doma for Roman citizens living in Judea.

Two men and a woman walked from a narrow lane and across the square through the mid-day heat. They led a pack mule behind them. The residents were either secluded in the shade of their homes or down in the markets enjoying the cooling breeze from the sea. No one noticed the trio seeking the oracle.

Lee Hammond was reminded once again that these structures were new at one time. Like most people, he had only the image of colorless ruins in his mind when picturing places in the past. The buildings facing the square were painted in colors that reminded him of South Florida. Pink and yellow and blue in various hues tinted the fronts of the multi-storied apartments. The shrine itself was a riot of colors that would have been at home in a Tijuana souvenir store. The eaves were decorated with outsized sheaves of wheat, bunches of grapes, and tree limbs weighed down with fruit. These reliefs were all painted in every color of the spectrum in gleaming enamels.

As they approached they could see the life-sized

statue of Ceres standing on a plinth within. She stood with an armload of ripe grain stalks and a hand held out in a gesture of benefaction. Her expression was open and vapid and genially smiling. The statue was painted in garish colors with the face grotesquely made up with heavy eye shade, rouged cheeks, and bright red lips. The goddess looked like she was ready for a night of hooking at a truck stop. She even had one breast exposed as a come-on. Let a thousand years strip away the enamel and artfully distress her and she'd be a revered work of art. To Lee's eyes she'd look tacky standing in a corner of a Bennigan's.

The granite dais at the feet of the statue was littered with the stems of long-dead flowers and baskets filled with black clumps of shriveled and rotten fruit. Rats skittered from the baskets at the sound of boots on the tiles. Ceres' devotees had been lax in their worship.

"Is this still here back in The Now?" Lee said.

"This will be a neighborhood in Tel Aviv. None of this is here then," Bat said. "But I think we're near a Pizza Hut I used to go to."

"I could go for a meat lovers," Chaz said, picking up a hammered copper bowl. A couple of tarnished coins rattled around the bottom.

"It won't get here for two thousand years so it'll be free," Bat said.

The scrape of sandal leather made them turn to see a woman draped in a black cloak shuffling from the dark behind the statue. She was bent with clawed hands. A strip of faded blue cloth was tied over her eyes.

"I'm guessing this is the Oracle," Lee said.

"What do I ask her?" Bat said.

"Don't ask her shit." The voice came from the blazing sunshine outside the shrine.

"She's not even blind and the arthritis is a fake," Jimmy Smalls said as they exited. He was dressed in a cotton kaftan and sandals. His jet hair reached his shoulders. One eye was covered with a strip of white cloth tied about his head. He smiled openly, holding his arms out for a hug from Chaz that lifted him off the ground.

"Ribs, you dumb bastard," Jimbo winced and Chaz set him down.

"Sorry, bro."

"How the hell did you find me?" Jimbo said.

"You know, I'm still not clear on that," Lee said, pumping Jimbo's hand in his.

"Bruce, it's okay, brother," Jimbo said, looking past them. He gestured to someone.

Byrus stepped from the alcove of a doma on the opposite side of the square. He wore a clean singlet belted with his sword girdle.

"He still hanging with you?" Chaz said.

"I wouldn't have made it without him. He hauled my ass away from some deep shit. I don't remember all of it. I was getting used to the idea of staying here."

"Your eye?" Bat said.

"Gone. I took a bad hit. Bruce had to cut it free. I remember that part. Wish I didn't," Jimbo said, making an exaggerated grimace.

"We'll get you back now. Have a doctor look at it," Lee said.

"We have a boat, a period accurate skiff tied up down at the harbor," Bat said.

"You have anything you need to take with you?" Lee said.

"Nope. All my gear that I brought back I dumped in the sea to rust. We're ready to go." Jimbo shrugged.

Lee and Chaz shared a glance. Bat laughed.

"Bruce goes with us. He goes or I stay." Jimbo's voice was flat. His eyes locked on Lee's.

Lee said nothing. He looked at the dusty street and ran a hand over his jaw.

"I owe him my life, Hammond."

"Look what followed me home, huh?" Lee said without looking up. "Does he know where he's going?"

"He's going with us. That's all that matters."

"Well, fuck it. So, we have a plus one going back," Lee said, grinning.

"The Taubers are gonna want to kill us," Chaz said.

"Never leave a man behind," Bat said.

Jimbo pulled a leather pouch from his belt and walked into the shrine to dump the contents into the offerings bowl. The old woman dropped to her knees and pulled off her blindfold to run her hands through the jumble of gold and silver coins.

Together they walked from the square toward the harbor and the boat waiting to take them to another place and time. Byrus trotted behind.

"Hey, so what was the outcome?" Jimbo asked.

"The decorations are up in the malls and they just ran *Charlie Brown's Christmas* on TV," Chaz said.

"Fucking A," Jimbo said.

New Sheriff in Town

Valerius Gratus was a broken man. The stranger, the white-haired foreign man who was the cause of all his troubles, never returned. The cursed man was an imposter. His every word a lie. He had neither the authority of the legate nor the imprimatur of the imperial house. His actions were not even sanctioned by the family Herod. And the damnable man did not return to Caesarea with more of the lovely morphea to help Gratus endure his own downfall.

The prefect of Judea was left without the warm embrace of the soporific that made his life tolerable. He was left to suffer the ordeal of seizures and chills that left him with a weakened heart and clenching bowels and, by far the worst of all, an unrequited longing for the welcome delirium of numbness the mystery draught offered him. He was abandoned now to the gnawing hunger for that which he could never have. Drink offered no solace. Lotus leaves were a poor substitute, offering only nausea and a burdensome ennui. Gratus was a vessel adrift with no hope of ever reaching shore.

The worst of his terrible deprivation was over. The tide of agonizing want had receded to a constant ache leaving him a lesser man. His teeth were gone except for a few blackened molars. He ran fevers. Sleep was restless and fleeting. His skin felt as though it belonged to another and was an ill fit. His flesh hung from his bones. His stomach roiled at the thought of food. Only honeyed fruit was tolerable and even that tasted of vinegar to his ravaged tongue. The other pleasures of the flesh held no appeal to him. His cock shriveled to a flaccid member useful only for urination which had itself become an increasing painful ordeal.

He had traded years off his life for a few days and nights of delightful delirium. It was a trade he would gladly make again were the elixir offered to him one more time. In truth, he would strangle without hesitation his most beloved for a moment's sweet release. That is, if the prefect had a most beloved other than his own miserable self.

The requirements of his office were left to others to perform. His lictor handled all administrative duties and correspondence. Gratus became detached from all that was expected of him except symbolic appearances at ceremonies and affairs of state. Even at these rare official obligations his participation was only to be seen and, if the mood struck him, to wave to others. Mostly he retired to his villa where he entertained few guests and lacked the motivation to do much beyond moving from his couch to a hot bath and back again all with the assistance of servants who were little more than substitutes for his own wasting vigor.

He opened his eyes at the urging of an irritating voice. It was his lictor speaking his name in an endless refrain to awaken him. The scribbler dared not lay hands upon the prefect to rouse him. Gratus enjoyed that much of what remained of his dignity. What was the man's name again? Did it matter?

Lifting his head from the cushion took his entire force of will. Rising to a sitting position spent what remained of his store of strength. The room was filled with long shadows. It was late in the day or early in the morning. A zephyr touched the sweat on his bare neck causing him to shiver at the icy touch. Waxing or waning, the sunlight through the shades failed to warm him.

The lictor, the chubby, oily excrescence, was still speaking his name, only more urgently.

"What is it, you foul issue of a donkey's cunt?" Gratus meant to growl but it came out a pitiable squeak.

"A visitor, lord prefect," the roly-poly bastard stammered. "He comes with a guard escort under the banner of the Senate."

"Fuck the Senate. Ass-licking parasites, the lot of them," Gratus struggled to stand, realizing that he was stark naked.

"A robe! Get me a robe!"

The lictor held up a white cotton wrap with a yellow border. The prefect punched his hands free of the sleeves and gripped the robe closed about his waist with a fistful of fabric. He staggered barefoot to a terrace that overlooked his courtyard in time to see a group of riders trot their mounts through the open gate. The scuff of steel shod hooves on the tiles made Gratus's remaining teeth grate painfully.

The shadows in the courtyard stretched toward the seaward end of the house. It was morning. No surprise then that his visitors were of the military class. Only soldiers were mad enough to be up and about at this indecent hour. The men dismounted, including an aquilifier bearing the red banner of the Roman senate topped with a brass laurel wreath and spread-wing eagle. The guard wore black leather smartly trimmed in white piping. The men stood whisking dust from their leather with the fly swatters made from horse's tails that were necessary accoutrements for any who traveled this pestilent land.

The last to step from his saddle had a military bearing despite his simple dress. He wore a common tunic of hemp that left his arms bare and the kind of leggings favored by legion cavalry. Only his fine soft-skinned boots gave away his station as the leader of this delegation. The only other feature that made him remarkable was a gleaming scalp entirely bereft of hair. The man shaved his head in the fashion of legion lifers. A man who commanded troops but wished to be seen as one of them.

A pandering fool, Gratus thought. How fitting he arrive under the banner of the preening whores of the Curia.

With the unwelcome assistance of the lictor, Gratus made it to his foyer in time for the entry of the bald man and a pair of his guard.

"To what do I owe the pleasure of this visit?" Gratus said in a tone meant to convey that the visitors' arrival was neither pleasurable nor welcome.

"The pleasure belongs only to the legate in Antioch, Valerius Gratus," the bald man said with a presumption of familiarity that the prefect found infuriating.

"What word does he send?" Gratus grumbled.

"That you are to vacate this residence and return to Rome by the swiftest conveyance and shortest route you can manage," the bald man said, handing a scroll tied with a purple ribbon to the lictor who accepted it with gravity.

An Imperial decree. Gratus's mind swung between anxieties over what being recalled to the capital upon orders from Tiberius might mean and a white hot rage at the impertinence of this bold stranger in his fancy boots.

"And who shall serve as prefect in my absence?" Gratus managed a snarl.

"I shall take that station permanently as of this moment," the bald man met Gratus's gaze with cold defiance.

"And might I know your name, you brazen bastard?" Gratus squealed, his fear taking voice.

"Pontius Pilatus," the man said with maddening authority.

Paris in the Now

An early snow fell like feathers from a slate gray sky closing low over the city. The flakes melted within seconds of touching sidewalks and rooftops and were hardly noticed by pedestrians except for a few who raised umbrellas purely out of reflex. Tires swished on the busy streets now made damp with melt. Passing cars created updrafts that lifted the flurries in swirls and eddies of white stipples. Drivers set their wipers at low to brush the swirling wisps from their view.

Daniel and Sydney Hochheiser of Alberta, Canada were wheeling a stroller past storefronts bright with the color and lights of seasonal decorations. Their son lay bundled and reclining in the basket of the stroller, looking up with wide eyes at the snowflakes dropping through the blinking multi-hued glow of bulbs strung over the street. Music played from unseen speakers playing songs of the season unfamiliar to the couple, such as "*Petit Papa Noël*" and others, like "*Le Petit Renne au nez Rouge*", recognizable by melody.

"I always hated 'Rudolph the Red-nosed Reindeer,'" Caroline said. "But it actually sounds lovely in French."

"I know what you mean. But no one murders rock and roll like the Frogs," Dwayne said.

She hugged his arm closer and pressed her cheek to his shoulder.

"You actually made good on your promise of pure

vacation time in Paris," she said. "And at Christmas."

"I don't remember ever making that promise. But we have a clean slate again. We're brand new Canadians. Let's enjoy it while it lasts."

"What do you think when you see the decorations and hear the carols?"

"I think mission accomplished."

"Morris says that there's really no way to tell if that's true or not. We can't know if events would have played out exactly as they did without the part the team played in it."

"Your brother will find his stocking filled with coal one morning."

"Morris isn't what I'd call a believer."

"I know. I've heard him and Chaz going round and round about it," he said, levering the stroller gently off a curb. They crossed a broad avenue, the tourist crowd swirling around them at a brisker pace. Dwayne and Caroline moved in their own time.

When they reached the opposite walk he tilted the stroller back. Stephen sat up, gripping the wall of the stroller to peek over the side. Caroline broke her grip on Dwayne's arm to press him back and recover him with the blanket. The infant tore the knit toque from his head and threw it to the damp sidewalk with a laugh. Caroline stooped to retrieve it and brush it on her coat.

"He's a terror," she said, pulling the cap tightly on Stephen's head and tying it in place under his chin.

"That's my boy." Dwayne grinned.

"Do you feel cheated? Stephen is eight months old. You missed all that time with him."

"I missed his first words. That sucks. But I knew married guys on deployments so long their kid was nothing but a belly bump when they left. By the time they got back the kid ran to meet them at the airport."

"Do you think it matters at this age?"

"To me? Hell, yeah. To him? Time means nothing."

"You can make almost any mistake right if you try hard enough. But you can never make up lost time," she said.

"You see that on a t-shirt?" He glanced at her.

"I heard someone say it. It stuck with me."

"Sounds like some gloomy shit, Caroline."

"Language," she said, nodding to the baby.

"Sorry. Gloomy *merde*. That better?"

They turned onto Avenue Bosquet and, midblock, Caroline stopped before Number 33.

"This is the place you told me about?" Dwayne said.

The ground floor was a storefront for a mobile phone store now. A second entrance had been added to allow access to apartments or condos on the floors above. A row of mailboxes were visible through the heavy glass of the entry door. A pair of bicycles leaned against a wall of the tiled hallway.

"It's not the same," she said. "Everything changes. That's the way it should be, I guess."

"Unless we have to change it back." He smiled but she didn't see it. Caroline could not turn to him, could not let him see her face. She knew it would betray her thoughts of the last time the two of them stood here; a time Dwayne would not recall as it had not happened to him yet.

"Excuse me," a voice addressed them in English. "I hoped to find you here."

They both turned. Dwayne stepped forward to place himself between the stroller and the man walking toward them from the shadows of a shuttered bakery.

Samuel.

Dwayne knew better than to offer his hand.

Samuel's gloved hands hung at his sides.

"I wanted to thank you for making sure Caroline and the baby got away safe," Dwayne said.

"Perhaps it balances the unpleasantness in Judea," Samuel said and met Caroline's pleading eyes. "In any case it matters a great deal that we keep your child safe from Neal Harnesh."

"We're good for now? Or are you here with another warning?" Caroline asked, eyes shifting to the street and behind them.

"This is a secure place and time. Sir Neal's agents are impeded for now. They will pick up the threads in time."

"We didn't just happen to run into you window shopping," Dwayne said.

"No. I am here to ask you and the others for a favor," Samuel said.

"I can't speak for the others but I'm here for whatever you need, Samuel. I owe you a debt I'll spend a lifetime repaying. What's the favor?" Dwayne said.

Samuel regarded them both with a grave expression before answering.

"To go back to Nevada and get my father."

Afterword

A Few Historical Notes

This is a work of fiction thus I made a lot of this stuff up.

There were no XXIII or XXX Legions in the Roman army. I wanted to spare any legion that did exist the embarrassment of having their ancient asses kicked by four guys and a girl. And to step around any true scholars who would race to point out that any real legion I might have chosen had never been in Judea or had been trudging through Hispania at the time of this novel.

Everything else about the legions is from all the reading I've done over the years. Blame Tacitus if I got something wrong. I think he has a Facebook page.

Little is known of Valerius Gratus, the Roman prefect of Judea at the time of Christ's youth. I'm sure he wasn't a heroin addict and have no proof he was a pedophile. But every good story needs a hero, a villain, and a wretch. Poor Gratus fills that last role. I'm pretty certain he wasn't a nice guy. Nice guys didn't get sent to Palestine back then.

And I have Pilate taking over for him a few years earlier than that actually happened.

The life of Jesus between his birth and his early adulthood are a tabula rasa. Other than ancillary legends (like the ones the nuns taught us) created long after the fact, we have no knowledge of his life. And we certainly have no idea of what he looked like. I have a sneaking suspicion he looked nothing like Jeffrey Hunter. I specifically avoided directly portraying Christ as it was not dramatically necessary to my story and I'm not out to offend anyone.

As for the siege of Paris in 1871, I took some liberties there. The events I portray did happen. The barrage, the horrific counterattack attempted by the citizens of Paris, the crowning of Kaiser Wilhelm I at Versailles are all real events. All I did was to telescope them into a shorter period of time. Things moved swiftly from siege to surrender but not as swiftly as I present here. And, moving beyond the events of the novel, the Prussians did eventually occupy part of the city as agreed upon in the very civilized surrender terms between the two armies. It was a brief occupation and France eventually agreed to pay an enormous amount of money to get the Germans to go home. Otto von Bismarck got what he wanted out of the war—a united German state. Things would not go so easily the next time these nations clashed.

And, unlike Lee Hammond, I did not read Bill O'Reilly's book.

Chuck Dixon

2014 AD

About the Author

Chuck Dixon is the prolific author of thousands of comic book scripts for *Batman and Robin, the Punisher, Nightwing, Conan the Barbarian, Airboy, the Simpsons, Alien Legion* and countless other titles.

Together with Graham Nolan, Chuck created the now iconic Batman villain Bane. He also wrote the international bestselling graphic novel adaptation of J.R.R Tolkien's *The Hobbit.*

His first foray into prose, the *SEAL Team 6* novels from Dynamite Entertainment, have become an ebook sensation. He currently scripts *Winterworld* for IDW publishing, which is being prepared as an eight episode event for Xbox Entertainment. He also scripts the *Pellucidar* weekly comic strip for ERB Inc.

He calls Florida home these days.

Visit the Dixonverse!
www.dixonverse.com